# THE INVISIBLE WOMAN
## A LESBIAN SUPERHERO STORY

# ANNETTE MORI

Vampire Pussy...Cat
Nicky's Christmas Miracle X3
(It's in Her Kiss, Affinity's Charity Anthology)
Donner Junior Saves the Day

**Series**
*San Diego Series*
Undercover Love
Politics of Love
Love Bonds

*The Next Generation Series*
The Next Generation Book 1
Love Hacks Book 2
Love Sins Book 3

**Co-authored**
The Organization with Erin O'Reilly

**Co-authored with Ali Spooner**
Humbug
Heart Strings Attached- TWC3
Free to Love
Trouble in Paradise -TWC4

# THE INVISIBLE WOMAN
## A LESBIAN SUPERHERO STORY

# ANNETTE MORI

Affinity
Rainbow Publications

2025

The Invisible Woman
© 2025 by Annette Mori

Affinity E-Book Press NZ LTD.
Canterbury, New Zealand

Edition first (1st)

ISBN: 978-1-991357-20-5 (paperback)
ISBN: 978-1-991357-21-2 (EPUB)
ISBN: 978-1-991357-22-9 (PDF)
ISBN: 978-1-991357-23-6 (KINDLE)

This is a work of fiction. Names, characters, places, and incidents are the product of the author's imagination or used fictitiously, and any resemblance to actual persons living or dead, businesses, companies, events, or locales is entirely coincidental.

Editor: A Koenig
Proof Editor: Sue Lee
Cover Design: Irish Dragon Designs
Production Design: Affinity Publication Services

## ACKNOWLEDGMENTS

A huge thank you to Ali Spooner, who was the only beta reader. I would also like to express my gratitude to Affinity Rainbow Publications—JM Dragon and Nancy Kaufman—other members of the Affinity Rainbow Publications team who provide assistance and support in so many ways. I am eternally grateful for the opportunities they give me to let my stories see the light of day. Thanks to Angie for her magic as the final editor to further tighten the story. She is a delight to work with. Inevitably, those pesky errors slip through, and I am thankful that the final proof editor, Sue Lee, who caught those before the book went to print. Thanks to Nancy Kaufman for the final cover. A huge thanks to all the other readers and fellow writers who have sent personal emails, written reviews, and posted nice things on Facebook (you know who you are). The Affinity authors are an incredibly supportive group and often share posts or send words of encouragement. Finally, my wife, Jody, continues her support even when it interferes with our time.

# TABLE OF CONTENTS

# PROLOGUE

Being the Invisible Woman isn't such a bad thing. I've been invisible all my life—metaphorically speaking. Now, I am the literal Invisible Woman.

It's easy to fade into the background if you're average. I was average in almost everything except my giant brain. I don't say that as a braggart; it was simply a fact. I liked being average. I had a few friends. It wasn't like the popular kids ostracized me. Mostly, they ignored me.

Unfortunately, people notice you if you're on the fringes, so I politely declined to be the valedictorian. My friend, Annalise, wasn't average and got picked on all the time. If you weren't one of the beautiful people, but you also weren't what society deemed ugly, life was bearable. Unfortunately, Annalise had scars from the fire that burned the entire left side of her body, including part of her face. She was on the fringe and scorned for something she had no control over. In

1

fact, most ostracized people don't have control over the reasons for banishment.

Annalise could have easily hidden the scars on her face with her hair, but that wasn't Annalise. She preferred a close cropping of her hair, signaling to the world she wasn't afraid of being labeled a lesbian. With her shaved sides, even though the scars on her jawline were visible, they didn't detract from her good looks in my opinion. Her arm and hand had taken the brunt of the fire and attracted the most attention, especially during gym class.

I became a scientist because I was determined to find a miracle cure for her scars. Practicality led me to forensic science, specializing in skin. Looking at the skin can tell a person a lot about the cause of death, the identity of the victim, and sometimes, when we're lucky, who is responsible for the homicide.

Annalise overcame all the obstacles and became an FBI agent. I think she enjoys unraveling puzzles, even though she's never been able to unravel the mystery of who started the fire that caused her scars. She's had to overcome all the rash judgments from others regarding her looks and almost didn't make it into the FBI, but Annalise is strong. Her perseverance is legendary. She says the same thing about me. I suppose she's right because, eventually, I found something that completely removed all her scars. And that is where our story begins.

They say most scientific breakthroughs are part tenacity and a healthy dose of old-fashioned luck. I quite literally stumbled on my discovery. I never dreamed of making a mark on the world like Annalise, so maybe that's another reason we kept the discovery hidden.

I wouldn't exactly say I'm an unlikely superhero because don't a lot of them tend to originate from outcasts and geeks? Most would undoubtedly consider me a geek, but transforming from average to exceptional seems a stretch. Annalise insists I was never average. We disagree on that point, which isn't unusual because, despite our affection for one another, we are very different people. Annalise believes in soul mates and love. I believe in science. But you aren't interested in our differences; you want to hear our story. It all started with the strange purple pod that literally glowed at night.

# Chapter One

---

"What are you still doing here, Doctor T?" my assistant Reggie asked.

"Psychotic killer still on the loose. Every minute counts, Reggie. I've been experimenting with a new chemical substance that might be able to lift prints on a badly decomposed body. I wanted to treat the tissues with my cocktail and see what happened. Why are you still here? I told you I didn't need you anymore tonight. I understand it is common for people to have dates on Friday night."

Reggie chuckled. "Can I ask you something?"

"Yes, of course. I am always happy to explain the science behind what we do. I'd like to think that being my assistant provides you the opportunity to learn and grow. Forensic science is an exciting field."

"It's not about work. It's about Agent Taylor."

I could almost feel my face contort in confusion. "Agent Taylor?"

"Yeah. Is she seeing anyone?" Reggie asked. "I know I'm no prize, but Annalise is nice, and that's all that should matter, anyway. She's also wicked good at her job, and that's incredibly sexy. Not everyone can be a beauty queen. I just think that maybe I'd have a shot because, you know…" Reggie's voice trailed off.

"You aren't suggesting that because Annalise still has visible scars that makes her less desirable?" My voice held a warning edge.

"No, no, sorry, Doctor T. I barely even notice them anymore. They seem to be less prominent. I'd like to ask her out, but I don't know if she'd say yes or no." Reggie stumbled over her words as her face flushed.

I tended not to feel comfortable with conversations in the workplace that weren't directly related to work. Still, my discomfort seemed unrelated to Reggie's line of inquiry, and I couldn't figure out why. Fortunately, I didn't need to analyze this too closely or answer Reggie because Annalise barged into the lab and interrupted our conversation.

"Tamara, come on, let's go. It's Friday night, and we have a Marvel movie marathon to get to," Annalise blurted. Her eyes turned to Reggie. "Oh, hey, Reggie. How come you're still here?" She jerked her head to me and stated, "This one spending her life in the lab is typical, but surely you have somewhere better to be on a Friday night."

Reggie blushed and stammered, "No, not really. My social calendar isn't exactly bustling with activity."

"Well, you could join Tamara and me if you want. We're just going to order pizza and watch a few movies," Annalise offered with a smile.

Something foreign bubbled up inside of me. At the time, I thought it had something to do with how insensitive Reggie's comments about Annalise's scars had been, but it was something far more unexpected. Whatever it was must have shown on my face because Reggie's eyes widened before politely declining the invitation.

"No, that's okay. I wouldn't want to intrude. Maybe another time?" Reggie asked hopefully.

Annalise shifted her eyes between us, and a wrinkle formed on her forehead. "Okay. Did I interrupt something here?"

I opened my mouth to say something, but Reggie was already heading to the door, waving and denying our previous conversation. "No, I'm honestly a little tired."

As soon as she left, Annalise asked, "What the hell was that all about?"

"Reggie wants to ask you out," I answered.

Annalise's mouth curled up on one side. "Really? Hmm, I never would have guessed that. She's nice but not really my type."

"You don't have a type. But that's good because I don't think you and Reggie should start seeing one another."

"I do too, have a type. Just because I haven't been ready to date again doesn't mean I don't have a type. I'm waiting until you find the miracle cream to eliminate all my scars, and then watch out, because I'll sow my wild oats like a freshman in college away for the first time." Annalise slung her arm around my shoulder. "After I'm done getting that out of my system, I'll force you to go out with me, and we'll fall madly in love, proving that love is not simply a chemical reaction resulting in an increase of endorphins."

"The notion of love is as silly as any organized religion that assigns an idol-like status to something a person cannot see, hear or touch." The familiar argument settled me. I knew what her next dispute would be, and the customary response further mended whatever was causing so much distress.

"Atoms can't be seen, yet scientists acknowledge their existence," Annalise argued as her arm dropped from my shoulder, and I felt the absence of her touch.

I chuckled. "Stop teasing me with the same argument. You know I can see atoms through an electron microscope." I began organizing my space, readying the lab to lock up and leave.

Annalise leaned casually against the table. "And you know scientists didn't always know they existed. Perhaps science has to catch up to religion. Never say never. Also, what about dark matter? Most scientists believe it exists but have never seen it."

After Reggie's earlier comment insinuating that Annalise had an inferior appearance, I studied my best friend. Objectively, Annalise had above-average looks, exceptional in some ways. Her dark, thick, slightly wavy hair would look good in any style, despite how she preferred it on the shorter side. A strong jawline and prominent cheekbones gave her a slightly masculine appearance that caught the attention of many young women on the rare occasions we would visit a gay bar, especially in a darkened room where her scars were less visible. But the features that generally charmed most women were her smoky gray eyes and cocky half smile. If she had more of a feminine appearance, I might describe her lips as almost pouty. They were certainly plump enough to satisfy our modern notion of attractiveness.

Yes, without her scars, Annalise might be considered an apex predator at the top of the heap, able to attract any mate she desired. Although I'd finally grown out of that awkward stage and did all right attracting women, especially those who preferred a more delicate appearance, I was an objectively less striking individual. Whoever said blondes had more fun wasn't scientifically accurate, even with my pale green eyes that many noted were particularly striking—probably due to the well-known fact that green was the rarest eye color. I mentally shook my head and returned to our debate.

"You're just trying to get a rise out of me. Well, it won't work." I laughed at our familiar discourse.

"I didn't have to try to get a rise out of you because you were already agitated. What's got your panties in a twist?" Annalise arched her brow.

"You know I don't wear panties. They're an unnecessary garment with the items of clothing I tend to wear." I grabbed my sling pack and headed for the door. "We're watching the ones with strong female leads, right? How about *Captain Marvel*, *Wakanda Forever*, *Black Widow*, and finally, *Thunderbolts*?"

"Duh," Annalise answered as she pushed off the table and followed me out of the lab. "Accept you forgot *Captain Marvel II, and w*e have to watch them in order. Oh, oh, oh, what about all the *Guardians of the Galaxy* movies? They could be a whole other marathon. Never mind. Stop changing the subject. You know you can't hurt my feelings, right? Let me guess, Reggie said something about my scars that you didn't like. It can't be that bad if she wants to date me. Nothing can compare to what everyone said in middle and high school. I've grown an exoskeleton that prevents harm no matter what anyone says or how they stare at me."

"Exoskeletons are wearable structures that support and assist movement or augment the human body's capabilities. They have nothing to do with how uninformed comments intended to hurt a person's feelings affect an emotionally vulnerable person. If you were more logical with your arguments, I wouldn't have to worry," I countered rationally.

Annalise burst into laughter. "If I didn't love you so much, I would take offense at what you just said. Forget it. I'm going to take it as a win that anyone wants to ask me out, regardless of whatever uninformed comment Reggie made."

We walked to the parking lot and got into our respective cars, mine a practical hybrid, hers a gas-guzzling monster SUV—a Toyota Sequoia SR5, what Annalise called a quality car with an engine powerful enough for a truck. I never understood why she didn't buy the truck with the same engine. It seemed more suited to her, but she insisted she didn't want to be a walking, talking, lesbian stereotype. The RV I planned on buying after I retired got better gas mileage. A fact that didn't seem to register with Annalise.

†

Annalise rested her long, lean form against her pride and joy, waiting in the extra paved space perpendicular to my driveway as I hit the remote to open my garage door. Her cocky smirk telegraphed her superiority at finding the fastest route and pushing the speed limit. I always groused about her knack of constantly wiggling out of those speeding tickets. Of course, having FBI credentials didn't hurt. She could have

9

easily opened the garage door and parked in her spot, but she wanted to goad me.

"Pizza should be here in about ten minutes," I called out.

Annalise pushed away from her car and greeted me inside my garage. Her brow furrowed as she shook her head in rebuke. "You really shouldn't order pizza while driving."

"Says the woman born with a lead foot," I parried, but with very little oomph. "I believe crashes related to distractions like texting make up thirteen percent of all motor vehicle accidents, while speeding is attributable to nearly one-third. You can lecture me all you want after you decide to drive the speed limit, Speed Racer." The familiarity of our recycled arguments helped to settle me again.

I didn't want to admit it, but the latest case had gotten to me. The body count was not only increasing, but the age of the victim seemed to decrease by one year with each new find. The last victim was two years younger than the previous one. Either the killer had slightly altered their pattern, or there was a missing body the FBI had yet to find. I believed it more likely they hadn't found at least one of his victims. The press had dubbed him The Hunter because he strung up his victims, gutted and skinned them. The killer had removed the victim's head, hands, and feet with precision, leaving what looked like slabs of meat attached to the tree with meat hooks. I'd yet to pull prints from the bodies, or rather skin, carefully hanging next to the body, meaning he'd probably used gloves. The forensic bone expert hadn't found any useful clues either. The only significant clue I'd discovered was an anomaly in the skin. After comparing it to the place of the body where it was apparent he'd removed something from the deltoid muscle, I suggested it might be a tracking device. The killer was hunting his prey using technology to give him the upper hand.

Annalise must have noticed the lackadaisical way I engaged her in the debate. "The facts are all present, but where is the passion? What's wrong?"

"Aren't you going to put your car in the garage?"

Annalise shook her head. "I'll do it later if I decide to crash here tonight," she absently responded.

I raised an eyebrow because Annalise usually stayed at my place when we had our movie marathons. I decided not to comment, and she followed me into the house after I pushed the button to close the garage door. Tossing my keys into my junk drawer, I turned to face my best friend, who looked at me with concern. "You're working The Hunter case. How do you do it? Remain unaffected," I clarified.

Annalise gently grabbed my arm and led me to my couch. She took my hand and answered, "Don't be so sure about that. Many things bother me, but I refuse to let the world see. I've been training all my life. Practically made it my own personal Olympic sport."

I saw the tenseness around her eyes and wanted to jump into a time machine and rewind the entire conversation. "Oh, goddess, I'm sorry."

Annalise smiled. "Forget about it. We're going to catch this psycho. I've no doubt you're going to help us with that. You always do."

My doorbell penetrated the discomfort I'd created. "Saved by the bell. Pizza time. Can you find the streaming channel with the marathon?" I pointed to the remote.

She maneuvered her body to enable her to shove her hand in the front pocket of her pants, pulling out two twenties. "Here, for the pizza."

I waved her away with my hand. "It's my turn. You never remember."

She shook her head and smiled. "Why fill my brain with unimportant details? I like to leave room for the critical facts." Stuffing the bills back into her pants, she asked, "Beer, cider, wine, or soda? I assume you have all those choices for us."

"Cider, please."

After I'd answered the door, paid the young delivery woman, and set the pizza on the coffee table, Annalise pressed the button to start the marathon. We began our usual commentary as the first movie played, debating everything from the ridiculousness of their superhero costumes to the disappointment that so few Marvel movies featured queer characters.

I wasn't sure what drew my eyes from the screen as we watched *The Marvels*. Perhaps it was the intensity of the light that I saw through my peripheral vision. I have excellent peripheral vision. But it wasn't something I could ignore. Once something catches my curiosity, I can't let go until I figure it out. I grabbed the remote and hit the pause button.

"Why did you do that? I'm still hoping Danvers and Rambeau will discover their love for one another," Annalise joked. "Screw the bone they threw us with the *Runaways* television series. I want a lead lesbian character in one of these damn movies."

I pointed to the glowing purple light barely visible through the window. "That's freaky. I'm going to check it out."

"Now?"

"You know I can't just let that thing glow without discovering what it is."

"I'm coming with. It could be radioactive or something. Then it'll zap you and turn you into some kind of freak mutant. I'm not letting you have all the fun," Annalise joked.

Before stepping outside, I rummaged around and found two sets of rubber gloves. Handing one pair to Annalise, we proceeded to my backyard and made a beeline to the soft glow. As we approached, the light began to pulsate and brighten. It appeared to originate from a small, round object about the size of an avocado pit. Donning my rubber gloves, I plucked the glowing item from the ground and placed it in my palm for inspection. It was dark out, and I could only see the pulsating light.

"What is that?" Annalise asked.

"No clue. I'm taking it back inside and examining it in my home lab. I'll put it under my stereo microscope. I don't want to do anything to harm it."

"It sounds like you think it's a living thing. I don't think aliens are that small," Annalise joked. "Maybe it's only a body part, like an eye or something. The poor alien might be blind now."

I bumped Annalise's shoulder playfully. "Cut it out. It could be a living thing. Maybe part of a plant or something. In Idaho, this biotech firm inserted genes from this bioluminescent mushroom into a petunia to create a new glowing houseplant called the Firefly Petunia. But it has a green glow, not lavender. Maybe they're expanding."

"You're pulling my leg," Annalise argued as she leaned in for a better look at the apricot-sized object in my hand.

I mimicked crossing my heart with my free hand. "No. I swear it exists. I'll order one, but right now, I can't wait to see this specimen under my microscope."

We hurried inside and rushed to my lab. Gently placing the glowing item under my scope, I adjusted one of my objective lenses and got my first look at the strange thing. "It's some kind of pod with multiple seeds," I exclaimed excitedly. "The membrane is translucent enough to see inside."

"Maybe we should plant one seed. Then, when it grows a huge beanstalk, I can be the one to climb it and steal the golden goose."

"Oh, I plan on growing these seeds. I'll have to experiment with different soils and plant foods to determine exactly what my babies need to flourish."

"Just don't prick your finger and start feeding it blood. Never forget *Little Shop of Horrors*." Annalise shuddered. "I refuse to capture a food source for a human Venus flytrap."

"Why not? It might save the taxpayers a whole lot of money. We'd only feed it serial killers, not your run-of-the-mill robber," I joked.

"Tempting, but no. Hey, are you going to tell anyone about your find?" Annalise asked.

"Nope. I'd rather wait and see if I can even get these seeds to grow. I'll start with different mixtures of potting soil and compost. Boiling eggs will leave us with an empty egg carton," I mumbled distractedly.

"I'll get the potting soil and compost while you continue to examine your find," Annalise offered.

"Can you grab my plant foods as well? I have all my gardening supplies in one section of my garage."

"Of course you do," Annalise teased.

14

As Annalise left to retrieve the items needed to grow whatever plants would emerge, I carefully sliced open the pod, revealing the tiny seeds, and changed to a more powerful objective lens to get a better look. The viscous liquid that spilled from inside the pod piqued my curiosity further. Close enough to detect an odor, I found the smell not at all unappealing. If a person combined honey, orange, vanilla, and pineapple in a blender, it might resemble the fragrance emanating from the liquid spreading slowly over the glass. I grabbed an eyedropper and quickly gathered my treasured finding, placing it inside a test tube for later examination.

Annalise sort of waddled into my lab, awkwardly carrying all the items I had requested. I chuckled as the various plant food and black plastic starter trays spilled onto an empty counter before she dumped the two bags of soil and compost.

"You could have made two trips, you know?" I shook my head at her.

"What's the fun in that? I'm always up for a good challenge. I found these starter trays, so we won't have to eat hard-boiled eggs for the next several days. You know how I hate eating the same foods every day."

"Help me fill the trays with a variety of mixtures. We'll start with all potting soil, decrease each by twenty percent, and fill the rest with compost. That will give us alternate 80/20, 60/40, 40/60, 20/80, and 100 percent compost mixtures to compare. We can add plant food to a couple to see how the seeds react but leave the rest alone."

"Do you have enough seeds for that?" Annalise asked.

"Yes, there are plenty of seeds to use. I may even put a couple of seeds in each mixture." I noticed a tiny droplet of purple liquid on my glove and frowned. Until I performed a few tests, I wasn't about to let the foreign substance touch my skin.

"How will you remember the differences? Don't you need to label them or something?"

"Nah, I'll remember. Especially since I'm going to start a new notebook and detail my experiment for later use," I explained.

"Hey, you got some of the alien goop on your glove. You know what it looks like?" Before I had a chance to answer, Annalise powered on. "Body fluids. You know, when the forensic geeks use their black lights, searching for blood and other stuff?" She reached out to touch the droplet on my glove.

I pushed her hand away. "Don't touch that. It might be toxic. And don't refer to the forensic scientists as geeks. You know I'm one of them." I pulled off my glove, pushing it into a container designed specifically for toxic waste.

"Maybe it has special healing properties," Annalise suggested.

"Or it could be corrosive. I'll need to run it through a few tests before even thinking of applying it to animals or humans."

Annalise scowled. "You mean use yourself as a guinea pig because I know you don't use rats, bunnies, or other mammals in your lab experiments. It's how you got that nasty rash when developing the cream for my scars. Promise me you won't put that on your skin."

"I promise to take reasonable precautions," I answered. I was already thinking of ways to pilfer small skin samples from any fresh bodies the FBI encountered, since I was always the first to be called to the scene. Skin and bone cells didn't die immediately, so I figured they'd be the perfect samples to test. As long as what I did would not compromise an investigation, what could it hurt? I quickly discarded that notion. It would be just as easy to scrape a sample of my skin onto a slide and see what happened when I added a droplet from my test tube with the viscous liquid I'd obtained from the pod.

Annalise helped me plant the strange seeds, and I put a grow light over half of the seed tray. After completing the task, we shuffled back to my living room and enjoyed a cold beverage, beer for her, and cider for me. Since it was so late, Annalise decided to crash at my place per usual. It wasn't like she was impaired with one beer; I often wondered if she just didn't enjoy spending the night alone. I almost asked why she was being so odd before when she said she might not stay, but I'm not the best at picking up on subtleties.

# CHAPTER TWO

---

The growth of the strange seeds amazed me. Annalise was so fascinated that she stayed at my place the entire weekend. It wasn't like this was unusual for her because she spent more time at my house than in her tiny condo, but I could tell this was different. She wanted to track the experiment's results every bit as much as I did.

It was a miracle neither of us received a call all weekend. No new dead bodies to examine with a questionable cause of death. Routine deaths always ended up with the coroner. The experiment's most fascinating aspect was that each tiny shoot grew at approximately the same rate. It didn't seem to matter which combination of soil or plant food I used. I guessed it would be another week before we detected any new pods. Not all plants flowered, but for whatever reason, I suspected this one would. I wasn't an expert on plants. Sure, I dabbled in gardening, but my aha moment came much later.

The strange purple object was very unusual. Several weeks later, I would deduce it was not of this world.

Late in the evening on Monday, we got a break in the Hunter case with a new body hanging from a tree in the dense forest. Two hikers had not only stumbled on the body but apparently startled the killer. His or her kill was incomplete. Although it was statistically more likely the killer was a man, I wasn't going to assume this. Equality and all that. The hikers had interrupted the unsub in the middle of their skinning process. If we were especially lucky, we'd find something to tie evidence to the killer once we caught them. Annalise was the one to discover the tiny piece of clothing on a blackberry bramble. Maybe we'd get lucky and find a bit of DNA. She carefully placed the thorny bramble into an evidence bag. Skin was my thing, so I called dibs on the evidence. I wanted to check for skin cells.

I pointed to the bag and declared, "That's mine."

Annalise grinned. "I wouldn't dream of giving this treasure to anyone else. Meet you back at the lab?"

"Only if you don't hover. I've already given you an estimate of the time of death. I don't believe it takes a rocket scientist or a forensic expert to tell you what you already know. A big clue is the fresh pool of blood in that bucket and partial skinning. The head, hands, and feet are still attached as well. That should make identification easier."

"Don't worry. I won't be there for a while. What I can't figure out is why these hikers were here. I'll be grilling them for answers. This is an extremely remote area of the forest. Every hiking trail is at least five miles away. Either they're highly experienced hikers and enjoy the more pristine locations, or they're foolish."

I looked at the two hikers, barely in their twenties, huddled together with their relatively small backpacks. "I vote for foolish. How did they even get here?"

"ATV," Annalise answered.

"Mmm, well, I suppose this is an adventure they'll never forget."

The new body kept Annalise and me extremely busy over the next week, and we barely dragged ourselves home in the evening. With everything going on at work, I'd almost forgotten about my experimental plants. The FBI was desperate to catch the killer and brought hundreds of samples of dirt, plants, bugs, and anything that could lead us to the maniac on a killing spree not likely to stop until we caught them. The FBI marked off a one-mile perimeter and ravaged the area for any clues. The forest had multiple places where scraped skin cells might linger after a killer made their rapid escape. The techs brought in anything thorny or with rough edges for testing. Nobody was going to get any sleep until we apprehended this guy or gal.

†

Finally, I finished with all the samples, but we were at another impasse with no DNA to test against and all leads exhausted. It especially disheartened Annalise because the investigation was going nowhere, fast. A week and a half had passed. Seeing Annalise look so despondent nearly broke my heart, so I invited her over for takeout from our favorite Italian restaurant. Spaghetti and meatballs, along with brownies and ice cream, were her favorite comfort foods. We were going to eat our worries away.

After stuffing ourselves, Annalise undid the top button on her jeans and groaned. "Why did you let me eat so much?"

I laughed. "You're a grown woman. Who am I to stop you from your gluttonous ways?"

"Hey, have you checked on your plants lately?"

I frowned. "I haven't. Think you can move enough to go to the lab? Or do you need to remain immobile while your food digests?"

"I hope you haven't let the poor things die. Don't you have to water plants every day?"

I shook my head. "They're on an automatic watering system. I've even varied the amount of water each plant receives, just in case that makes a difference."

"Of course you have." Annalise chuckled. "I might need a little help getting up, but I think I can waddle my way to the lab. I'm curious to see how much they've grown."

"Me too." I held out my hand and tugged.

"Omf. I'm going to need to spend extra time in the gym." She refastened the top button on her pants, and I glimpsed her muscular torso.

I raised one eyebrow. "I doubt that. I've never seen a flatter stomach or a more toned body."

Annalise grinned and flexed her biceps. "Like what you see, huh?"

I decided to change the subject and ask about something that had bothered me ever since I saw Reggie fawn over Annalise. "So, did you ask Reggie out yet?" We started walking to my lab.

Annalise furrowed her brow. "What? No. I told you she isn't my type. Why are you suddenly so interested in my love life?"

"I just think you have a lot to offer. You have no social life, and that isn't healthy," I insisted.

Annalise chuckled. "Says the pot to the kettle. When was the last time you went on a date?"

"I've been busy. Doing important work." I opened the door to my lab and gasped when I saw the starter tray. Roots grew from the bottom, spreading like an overgrown vine across the table. Small purple buds glowed in the dim light.

"Holy shit," Annalise exclaimed.

"Will you help me transfer these to larger pots?" I asked.

"Sure, sure. Do you have enough pots?"

I frowned. "No, I don't. Okay, new plan. Let's take this out back and dig a garden for them."

"Now?" Annalise asked with a fair amount of incredulity.

It was pitch dark, and the only light we would have, came from the tiny buds and anything I might be able to dig out from my camping gear.

"Well, shit. It's not like we have a ton of time when it's light outside. This case is killing any free time I might have."

Annalise let out an exaggerated sigh. "Fine, I'll help. Please tell me you have some powerful light to shine in your backyard and a rototiller or whatever to dig up the soil."

"It won't be that hard. I was going to plant a vegetable garden and already started preparing the ground." I turned to look at Annalise, who didn't even try to hide her skepticism. "Don't look at me like I've just grown two heads. Yeah, yeah, I know it's a little late to plant, but you know how unpredictable the weather is. I've been busy," I insisted. "Besides, I have a place I go to that gives me mature plants, so I'm not starting from scratch. I was going to devote the upcoming weekend to the task."

"No, you weren't. Why didn't you just hire someone to do it?" Annalise asked.

"I did hire someone. Why do you think the space is ready for plants?" I grinned. "Grab that extra potting soil and compost. I'll find us some light. The glowing buds should give you enough light to navigate to my garden spot. You can't miss it. It's a large rectangle with freshly overturned dirt."

While I listened to her grumbling, I headed to my garage and the corner set aside for my camping gear. I prayed the batteries were fresh, or I'd be looking for new ones. I wasn't sure if I had any that large. The main grocery store might carry batteries, but I didn't relish making a trip to the store.

By the time I'd found my lantern and a portable spotlight that I had thought was too cool to pass up on one of my foraging trips for new tools at the local big box hardware store, Annalise had already dragged the starter tray and bags of soil to the spot. I also grabbed a few gardening tools to help us dig the large holes needed to plant our curious plants. After setting up the spotlight that produced an impressive amount of light, I handed Annalise a large trowel.

We worked diligently for two hours, spacing the plants several feet apart to allow ample room for more growth. I wasn't sure how large the plants would get, but I didn't want to stifle their growth.

Out of the corner of my eye, I caught movement and noticed a pair of glowing yellow eyes. I'd seen a stray cat lingering around my property for the past week and had set out water and food for the poor thing. So far, the feral cat had not deemed me trustworthy enough to get any closer. I wondered if the cat was just as curious about the strange plants as we were. I hoped they weren't toxic to the scraggly feline because I planned on slowly gaining its trust. My previous cat had passed six months ago, and I was sure the universe would bring me another. It always did.

Annalise stood and stretched her back. She glanced at her smartwatch and asked, "Can I crash here tonight?"

"Of course you can. You know you don't have to ask. You have your own room, filled with spare clothes and everything. I'm not even sure why you bought that condo. You spend all your time at my place."

"I didn't want to cramp your style when you started dating what's her face," Annalise mumbled.

"What's her face?" I chuckled. "You mean Stacy? We went on exactly three dates. It's not like I asked her to move in. I wanted you to share the house with me. That made more sense. You're used to my quirks." I laughed. "We should make a pact. If neither of us is married by the time we hit forty, we'll give up on finding a mate and become two spinsters, living together forever. I think we both know it's improbable I will choose a mate, but one never knows." I was only half joking because I could see spending the rest of my life with Annalise. We might not agree on much, but we were compatible in all the ways that were important to me. It wasn't like I believed in marriage and true love, but I was very fond of Annalise. Unfortunately, Annalise wanted the whole ball of wax: soulmates, true love, and all that malarky. I couldn't deny her that dream simply because I believed love was a chemical reaction. Yet, that didn't stop me from making this outrageous suggestion.

Annalise shrugged. "I could do worse." She smirked.

# CHAPTER THREE

---

Annalise bounced into the lab the next afternoon, vibrating with energy. It was late but not excessively so. I'd been known to hang around at work much later.

"What's got you so excited?" I knew when Annalise was like this, I had no choice but to begin tidying up and preparing to leave with her.

"Come on, time to go, Tamara. I need that big brain of yours. Thai okay tonight?"

"What are you talking about?" I asked as I continued to put everything in order. Reggie had already left for the day, so at least I didn't have to watch her mooning over Annalise. There was only so much blatant flirting I could take.

Annalise agitatedly tapped the stack of folders in her hand with the pen she had retrieved from her ear. "I think I may have discovered a pattern."

"So, talk it over with your colleagues."

"They're misogynist pricks, always disregarding my contributions, and this guy is smart. If we're going to catch him, I need someone more intelligent than myself to weigh in on possible theories," Annalise answered.

"What about that entire division in the FBI devoted to profiling?" I sloughed off my lab coat and tossed it in the cloth bag I set aside expressly for soiled clothing.

"I guess they know their shit, but they aren't perfect. Come on, you owe me after last night."

"True. All right, but if you don't want me to use my phone while driving, you'll need to call in the order before you head to my place. I'm starving."

Annalise grinned. "Already done. If we leave right now, we should make it to your house before the delivery guy gets there."

"Sneaky. I'll meet you there. I need to stop at the pet store for more food and maybe a new cat house. The new feral doesn't like the smell. Madam Curie's scent is all over the old house."

"You're losing your touch, huh? Haven't tamed him yet?" Annalise goaded.

"I'll admit, he's more skittish than Madam Curie. Maybe male cats take longer to tame," I reasoned.

"I doubt it. I had a male cat growing up, and he was a lot more Zen than the female we had. It's likely due to how long he's been on his own and the kind of past experiences he's had with humans." Annalise gave me a tiny push. "Come on, chop, chop, we need to go."

I smiled. "See you soon."

†

It amused me to watch Annalise stuff food in her face, attempting to hurry along dinner so she could start talking about her case. By now, she knew the rule. No work conversation until after dinner. I had digestive issues, and discussing murder and mayhem while eating tended to cause problems for me. Just to rile her up, I took my time, wondering when the explosion would occur. Too bad I didn't have someone else to bet with. I figured I had five minutes until she detonated. To my dismay, she refused to play my game.

"Stop baiting me," Annalise said. "I know exactly what you're doing. It won't work."

I grinned as I plucked another piece of chicken from the takeout container and placed it in my mouth, chewing slowly. "This is really hitting the spot. I feel like every morsel needs savoring to appreciate the full genius of the dish. The absolute mastery of the spices is a truly marvelous thing of beauty."

*Five, four, three, two, one…*

"Dammit, you win. Will you finish dinner already so we can start talking about the case?"

I closed the container and carried it into the kitchen to place in the refrigerator for snacking on later. Leftovers never bothered me. Annalise didn't usually have any, mainly because her excessive need to exercise burned enough calories that she'd demolish any meal set in front of her. Sometimes, she would eat my leftovers, but not tonight because she was too excited to start discussing the case.

As soon as we'd cleared the table, Annalise set out the folders, opening each one for me to inspect. "So, do you notice anything interesting?"

I took my time to look at the photos and read the details, synthesizing the information. Finally, I saw what I suspected Annalise had picked up on.

"Each death occurred shortly before the victim's birthday," I stated.

"Yes! When we've been able to pinpoint more accurately the time of death, it's been exactly one day prior to the victim's birthday. That's not a coincidence."

"Not likely, no," I answered.

"The question is why? Does he want the victims to not celebrate their birthdays? Did something terrible happen to him on his birthday?"

"What have the profilers said about him? I'm assuming they believe it is a man. Normally, I prefer not to make assumptions about gender, but I suppose the evidence is overwhelming that it is most likely a man." I studied the photos carefully.

"He's meticulous. The blood and guts are absent except for the last crime scene. The head, hands, and feet were missing, as though he couldn't stand to look at their eyes or anything that would suggest the victim was a living being."

"Exactly! At first, we thought it was a way to remove evidence that could tie him to the murder and make it nearly impossible to identify the victim. But then we found his fastidious burial site for the head, hands, and feet at an exact distance from the rest of the body for what we presume are his first two victims." Annalise frowned. "The rest remain missing, and we can't figure out why the pattern changed."

"Maybe he started out as a hunter but a reluctant one, and now he's evolved, getting more comfortable and gaining confidence with his kills," I suggested.

"That makes sense. Ugh, maybe he kept them as trophies." Annalise shuddered before pulling out a large map of the forest with red dots for each of the dump sites. "Notice anything here?"

I studied the map for a pattern, tilting my head, trying to see the image in my mind. "A star, or perhaps a pentagon." I shuddered. If this was some ritualistic killing, I wanted no part of it. "It's incomplete." I traced the map with my finger, connecting the red dots. "He isn't finished yet."

"Damn, you're good. So, how is The Hunter getting their age and birthdays? Who would have access to that information?" Annalise asked.

"Lots of people. Every time I check into a hotel, I have to show them my license. The DMV, of course. Computer hackers who want to steal people's identities need birthdays. Bars that card people. There are so many places that we present our IDs. Whenever you fly, you're required to show either your passport or ID. Both have a person's birthday. Unfortunately, the list is endless."

Annalise sighed. "Yeah, I know. But this guy has to be local and someone who knows that forest like the back of his hand."

I pointed to potential areas on the map that would complete his star. "Consider staking out here and here."

Annalise slumped back against the sofa. "They'll never authorize the resources for that. We don't know when he'll take his next victim. It could be days or hours before he kills them. With the exception of our theory that he kills them one day before their birthdays, the time between killings has been random."

"Maybe that's because there isn't a consistent mechanism to choose the next victim, which would probably rule out the

DMV or a hacker. The last guy was about to turn thirty-three, right? Except for the two-year difference between these last two victims, the pattern has been one year apart and getting progressively younger with each new victim. Unless it really is a change in pattern and not due to a missing body, look at any missing person who is thirty-one and on the cusp of turning thirty-two. He'll likely perform his ritual then," I theorized.

"Brilliant. See, I knew you could help. Okay, enough work. Want to check out your plants?"

"Hell yeah. At the rate they've been growing, those buds may turn into flowers any day now." I jumped up from the couch, grabbed my spotlight, and headed for my sliding glass door to the backyard, with Annalise nipping at my heels.

After flipping the switch to the portable light, I saw Einstein's scarred ears twitch before movement in my bushes revealed one of his hiding spots. Since I was sure the feral cat was a male, I'd named him Einstein. Kneeling to inspect the plants, I found fresh kitty prints and evidence of gnawing on the leaves.

The plants had bloomed overnight with small purple flowers and what looked like a tiny pod in the center. It was at this point in the plant's growth cycle that I began to question if I had gotten it all wrong and the pod we found earlier was some kind of edible fruit. I'd just assumed it was a seed pod, but this plant continued to behave vastly different from any earthly variety. It wasn't like anything I'd ever come across in my limited experience. I should have deduced the pod was fruit after slicing it open and detecting the sweet, citrusy odor.

Next to one of the plants, it looked like Einstein had eaten one of the small flowers, fruit and all, then promptly thrown up.

I wagged my finger at the bushes. "Bad kitty. I really hope these plants aren't poisonous. Poor Einstein. He really should have waited until they were ripe," I joked.

"Einstein?"

"Yeah, that's his name. I'll look for him tomorrow morning to make sure he's okay. I'm pulling out the big guns, tuna, yogurt, and that leftover salmon. I'm sure one of those items will entice him out of hiding. I'll put all three in the brand-new house."

Annalise squatted next to me as I examined the barf. "Gross. Please don't tell me you're going to scrape that from the garden and inspect it under a microscope."

"Of course I am, along with one of the petals from the flower. They're rather thick, a little like a cactus or an aloe plant. Maybe they'll have curative properties," I joked.

"Well, sign me up for testing!" Annalise exclaimed.

"If nothing bad happens to Einstein, I might use myself as a test subject. Early days. I want to let them reach their maturation point before we even consider any testing." That sounded like a perfectly reasonable approach to me.

I ran back into the house to don my rubber gloves and gather a test tube and eye dropper for the specimen left behind in the dirt. Equipped with everything I needed to conduct further tests, I made a beeline for the garden. Before I collected the sample, I stuck my finger in the small mess left behind and lifted it to my nose. Taking a deep breath, I noted the faint smell.

"Ew, why did you do that?" Annalise asked.

"Specimen examination should include all five senses. A person would miss quite a bit by not exercising everything provided to a scientist to unlock the mysteries of the world."

"Animals make sounds, but I seriously doubt plants do," Annalise argued.

"Au contraire. The buds of rhubarb crack open and creak during the growing season. You can often hear corn grow, too. It's like a cracking sound, similar to the sound of corn breaking."

"You're pulling my leg," Annalise insisted.

"No, I'm not. Honest." I sniffed again. It was more acidic than when I had noted the aroma before, but I couldn't tell if that was due to Einstein's digestive juices or the premature picking of the fruit. To be safe, I plucked another fruit in the center of a blooming flower to dissect and examine thoroughly, including the smell. With my bounty of specimens, I walked straight to my lab.

Annalise followed me and sat patiently in what she had designated as her chair. While I inspected each sample collected, she scrolled through her phone. She had joked about adding a dating app, and I wondered if she was checking out prospective mates. I didn't like that for reasons that were just beyond my reach at this point.

# CHAPTER FOUR

The previous evening, I had run the samples through every conceivable test. I wasn't any further along in my analysis regarding the safe handling of the substance inside the pod or the petals. Even the leaves of the plant had a sort of gooey, purple, paste-like substance when I cut into them. I hadn't managed to sleep much as I tossed and turned, wondering what my steps would be. Giving up on getting any sleep beyond a couple of hours when I'd managed to enter dreamland, I slipped from my bed to check on the plants and Einstein. I had to run further trials but was adamantly opposed to animal testing. What I saw would change my life forever.

Attempting to be quiet so that I wouldn't wake Annalise at the crack of dawn, I tiptoed into the kitchen to gather the tasty treats for Einstein. I arranged the three items on a small plate, hoping at least one would bring the streetwise cat from his hiding place.

Einstein was alive and well, licking his paws. I must have interrupted breakfast. I'd left a tiny amount of dry food the night before, but not enough to satisfy him since I hoped the tuna, salmon, and yogurt I planned to put out this morning would cause him to enter the giant carrier. But something astonishing had happened to him. The only way to describe his appearance was to say he looked like a space-age hologram. He was there but in a sort of shimmering, translucent form.

I rubbed my eyes and blinked, thinking I might still be half asleep and not seeing what was right in front of me. Nope, still there and looking like an experiment gone wrong.

"Holy shit!" I exclaimed. This caused Einstein to flee to his favorite bush. I needed to stop scaring him away. Crouching in front of the specially designed cat carrier I'd set on the deck, I placed the dish inside and waited on one of my deck chairs, speaking in low tones, hoping to entice him out of hiding. "I promise, Einstein, I'm not going to hurt you. Come on out, you know you want to sample the goods."

Staying as still as possible, I waited. His tiny nose peeked out from the bushes, and he cautiously approached the carrier. I remained sitting a respectable distance until he slinked inside.

"That's a good boy," I encouraged. I slowly pulled the remote for the carrier from my pocket and pressed the button, activating the wire door. Einstein backed into the far corner, blinking his green eyes and watching my every move as I made my way to the carrier. He was a lot smaller than I originally thought, probably the runt of the litter. Now that I was close enough to get a good look at him, I discovered his ears appeared to have fully healed, forming two perfect triangles. Even from a distance, I'd noticed that, prior to this morning, one ear had a deep split, and the other appeared as though someone had chewed the edges.

"What the hell," I muttered to myself, grabbing the handle at the top of the carrier.

I needed to find a small space where I could let Einstein out of his carrier and simply sit with him until he got used to my presence. So far, he hadn't shown an ounce of aggressiveness. I was willing to take a chance that he wouldn't scratch or bite me once I let him out. My master bath was large enough, so I headed in that direction, engaging in what I hoped was soothing conversation, albeit of a one-sided nature, hoping to settle him.

"I promise, sweet boy, you're going to learn to love the life of an adopted kitty. After we bond a little, I'll even let you go outside whenever you want."

Before I reached my master bath, Annalise emerged from the guest bedroom, yawning and stretching. I should have known she would wake up despite my efforts to avoid disturbing her. Annalise was a very light sleeper.

"Why are you up so early? Oh, hey, you caught him. Can I see? How come there's a purple glow? Did he grab one of the flowers again?"

Apparently, my body was blocking her from getting a good look at him, and all she saw was his muted glow. "Um, not exactly." I set the carrier in front of me and waited.

"What the hell is that?" She bent to get a closer view.

"Best guess, even though he upchucked most of the flower and pod, eating the plant had some unusual side effects. On the plus side, it must also have curative properties because his ears are all healed."

Annalise stood to her full height. "Wow! So, how will you test the plant for potential healing properties?"

"I don't know. You know how I feel about animal testing. But ingesting and likely being exposed to every part of the plant hasn't negatively affected Einstein, so I might be inclined to test on a few lab rats," I answered. "I suspect either the leaves or flower petals are responsible for his healing. He may have gotten it on his paws, then started cleaning himself, causing the regeneration to occur."

Annalise glanced at her severely scarred left hand and stated, "My scars can't get any worse…"

Before I could stop her, she hurried to the backyard, plucked one of the flower petals, and broke it open, letting the gel-like substance ooze over her left hand.

"Wait!" I yelled, but it was too late. I watched in horror as the purple light seemed to glow more brightly.

"It tingles, but I'm not in any pain." Annalise stared at her hand in amazement.

Too shocked to do anything but watch, I forgot every principle of conducting a proper experiment. I couldn't tell you exactly how long it took for whatever substance was inside the flower petals to heal the patch of skin Annalise had exposed to the substance. Sixty seconds sometimes feels longer than it actually is, but I guessed that was how long it took.

"You crazy woman. You shouldn't have done that. What if you turn all glowy too?"

Annalise grinned. "I'm not a scientist, but I don't think whatever is inside the petals caused Einstein to become a hologram. Maybe it's the pod he ate and promptly spit up."

"I'm starting to think it might not have been a seed pod he ate. I believe they're fruit, and Einstein picked the fruit too soon. It was probably bitter tasting because it wasn't ripe yet."

Annalise rotated her hand, examining it from every angle. The soft purple glow had faded, leaving only the area where the curious substance had made contact with her skin, now free from scarring. "I don't suppose you're going to let me bathe in that, are you?" Annalise pointed to the flowers that were now twice the size they had been on the previous evening.

"I'll make you a deal. Let me take a small skin sample and examine it under the microscope, maybe perform a few tests. Then if you don't have any nasty side effects after a few days, have at it."

Annalise grinned. "Works for me." She jerked her head toward the flowers. "The fruit in the center is almost the same size as the pod with the seeds that we planted. I'm confused, is that a seed pod or fruit?"

I shrugged. "I don't know. We may not have found a seed pod after all. Most likely, it was an unripened fruit. It's obviously not like any plant I've ever seen before. I don't like leaping to conclusions, but I have no other explanation than the plant is not of this world."

"Cool. An alien plant. Do you think it'll be ripe enough to eat soon?"

"Why? Are you planning on trying one so you can become a human hologram?"

Annalise shook her head. "Nah, I've been attracting attention because of my scars all my life. I'd rather not become a lab rat for unscrupulous scientists."

"Whatever is causing Einstein's glowing form, it's either permanent or a long-lasting effect. We'll see if it fades over the weekend. I need to set him up in my bathroom and get him acclimated to the good life. I hope it won't take too long to tame the feral out of him."

Annalise crouched in front of the cage. "He looks scared but not too aggressive. Want me to make you some breakfast and bring the carrier into the bathroom while you two bond?"

"Thanks. That would be awesome. You're the best. Before we settle Einstein in the bathroom, will you come to the lab with me while I scrape a few of your skin cells for examination?"

Annalise grinned. "Hah. I know you. You aren't going to be able to resist doing your thing right away. After you get your skin cells, I'll settle Einstein in the bathroom, then make breakfast and bring it to the lab."

"Yup, you do know me so well. You're the best."

†

After several hours of testing, I couldn't find a single abnormal thing about Annalise's newly healed skin cells. I nibbled on my breakfast and pondered the ethical dilemma before me. Should I involve other scientists in my discovery? Perhaps get financial backing and thoroughly explore the plant's benefits to society? Yet, there was the side effect we'd witnessed in Einstein. There were still too many unknowns. I needed to weigh the potential benefits with the possible risks. Sometimes, scientific breakthroughs were used for purposes not originally intended. Although a lot of people could benefit from the plant's healing properties, there were still too many unanswered questions. It was looking more and more like the plant was alien in nature, and if the wrong branch of government wanted to get involved, our lives would never be the same.

I didn't know where Annalise had gone off to. I was sure she hadn't left my house. "Annalise," I called out.

"I'm in here," she answered from my master bath.

Of course she was trying to bond with Einstein. She loves cats as much as I do. Although, I didn't know why since she seemed more of a dog person. I, on the other hand, was perfectly suited to the aloof nature of cats.

My previous cat, Madam Curie had taken a special interest in Annalise. Whenever she'd come over, Madam Curie would scramble to greet her, wind herself around Annalise's legs, and wait until Annalise settled on the couch so she could curl up in her lap. Annalise was heartbroken when we'd taken her to the vet to be put to sleep. In all honesty, I'd waited too long, but I just couldn't make the decision. She was my baby. Annalise had to be the one to convince me it was time. She knew I hadn't wanted to see her suffer anymore.

I carefully opened the door and noticed right away that Einstein appeared less translucent. Annalise had gathered the lambswool from the new cat house I'd purchased for Einstein and set it on the floor next to her. Einstein was curled up on the soft material, and I swear I could hear him purring. Annalise stroked his fur. His green eyes blinked open, but he remained rooted to the bed.

I slowly settled on the floor next to Annalise and cautiously reached out to stroke his head as gently as I could. "I'm dubbing you Cat Whisperer. Nicely done."

"He's a sweetie. It didn't take long. Especially after I raided your refrigerator for more tasty treats. Grilled chicken is his favorite."

"Over salmon?"

Annalise nodded. "I know, go figure."

"The glow is fading. He's becoming more…present." I wasn't sure how to describe how Einstein seemed to look less like a hologram.

"Yeah. I noticed that too. Did you learn anything new about my skin cells?"

I shook my head. "No, they appear to be perfectly normal. Better than normal. You know how our skin changes with age. If I didn't know better, I would assume these skin cells were from someone a few years younger. This plant might be the ultimate anti-aging cream, but it's too early to tell."

"Hey, I'm still young and vibrant. No visible wrinkles to speak of."

"I was just telling you what I discovered microscopically. You haven't noticed any changes to the patch of skin on your hand, have you?"

"Nope. All good. Do you think we can let Einstein out yet? The sooner he can explore his new home, the better."

"Sure. I think I still have leftover cat litter. I'll fill the litter box, and you'll be responsible for making sure he learns where to pee. We need to get him fixed, too. The last thing I want is him spraying all over the place."

"Why do I have to teach him?" Annalise whined.

"Because you're the Cat Whisperer."

"Fine. Challenge accepted."

## CHAPTER FIVE

Another week passed, and Einstein had completely returned to his previous appearance, with the exception of his ears. Apparently, the healing that occurred was permanent. This all made sense because Annalise's test patch of skin also remained smooth and unblemished. It took a lot of convincing, but Annalise agreed not to treat her skin with any more of the gel or whatever oozed from inside the flower petals. I didn't reveal the small tests I had performed on my own body. She would have undoubtedly called foul.

First, I deliberately burned my finger using a hot pan, creating a painful blister, then promptly applied the miracle gel. The result was almost instantaneous. I felt the tingle that Annalise had described, and my pain immediately subsided. Within thirty seconds, the blister was gone. My second test took a great deal of willpower because I'd been known to faint at the sight of blood. But sacrifices were needed in the pursuit of knowledge.

Using my sharpest knife, I sliced the tip of my forefinger deep enough to require stitches. I had a towel ready to stop the flow of blood and watched in fascination as the gel mixed with the blood, quickly closing the wound before all evidence of injury disappeared, leaving only a small blood residue behind. Wiping away the blood, I inspected my finger with high-powered magnifying glasses. But I wasn't satisfied with these results. I wanted to see the healing process in action.

Friday was the perfect day to use the electron microscope at work. Most of my work colleagues left early on Friday, leaving me alone in the lab. I snuck in several flower petals and leaves to repeat the tests I'd done at home. I wanted to get an up close and personal look at how the miracle gel worked.

Needing to improvise, I used a glass test tube and heated the glass until it was hot enough to create a burn. I was in the middle of performing my first test when Annalise burst into the lab.

"What the fuck are you doing?" she asked.

I gestured for her to go away and stop interrupting me. After applying the gel, I put my finger under the scope and observed. It was the most astounding thing I'd ever seen. Microscopic objects, looking very similar to a virus, vibrated on my finger while simultaneously pulsing tiny bursts of purple light.

"Incredible," I exclaimed in awe.

"You are unbelievable. Chastising me for putting that stuff on a small section of my hand, and here you are, actually injuring yourself to see what happens. Well, have you learned enough to declare that stuff safe for me to use?"

"I think so, but I'm not too happy about observing something ridiculously close to what a virus looks like."

"I haven't turned into a flesh-eating monster yet, nor has my health taken a nosedive. I think I'm safe. It's been seven days."

"You've had those scars for twenty years. A few more weeks won't kill you. I'd feel horrible if something bad happened to you," I argued. "One more week to ensure you don't suffer any unforeseen consequences for your rash actions." I held up my hand. "Nope, don't go lecturing me on my carefully constructed tests."

"Fine. But are we going to do any experiments on the pods or fruits? Einstein seems fine. He recovered from whatever he ingested fairly rapidly. It'd be kind of cool to turn into a human hologram for the weekend."

"Nope. My turn to be the guinea pig. One of us should be free of any alien influence in case something goes wrong."

"You've decided it *does* come from an alien planet," Annalise stated excitedly. "How cool is that? I hope the aliens are friendly. I'd like to think they are. Why else would they leave behind a miracle healing plant?"

"It's a possibility. Can you give me a few more minutes to run some more tests, please? I'll meet you at my house. Order pizza for us, will you?"

"All right, but can you please not lose track of time again?"

"Half an hour, tops. I promise." This was a promise I intended to keep because Annalise had planted a different kind of seed. I was going to taste one of those alien fruits. They'd grown to the size of a tangerine, and I was dying to try one. Since their growth seemed to remain that particular size over the past three days, I surmised they were ready to pick. At least, that's what my logical brain was telling me.

†

Annalise was lounging on my sofa when I entered my house. Einstein seemed content to settle next to her and barely lifted his head in acknowledgment. He'd taken to indoor living quite well, preferring to remain inside. I suppose his old life was just too hard, and now that he was pampered by both of us, he had decided he had no need to return to the wayward life. She had a sheepish look as she brought a large piece of pizza to her mouth.

"Sorry," she mumbled around a bite of pizza, "I was hungry, and you broke your promise." Chewing quickly, she continued, "But I forgive you because this time, it was only by about fifteen minutes. That's within the margin of error but not within the parameters of my growling stomach."

I settled next to her on the couch and grabbed my own slice. "Thanks for getting my favorite even though I was a tad later than I promised."

Annalise shrugged. "It's not like I hate arugula and goat cheese pizza. I simply crave meat sometimes. By the way, I checked on the alien plants, and the fruits are huge."

"A little hyperbole. They're the size of tangerines," I corrected. "It's actually a small fruit by comparison."

"Compared to the original pod or fruit we found, they're huge. If you set one next to a watermelon, it's small but enormous compared to practically any berry."

"I think the fruit is ready to harvest. The size hasn't changed in the last couple of days, and they're a deep purple

44

now versus the lighter lilac color. The light seems a little brighter, too." I grabbed the cider Annalise set out for me and took a large sip. "Thanks for the cider."

"I debated whether to have one ready for you, knowing how you get involved in projects and lose track of time. But then I figured drinking a warm cider would serve you right if you were too late."

"Such a sweetheart. How kind of you," I responded, my voice dripping with sarcasm.

She grinned. "Most welcome," she tossed back. "I presume you'll conduct your tests on the fruit tonight."

I took another large swig of my drink. "Yup, sure am."

"Aren't you afraid that whatever is in the fruit might negatively react to alcohol?" she asked.

"Hmmm." I frowned. "I hadn't really thought of that. I suppose it would be prudent to conduct two tests, one with the presence of alcohol and one without. Good thought. See, you can think like a scientist."

"Comes from years of hanging around you."

I was hungrier than I thought, and we finished the pizza in record time. Together, we cleared the area, and I took a few minutes to scratch under Einstein's chin. I didn't want him to think I was ignoring him. But now I was ready to begin the second level of tests.

"Head to the lab, and I'll meet you there," I directed. "I'm just going to select two of the darkest-hued fruits."

Annalise saluted me. "Rightio, Chief."

"Stop that. I just meant I don't need help to select two samples."

Annalise chuckled and ambled down the hallway to my lab. It hadn't turned pitch black yet, so there was enough light to see, especially with the glowing fruit as a massive beacon for any curious onlookers. Good thing I lived miles away from civilization and had a fenced in yard. I found what I believed to be the two ripest fruits and twisted them until they came free of the large flower. This was another odd characteristic of the plant. Flower petals always fall off after pollination. These petals simply widened to allow the fruit to grow in the center of the flower.

Annalise sat relaxed on her chair, but this time, she had brought her tablet with her and was scrolling through the news. "The press is killing us on their coverage of The Hunter. I can't wait to catch that son of a bitch and shut them the hell up about the incompetence of law enforcement."

"Mmhm," I replied absently as I went to the table and sliced open one fruit. The biggest difference from the unripened fruit that I mistook for a pod, was the consistency. It wasn't exactly solid, but it wasn't the same viscous liquid I had inspected under the microscope. The closest description I could think of was that it reminded me of passion fruit, only with slightly smaller seeds. I brought my nose close to the fruit and sniffed. The same pleasant odor emanated from the fruit, albeit a tad more powerful.

"Wow, I can smell it all the way over here," Annalise said. "It's quite enticing."

I put the tip of my finger on the gelatinous pulp and placed it on the tip of my tongue for a taste. "It's sweet. Quite good, actually. I'm not sure I can make a comparison to any known earth fruit."

Annalise pointed to me. "Um, your face is glowing. Wait, can you stick out your tongue?"

I pushed past Annalise and went directly to the closest bathroom. I found the mirror and stuck out my tongue. Sure enough, it was glowing in that same translucent manner that Einstein had glowed for approximately twelve hours.

"That's freaky," I said, stating the obvious. I kept inspecting my tongue, then jumped back when my entire tongue disappeared.

Annalise was right behind me and screamed. "It ate your tongue. Oh my god, oh my god, oh my god."

I could still feel my tongue as I rolled it around in my mouth. "Chill. I can still feel my tongue. It isn't gone, it's just invisible."

"Can I touch it?" Annalise asked.

I stuck out my tongue as Annalise brought her finger close until she came into contact with my tongue. "Damn, that is the freakiest thing I've ever seen. Just imagine what you could do if you went completely invisible? Talk about stealth. You'd be the best person to send on a stakeout," she joked.

"I feel completely fine. I'm going to eat the entire fruit. It's the only way to see what happens with the rest of my body."

"Um, okay. Are you sure? I mean, what if you become the invisible woman or something? How will you explain that to your colleagues?"

I shrugged. "Maybe the effect has a shelf life. What happened to Einstein would suggest that's exactly what occurred."

## CHAPTER SIX

That Friday evening, after stuffing ourselves with pizza, was the day I officially became the Invisible Woman. Sure, there were a few fits and starts. I hadn't yet learned how to control this new power. Nor did I realize just how capable I would become. It turned out the alien flower had more secrets to reveal. Also, like any drug, certain side effects surfaced in some results while remaining dormant or nonexistent in others. That was the only way my scientific brain could wrap around the fact that when Annalise eventually tried one fruit, she had a different reaction—one that was slightly less beneficial to our ultimate pursuit of justice but nonetheless saved my bacon as I learned the edges of my powers.

I'll never forget the feeling when I finally scooped the insides of the fruit, eating it like a piece of passionfruit. It was like a power surge or an electrical charge but not at all uncomfortable. Annalise watched wide-eyed as each exposed part of my body slowly disappeared.

I wanted to experience every sensation and stood still as the immense power flowed over my body, reaching the very tips of my fingers and toes. Standing nearly still, Annalise gasped.

"Tamara, um, you're ripped. I can see the definition in your biceps pushing against the sleeves of your shirt."

"What?" As an automatic reaction, I flexed my muscles.

"Holy shit, I can't see the sleeves of your shirt anymore. They've gone completely invisible," Annalise exclaimed.

I looked at my arms, and sure enough, where my shirt felt tight, that part was invisible. I twisted and flexed as many muscles as possible and saw a patchwork of clothing still visible, but the places where my clothing was more form-fitting, it had also turned invisible.

"Interesting," I said, as if this were merely another routine experiment, and I found the findings slightly noteworthy.

"It's kind of freaky," Annalise said. "Do you feel stronger?"

"I guess so. It's hard to describe, but there was this kind of power surge after I swallowed the fruit," I answered. "Maybe the fruit sparks an adrenaline spike. Hang on, I'm going to do a little test. Follow me to the garage."

Jogging to the garage, I tested my strength by taking hold of the bumper of my car and lifting it as if it were made of cardboard. At first, I used both hands, then I tried lifting with just one hand, and the car easily came off the ground. More sections of my clothing disappeared after my muscles touched the soft fabric of my pants, probably due to jogging to the garage.

"You're like a superhero, Tamara. I bet if you stripped out of your clothing, you'd be completely invisible."

"Or, if I wore a Lycra outfit that is completely form-fitting." A vague idea began forming.

Annalise chuckled. "You should design an outfit. Every superhero needs a proper outfit. This is so cool. I want to try it. Can I please eat one of the fruits now?"

"I'd really rather you not. Let's see what happens to me over the weekend. If I haven't suffered any negative consequences, we'll test out the effect of the fruit on you next weekend. I want to make sure I go back to a fully formed human that everyone can see. My theory is that it will take between twelve to fifteen hours if the effect is similar to what happened to Einstein."

"Aw, you're no fun," Annalise whined.

"Safety first."

"Please, I didn't see a whole lot of safety on your part with you gobbling up that fruit like it was your last meal on Earth," Annalise grumbled.

"You're just mad that I probably have a six-pack now without spending a single minute in the gym," I teased. "I have better things to do than waste my time on that dribble."

"Yeah, too bad no one can see it. It'll probably go away as soon as you become visible again. There are no shortcuts to losing weight or sculpting one's body," Annalise argued.

Annalise's cell phone interrupted our debate, and she answered, "Taylor." She paused as she listened to the person on the other end of the phone. "Thanks. You just earned a gooey pastry, Leslie. I guess my weekend is shot. Nah, just following up on a hunch. I'm going on a little stakeout." Annalise ended her call and grinned.

"Stakeout?"

"I put one of the data techs on an assignment, watching for any hits on missing persons in our specific age range. We just got a hit. I think I'll go camping this weekend. Can I borrow your gear? It's a lot better than mine."

I nodded, but of course she couldn't see that, so I answered, "Of course. You know whatever is mine is yours."

Annalise frowned. "The only problem is that there are two possible locations to stake out, and I can't be in both places at once. If what you said is correct, he's going to leave the body in one of two locations. I'm hoping to catch him before he kills another victim. I just don't know if he transports their bodies to the dump site. He might kill them prior to gutting them and presenting their bodies for the world to see his handiwork. If this missing person is his next victim, she's going to be slaughtered tomorrow. Her birthday is Sunday, and she turns thirty-two."

"Maybe I can help," I suggested.

"No. It's bad enough I have to leave you alone. I don't exactly feel great about that. What if you get sick and I'm not here to monitor you? I'd never forgive myself if something happened to you. I have a fifty-fifty chance of catching this guy."

"You should have backup. Can't you pull in another team?" I asked.

Annalise shook her head sadly. "I'm supposed to let the profilers do their job and not muck around in their territory. Idiots. They wouldn't even let me present my findings. I tried to arrange a meeting with Gary and the behavioral analysis unit. It was a no-go. My asshole boss waved me away as if I were an annoying fly and then assigned me to a crap case as punishment. I wasn't supposed to take the files home because Gary only reluctantly assigned me to the task force."

"You should have been the one they promoted. Everyone knows how incompetent Gary is. Perhaps I could have a little fun with him in my invisible state," I stated evilly.

Annalise chuckled. "Now, now, don't you go turning into some evil villain."

"That reminds me. I don't think I have to explain how dangerous this plant could be in the wrong hands. No one can know about it. It's sad to say, but I don't trust our government."

"Me neither, and I work for the government. It's too bad. Because that gel could help a lot of people."

"I know." I felt the pit in my stomach. "It's an ethical dilemma I've been wrestling with. But it's still premature. More testing needs to be done before I deem it safe to use. I have to admit the results are promising."

"It's really hard being patient. I want to slather that gel over every inch of my scars." Annalise looked away and wouldn't meet my eyes. I should have known at this point, but I ignored that niggling feeling of guilt.

"I know. But have you considered what you plan to tell people about your miraculous healing?"

Annalise shook her head. "Shit, I hadn't considered that."

"All the more reason to wait until we come up with a reasonable explanation."

"I'll quit the FBI and move across the country if I have to, but there is no way I'm giving up the chance to be normal. I'm tired of everyone staring at me like I'm some kind of monster."

"Oh, hon," I stroked the left side of her face where the scar was visible. "You are normal and beautiful. I never realized you thought you weren't. You've always been so defiant, never caring what anyone thought or said."

"Yeah, well, it's an act. A coping mechanism that allows me to separate the assholes from the angels." She smiled at me, and I saw something in her look that caused a small flutter in the pit of my belly. If I didn't know any better, I would describe the feeling as a rush of love. But I didn't believe in the notion of love, at least not in the way that most people described this emotion.

"You're one of the angels." She coughed. "Back to the stakeout. Are you going to be okay on your own this weekend while I catch a serial killer?"

"I am. I'll call if anything goes awry. And *you* need to promise to call if you run into any trouble. Let me know which location you plan on staking out."

"Deal." She held out her hand for me to shake. "Damn, this is going to take some getting used to," she exclaimed as it appeared as though she was shaking thin air.

†

After Annalise had gathered my camping gear and placed it in the back of her SUV, I told her to be careful and watched her drive off. She was an experienced camper and FBI agent. I knew I shouldn't worry, but I couldn't help myself.

Before returning to my lab, I removed the full-length mirror from my bedroom and hung it in the lab. I needed to record every change in my appearance. Einstein had woken from his nap and was following me around. I didn't have the heart to kick him out of the lab, so when his fur brushed against my leg as he scrambled inside, I let him enter.

53

Then I decided, on a lark, to rifle through Annalise's clothing, knowing I would find workout gear. Annalise was slightly larger than me and certainly more muscular, but perhaps her Lycra shorts and cycling shirt would work in a pinch. I grabbed my one-piece bathing suit in case her workout gear didn't perform as expected.

I rushed back to my lab to conduct a series of tests. Stripping from my loose-fitting outfit, I donned Annalise's borrowed clothing after carefully setting my phone on the table. Either I'd gained thirty pounds, or the fruit had buffed me out because the clothes fit snugly against my skin. When I lifted my eyes to the mirror, the only things that remained were my earrings, rings, and smartwatch. They all seemed to hover in space, moving only when I waved my arms or shook my head. *Truly mesmerizing.* It was starting to set in how remarkable all of this really was. Having a tendency to view most things with a higher level of dispassion than most, I was finally allowing myself to feel something beyond bland clinical interest. A rush of excitement flooded my core.

I removed all my jewelry pieces and set them on the table. Einstein meowed loudly, letting me know this was something new and frightening to him. I suppose it was barely acceptable when he saw patches of clothing and my rudimentary accessories, but being completely invisible was not something he could get behind.

"It's okay, my sweet baby. I'm still here. I know you can smell me." Squatting in front of him, I cautiously touched the top of his head. It was like I had to tame him all over again. At first, he startled, then leaned into the touch and began purring. "See, this isn't so hard to get used to."

Annalise's special ringtone startled both of us. Not wanting to scare Einstein, I stood slowly to retrieve my phone from the table. It was beyond freaky how it moved through the air, reminding me of those horror films where someone had the power of telekinesis or a naughty ghost was playing a trick on unsuspecting guests.

"Hey, what's up? Are you okay?" I asked.

"Yeah, just letting you know I'm almost at the first location. I might scour the area and see if anything seems amiss before checking out the other spot. Also, I wanted to let you know that my hand tingled like thirty seconds ago. I haven't felt a single thing since the gel touched my hand a week ago. I thought it was something you'd want to note. Also, you'll think I've gone bananas, but I could swear I had this rush of emotion that I can only describe as astonishment or intense excitement. Then, shortly after, I felt not exactly scared but more like unsettled. Although I probably would not have noticed if I hadn't felt the prior emotion so intensely. The fear almost felt like a muted echo because it lacked the same intensity. Forget everything I just said. Now that I've verbalized it, it sounds completely nuts."

I let what Annalise just said sink in. This was something new to record. It might be important later on. "You aren't experiencing any pain or other negative effects, are you?"

"Nope, just the tingle and rush of feelings."

"Maybe you should return to the house so I can closely monitor you," I suggested.

"No way. I'm not letting this asshole take another victim."

*Anger.* I felt a tingle, and then it was like I could almost see a rush of anger—a pulsating red glow. Sure, I knew Annalise so well that I was in tune with her emotions most of the time, but this felt different. A theory was beginning to form, but I needed more data.

"All right. But be careful, please," I soothed. The anger dissipated slowly like a helium balloon, gradually losing air. I didn't just think this was happening. I could feel it. This flooding of emotion caused a rush of panic. Holy shit. If my theory was correct, the shared use of the alien flower had somehow connected Annalise, Einstein, and me. If we couldn't control this, every tiny emotion would flood and overwhelm us.

"Tamara! What the hell is happening to us? I don't panic. Ever. But at that precise moment, that was all I could feel."

Concentrating on modulating my emotions, I took several deep breaths. "We'd better learn how to control our emotions. I think we're connected."

"Connected? How?" Annalise asked.

"By the alien flower."

"Okay, that's not the worst thing," Annalise answered reasonably. "At least I'll always know when you're in trouble. Besides, it wasn't exactly uncomfortable. A small tingle and then a kind of muted message."

I laughed. "Only you would see the silver lining. I suppose I'll have to add some experiments to measure the effectiveness of certain forms of meditation, deep breathing, biofeedback training, and such that will help us control this new wrinkle."

"Yeah, you do that. I'll do what I always do when entering a dangerous situation. It's a little internal mantra I've mastered that never ceases to calm my senses and create a sort of bubble of calm. Not to be offensive, but since you rarely show intense emotion, I'd like to think this will be a piece of cake for you."

"No offense taken. Let's hope that Einstein's emotions are only amplified when he's in close proximity to one or both of us. Otherwise, we're going to feel whenever he's afraid. Good thing he seems to be relatively chill most of the time."

"All right, you get back to your mad experiments, and I'll continue my quest to catch the bad guy," Annalise said before ending the call.

I tamped my excitement down, but I was eager to begin a whole new set of experiments. I needed to test my strength and perhaps even my speed. Could I run fast? So far, I had invisibility, super strength, and a form of telepathy. Would rapid healing only occur when I used the gel from the flower petals? Or, by consuming the fruit, did that change my body chemistry in the same manner, activating a self-healing process?

Picking up the scalpel I'd used to slice open the fruit, I attempted to make a slight cut on my finger, but it was hard to see my invisible hand. I felt the slice but didn't see the blood. I suppose that was a bonus since I really didn't tolerate observing blood spillage. However, I needed to know if the wound was still bleeding. Looking around for something that might capture the blood and become visible to me, I spotted the hand towel I used to dry my hands after washing. I'd have to sacrifice a perfectly good hand towel for the experiment. *Oh well*. The pursuit of science was worth it.

Pushing the towel against my hand and wiping every inch I could feel, I waited to see if a blood stain would emerge. Nothing. In case I missed the cut, I imagined using the towel to dry my hand, arm, and any area I may have sliced. Still nothing. *Could my blood be invisible, too?* I tossed the towel into the bin I kept for soiled biohazard materials and didn't give it another thought.

Tampering the small joy I felt at learning that the fruit also had healing properties, I wondered how far I could take it. Was I willing to shoot myself to see if the bullet would pop out and allow for healthy regrowth once my body expelled the foreign object? Would broken bones self-heal? There were so many other tests to perform, but I needed to wait for Annalise. It wasn't safe to perform more aggressive testing without someone there to take me to the hospital should the test fail. With nothing better to do for now, I changed into loose-fitting clothing. I was still getting used to the invisibility. Because this affected my hand-eye coordination and caused a form of vertigo, I added a pair of gloves. I settled into my favorite reading chair, and Einstein crawled into my lap as I read my latest romance novel. The spicier, the better. It was a guilty pleasure of mine and totally out of character.

# CHAPTER SEVEN

I must have nodded off in my chair because I was startled awake after experiencing a jolt of adrenaline. *Annalise*. I couldn't tell if she was in trouble, but I would not take any chances with the well-being of my best friend.

Grabbing a ball cap and slipping on the walking shoes I left next to the door to the garage, I rushed to my car. I almost forgot my car keys but remembered them at the last moment and hurried to the kitchen to retrieve them. It was a good thing I was a creature of habit and knew just where to find my car keys. Although I classified the drawer as my requisite junk drawer, I'd taken the time to organize it, complete with a molded plastic tray similar to a silverware organizer. However, my tray contained compartments of various sizes and shapes designed to accommodate frequently used items.

The tingle intensified the closer I got to the dense copse of trees. When I found Annalise's car parked at the edge of the forest, I practiced deep breathing. She didn't need to feel my emotions along with her own. I surmised that invisibility might be to my advantage if Annalise had somehow found The Hunter and was in trouble. Quickly stripping, I scrambled from the car, unseen by predators but not completely absent from their senses. Animals have a keen sense of smell and enhanced hearing. I didn't even try to mask the sound of my feet running through the forest toward the heightened tingle.

The second thing I noted was my ability to see despite the absence of light. I wasn't a runner, but I registered how quickly I moved through the forest—certainly not in stealth mode as I crashed through the foliage, disturbing everything in my path. I didn't believe I had super speed, only that I felt more athletic traveling through the dense vegetation. I barely noticed the brambles and thorns that tore into my skin but knew I would emerge from the forest without a single scratch.

I found Annalise crouched in the forest, low to the ground but moving steadily through the dense foliage. Her head swiveled quickly in my direction as she lifted her gun and took aim.

"Don't shoot," I whispered. She might not be able to see me, but she could see movement in the ferns and leaves.

"Tamara?"

I tentatively touched her shoulder and whispered in her ear, "Yeah. I felt you. I thought you might be in trouble."

"He's taunting her. I heard a shot ring out," she said.

"How do you know he hasn't already killed her?" I asked.

"Because right after he discharged his shotgun, he yelled, 'Run, little rabbit, run.' Sick bastard," Annalise hissed. "I can't figure out how he transports them to the forest. I've searched for a vehicle, and I can't find one. Either he's incredibly strong, or maybe there's two of them? We know he drugs his victims because the tox screen confirmed that, but then what? Does he drag them into the forest, wait patiently for them to wake up, fire a warning shot, then hunt them for sport? It's like he's imitating that *Criminal Minds* episode but with his own personal twist."

"You mean the birthday thing?" I asked.

"Yeah. You shouldn't be out here. The last thing I need is for you to catch a stray bullet. If I could hear you trampling through the forest like a clumsy elephant, I'm sure he could as well."

"Maybe that will scare him off, and we can find the missing woman," I suggested.

"Or he could shoot at whatever is moving despite being unable to see you," Annalise retorted.

"Good point. I'll move more cautiously. But I have a feeling he's made a hasty exit, especially with me crashing the party rather ungracefully. Since he left the last victim unfinished, I think he's a coward. He'll cut his losses." I stood and cautiously moved away from Annalise, scanning the area for anything out of place.

I'm not sure if I heard the noise before Annalise, but my head turned just in time to see a naked woman staggering toward us. I'll never forget the panicked look on her face. I swiveled my head to get a better look and narrowed my eyes, barely detecting the outline of a man holding a shotgun. I wanted to shout for her to watch out, but by the time I opened my mouth, a shot rang out, and I stumbled to the ground. Lifting my hand to my shoulder, I felt a sticky substance ooze from my body before the intense tingle I'd come to recognize.

Annalise must have returned fire, practically emptying her gun in the direction of where the single shotgun blast originated. I saw him run in the opposite direction, but he was limping. Annalise had gotten a piece of him. I was sure of that.

"You nicked him. He's limping," I whispered.

I felt Annalise's moment of indecision before she rushed to the woman and commanded, "Stop. FBI. I'm not here to hurt you." She fumbled in her pocket, pulling out her badge. "Are you hit?"

Although her eyes were wide with fear, the woman shook her head.

I remained quiet while Annalise took control of the situation. I suspected it wasn't much comfort, but Annalise removed her light jacket and draped it over the woman. That's when I noticed that not a trace of scarring remained on her left hand and arm.

"My campsite is a little ways away. Can you walk? I'll get you some clothes. Then we'll head to my car, and I'll take you to the hospital. Okay?"

The woman nodded. "He's still out there. He'll hunt us down."

"I don't think so. He's wounded. He'll retreat. What's your name?"

"Carmen Hardgrove." Carmen squinted her eyes and turned her head to the right. "Someone else is here. I heard her. Don't you need to check on her, too? He must have been hunting both of us."

It was at this moment that I discovered my final power. I closed my eyes, and with tremendous concentration, the outline of my hands, feet, and the rest of my body materialized. Within less than a minute, everything was visible. Fortunately, both Annalise and the woman faced the opposite direction. I lay on the ground in all my naked glory. Before pushing myself to a standing position, I felt the large slug that I knew had ejected from my body. I palmed the evidence before Annalise or the woman could see. I didn't give a second thought to the blood left behind, believing it would remain invisible. Both turned at the same time. I subtly shook my head, hoping Annalise would catch on.

"I'm okay," I reassured them. "I'd rather not go to the hospital, but some clothes would be nice. I'm in a lot better shape than you are." Pointing to the scratches all over the woman's body, I calmly explained, "You were his first target. I had more time to hide." She looked down and noticed blood oozing from a particularly deep cut, and her rapid breaths increased. Obviously, she didn't fare any better with blood than I did, as she crumpled against Annalise.

Annalise stared wide-eyed at my naked form, before catching the poor woman as she tumbled to the ground. As soon as the woman regained consciousness, I slipped her arm over my shoulder, taking half of the weight.

"Come on. I've got her other side. How far is your campsite?" I asked.

Annalise blinked twice. "Not too far. And I have a change of clothes that should fit you."

Undoubtedly too shocked to say anything, the woman let us half carry her as we made our way slowly through the forest. She didn't say a word about the strange car next to Annalise's SUV.

†

After we'd transported Carmen to the hospital, Annalise told her she would be back to ask her a few questions. Carmen had provided her name and address but insisted she couldn't tell Annalise much. Carmen hadn't seen his face. The only thing she was positive she'd never forget was his voice. Annalise assured her that she might know a lot more than she thought, and Annalise would be back to do a guided interview. The smallest detail might help. As The Hunter's only known survivor, Carmen might be key to catching him, but Annalise didn't tell Carmen that, letting her think I was another victim.

The minute we were alone, Annalise barked, "How in the hell are we going to explain your naked ass in the forest with me? They're going to want to interview you."

I shrugged. "Just tell them I was uncooperative and slipped away while you were dealing with Carmen." I held out my hand and revealed the slug. "This popped out of my body."

"What?"

"I suggest we clean it up, just in case DNA isn't as invisible as blood. There can't be any traces of my DNA, but at least we can examine the evidence. Perhaps it will provide another lead."

"You know, you've completely fucked up my investigation."

"I know. I'm sorry. But that slug was meant for Carmen, and if it weren't for me, she might be dead or seriously injured."

"By the way, are you going to tell me how in the world you managed to control your invisibility?" Annalise asked.

"It's kind of hard to explain. It's like I can control it with intense concentration."

"Does it work both ways? Can you become invisible again?" Annalise asked.

"Don't know. I haven't tried that yet." I grinned.

"Um, don't you think that's an important experiment to conduct?" Annalise grunted. Clearly, she was frustrated with me.

"I think I should wait until we return to my lab. I was going to ask you to shoot me, but now I don't need to perform that test."

"Are you out of your fucking mind?" Annalise shook her head in exasperation. "Never mind. You're just nuts enough to suggest that."

"Do you want to know what I've discovered so far?"

Annalise sighed. "Sure."

"In addition to the invisibility and my ability to control that, I have super strength, enhanced vision, a type of telepathy with you, and self-healing capabilities."

"Well, sign me up. I'm eating one of those fruits the minute we return to your place," Annalise insisted.

"I'd really rather you not until I conduct more experiments. Besides, body chemistry matters. You shouldn't expect the same results. Although I should ask if you've already given it a try." It was time to confront her.

"You saw, didn't you? When I gave Carmen my coat," she added.

"Yeah, your chivalrous side got in the way of hiding what you'd done from me." I glared at her. "I should be furious with you."

The corner of her lip turned up in a lopsided smile. "But you're not. You love me and will always forgive me. I wanted to see if it worked on the rest of my body. It does," she exclaimed. "I left my face alone because I didn't want you to know just yet. Although you may be right about different body chemistry because I inadvertently scratched my arm, and it hasn't healed."

"Not necessarily. Perhaps the gel only works on old scars. The self-healing may come from the fruit," I offered as an explanation. "No more testing. I'm exhausted."

She pulled in next to my car and told me she would meet me back at my house. I climbed inside and noted the time on the dashboard. Five in the morning. No wonder I was tired.

# CHAPTER EIGHT

I waited several hours for Annalise to return and began to worry, but figured she'd gone back to the hospital to interview Carmen. While I waited, I experimented a little with my new abilities, and after a considerable amount of trial and error, I mastered the ability to turn off and on my invisibility. It was like I sent messages to my body in the same manner the neural network directs movement to our limbs.

Periodically, I would pick up on Annalise's emotions, but nothing specific. It was like they were all over the place. Frustration, anger, a sense of defeat. Something was happening, and it wasn't good. When, finally, she dragged herself inside, I took one look at her face and knew something was amiss.

Clearly, this wasn't the time to talk about Annalise's deception. As far as I knew, Annalise had never lied to me before. Perhaps she would argue she hadn't technically told an out-and-out lie. She had to know that both lies of omission and tossing something out that let me draw an alternate conclusion were still falsehoods in my book. That whole speech about how hard it was for her to be patient and wanting to be normal was the ultimate cherry on top of her mound of deception because it generated an unwelcome rush of emotion.

"What happened?"

"I just got my ass handed to me by Gary."

"Why? That doesn't make any sense. You have your first survivor. Isn't that an enormous breakthrough in the case?" I patted the sofa for her to sit next to me.

"Acting like a fucking cowboy. No authority to go out there on my own. Losing a potential witness. Blah, blah, blah. I'm off the case and on suspension for not following protocol," she explained.

"Did they take your gun?"

She grinned. "Yeah, but I have a backup."

"You're not going to stop pursuing him, are you?"

"Hell no. I plan on combing through every inch of that section of forest. There has to be something."

"Won't there be FBI techs doing that today? I'm surprised they didn't ask you to show them exactly where the firefight took place, especially since you're sure you hit the guy."

"Since we'd already mapped the two areas where he most likely would display his next victim, I pointed them out on the map. I wouldn't exactly say I gloated about being correct, but I suppose Gary might have interpreted my tone of voice as insubordination." Annalise shrugged. "I don't think that helped my cause."

"I take it you didn't get anything more from Carmen?"

"A few nuggets. He wore a mask and gloves. She felt a nudge to her side and woke to him hovering over her with his shotgun pointed at her head. Apparently, all he said was, 'I suggest you run now.' I asked the hospital to check for something embedded in her deltoid, and sure enough, they found the tracking device. I suppose that's something. One other thing, he kept her somewhere else before transporting her to the forest. She described it as a cement holding pen, like a bomb shelter or something. But she was a little fuzzy on that because as soon as she drank the water he left for her, she went out again and didn't wake until he jostled her awake in the forest."

"Did she say how long she'd been running before we ran into her?"

Annalise wrinkled her nose. "She wasn't sure, but it felt like forever to her—several hours. She did mention something that was rather strange."

"What?" I asked.

"She said that every so often, he would step from the brush and say, 'Wrong way.' She mentioned it felt like he was herding her in a specific direction."

I nodded. "Can you pull out the map again? The one where you marked the dump locations."

Annalise frowned. "I don't have it anymore. I took it back to the office."

"Do you think you could access Google Earth to create it from memory? We can use my printer and add the markings," I suggested.

Annalise smiled. "I can do better than that. I'll have Leslie send us a pic of the map. Why? What are you thinking?"

"Leslie, huh? She's the data tech that you have wrapped around your pinkie." I laughed. "She has a crush on you just like Reggie. I'll bet she's the data tech you had looking for missing persons with the specific criteria you gave her. Sweet talker."

"Never mind that. You have something rolling around in that big brain of yours. What is it?" she asked.

"It occurred to me that a star or a pentagon has a center. What if this bomb shelter or cell, whatever the hell-demented place he puts them in, is located in a central location to his hunting ground? Find the location and you may be able to catch him unawares."

Annalise grabbed me, pulled me into an embrace, and smacked me on the lips. "Brilliant."

I was too shocked to react, but I couldn't say it was an unpleasant sensation. However, I am nothing if not consistent. The Queen of Denial surfaced quickly, and I blurted, "Do you think we can get some sleep before exploring the forest?"

"Right. It would be better to tackle this after we've rested." Annalise grabbed both of my hands and captured my attention. "I'm sorry I lied to you before. I know a lie of omission and a deliberate redirection are just as bad. Maybe worse. I promise I won't do that again. I don't know what came over me. The only thing I can offer is that I wasn't lying when I told you I was tired of not being normal and how hard it was to exercise patience. The fact that I failed to mention I hadn't waited like you asked was wrong."

"Apology accepted. Considering your inability to practice restraint, I'll only take a nap for a couple of hours, and then we can go on an adventure together."

"Perfect. You know, as soon as we wake, I'm going to want to eat one of your alien fruits and smear the gel over the scar on my face," Annalise declared. "You said it, not me. I have an inability to practice restraint. I believe I went beyond your expectations by waiting as long as I did to heal the scars on my body. Maybe that asshole Gary gave me a gift. A suspension offers a viable explanation for my miracle cure. Breakthrough plastic surgery! I have no qualms about lying to him."

"Incorrigible. You're taking advantage of my exhaustion."

"Damn right I am. It's not too often I have an advantage over your brilliant mind," Annalise stated.

Once we'd retired to our respective rooms, I touched my lips and sighed. *Damn brain chemistry.*

†

The sun streamed irritatingly through my closed blinds, and my eyes blinked open, but not before I heard Annalise stirring in the kitchen. Reluctantly, I tossed aside my covers and stumbled, still half asleep, into the kitchen. Annalise looked like she'd been up for a while. I noted her sweat-soaked workout gear and figured she'd gone for a run.

"Morning, sleepy head," she chirped.

Einstein, relaxing on one of the kitchen stools, blinked his green eyes as if he didn't have a care in the world. I glanced at the clock on the stove. It was just shy of noon.

"Don't you require sleep at all?"

"Stuff to do, people to see, forest to explore," she answered. "But first, I want to see if I can make myself invisible like you. If that's possible, then I could search the forest at the same time our FBI techs are collecting evidence. Even better, I can listen in and ascertain if they've found anything of significance." She bounced on her heels like an excited puppy ready for her walk.

I rubbed my eyes and grumpily stated, "For the record, I haven't exactly agreed to your plan. And I need coffee first."

Annalise poured coffee into a mug, adding creamer in just the right amount, then pushed the cup over as I plopped onto the high-backed chair in front of my breakfast nook. She knew me so well.

"Want me to fix you a bagel?" she asked.

"Sure, why not? I don't suppose I can talk you out of sampling the fruit?" I sipped my coffee and sighed. There was nothing like that first sip of coffee made to perfection.

Annalise shook her head. "I hope the fruit is healthy because that will be my breakfast," she teased as she put the bagel in the toaster.

"Please tell me you aren't planning on scarfing down more than one piece of fruit."

Annalise shrugged. "You said it yourself. Body chemistry is different from one person to the next. I used to be bigger and more muscular than you. It might take more than one piece. Although, I kind of hope I don't get too bulked up or turn green like She-Hulk."

"Hmm." I sipped my coffee. "Veterinarians adjust for weight, and there are vast differences between child and adult dosages, but I doubt thirty pounds makes much of a difference in humans."

"All I know is that I can consume twice as much alcohol as you. Lightweight," she taunted. The bagel popped up and Annalise retrieved the cream cheese from the refrigerator and proceeded to spread it on both sides of the bagel, slapping the two pieces together to form a sandwich. She handed me my bagel.

"You have more practice than I've had. I never quite entered that wild stage in college." I took my first bite. "Thanks, this hits the spot."

"I don't mean to rush you or anything, but daylight's a-wasting."

I was about to argue with Annalise when I finally noticed her face. She'd already gone and applied the gel to her final scar. "Well, far be it from me to keep you from doing exactly what you want, damn the consequences," I sniped. "Clearly, you didn't wait to lather the gel all over your body and face."

She waved her hand in the air. "I did that last night as soon as you toddled off to bed. I already know I don't have any negative side effects after using the gel. The alien fruit is an entirely different breed of cat."

"But it's not a different taxonomic genus."

"Don't be so literal, Tamara. It was just an expression. To be honest, I want you there when I eat the fruit, in case something goes wrong," Annalise sheepishly admitted.

"Now that is the first logical statement you've made all morning. Honestly, I don't know why we're such great friends. You are reckless," I chastised.

"Don't get high and mighty with me, Tamara Childs. I watched you eat that fruit, get all glowy, bulk up, and then disappear. How was that not reckless?"

I wrinkled my nose. "You've made an excellent point. I admit my need for quick answers outweighed any logical thought process. All right." I grabbed the rest of my bagel and coffee and stood. "Go pick a fruit and bring it to the lab. I have something to counteract an allergic reaction if that should occur. However, I insist that we repeat the process I used, by starting in the same manner as my experiment with the fruit. You need to place a small amount on your tongue, and I'll observe your body's reaction before we proceed."

"Works for me," Annalise responded as she bounded off to the backyard.

†

Using one of my sterilized scalpels, I sliced open the fruit that Annalise handed to me. There was a split second of hesitation before Annalise picked up one-half of the fruit. Instead of dipping her finger inside the pulp and putting it on her tongue, she dipped the spoon into the gelatinous liquid and brought it to her mouth, snaking out her tongue to taste the small amount on the spoon.

"It's sweet," she announced.

"Keep your tongue out," I directed.

A very feint purple glow appeared, but Annalise's tongue remained visible.

"Iz muny tongue inbvisibl yet?" she mumbled.

I broke out in a fit of laughter. I couldn't help it.

Pulling her tongue inside, she asked, "Why are you laughing?"

"Sorry, sorry. You sounded funny trying to talk with your tongue out. I only detected a minor change in appearance. How does it feel?"

"I don't feel much of anything. Maybe a slight tingle," Annalise answered.

"Okay, scoop out a small amount. Let's see if we can generate a more robust reaction," I directed.

Annalise followed my suggestion and swallowed a spoonful of fruit. "This is fantastic, you know. I could actually eat this for breakfast," she joked.

The seconds ticked by, and Annalise resembled Einstein on that first night that we noticed his opaque appearance. But she didn't bulk up much, and she certainly did not become invisible. "Let's give it a few minutes."

Annalise looked down at her glowing form and answered, "Okay." I could tell she was disappointed. The emotion surged inside me, and I knew I was picking up on her feelings.

We spent the next hour in the lab, but after consuming three fruits, Annalise merely glowed and became a human hologram—still visible to the naked eye. I knew if I wasn't able to work with Annalise to enable her to control the glow, this would be a far worse outcome, because she couldn't go out in public looking like this. Maybe the light would fade, and she would return to normal like Einstein.

"You have to concentrate, Annalise. Order your body to return to normal."

"I'm trying," she barked.

And then it happened. The glow faded, and everything appeared as before, except her body, which looked even more sculpted than before.

"It worked! I think your spark of anger triggered a response. Um, you may not be able to turn yourself invisible at will, but I suspect you've developed super strength like me. And bonus, I practiced invisibility at will before you returned to the house this morning and can turn it off and on, but my strength remained. Maybe the same will hold true for you."

Annalise grinned. "I'll take it."

"We should test that. Also, we should test your vision."

"You can make yourself invisible on command? That's so cool. Show me."

I proceeded to blink in and out of existence for Annalise like some sort of freak sideshow at a circus. Later, I would learn invisibility was the one power to diminish over time—at least until I had enough of the chemical within my cells to activate its self-generating properties. Just shy of twenty-four hours after ingesting the fruit, I could no longer become invisible. Unfortunately, I would discover this inconvenient fact at a most inopportune moment.

I became worried when Annalise grabbed her chair and wobbled as if she might pass out. She grabbed her ears and closed her eyes. "Too much," she screamed.

"What's happening? Talk to me, Annalise."

"Air. I need air. Help me outside."

She kept her eyes closed, and I guided her to my backyard. She rambled about the sights and sounds overwhelming her. I blamed myself for allowing her to eat so much of the fruit. It seemed her neurons were firing too quickly for her to control.

I spent the next two hours helping Annalise control her new abilities. Then, we moved on to the next phase and began testing her strength, vision, and hearing. Maybe she couldn't make herself invisible like I could, but her hearing and vision far exceeded my capabilities. At first, the flood of sensations nearly incapacitated her until she learned to control them in the same manner that I manipulated my invisibility. Somehow, Annalise could tell if a single leaf had recently been disturbed. She tried to describe what she saw, but since this wasn't a superpower I possessed, it was more difficult for me to understand.

"It's like an echo presenting as a sort of dream. You aren't seeing the leaves or plants move, but I am." She pointed to the large birch tree in my backyard. "A bird landed on the third branch from the top, sat there for maybe ten seconds, then flew to that bush. What I can't tell you is how long ago it happened. You have an awful lot of bees and wasps out here, and their patterns of movement are fascinating. If they're the pollinators, I wonder why they aren't glowing like the flower. They haven't been, have they?"

I shook my head. "Not that I've noticed."

"That's good. I'm glad they aren't. Can you imagine if there were a bunch of glowing wasps and bees lighting up the night like alien fireflies?" Annalise shuddered. "I know I've been given this incredible gift, but I need to block it now. Can we take a break?" she asked.

"Goddess, Annalise, you don't need to ask me that. No more gorging on fruit."

"Give me a few minutes to relax, then I'd love to check out the forest. Maybe I can pick up a trail or something. Find The Hunter's holding pen in the center of that creepy pentagram."

"I don't know if that's such a great idea," I cautioned.

"Why not?"

"Considering you freaked out a few hours ago and can barely control the surrounding stimuli, don't you think this can wait?" I argued.

"No, I don't. Besides, I'm getting pretty good at controlling this." She grinned. "I'm a fast learner. You can come with me. Keep me out of trouble."

I sighed. "You're going to do this whether I like it or not, aren't you?"

"Mmhm. There's a psycho out there. I don't know how long these echoes last. I've got to take advantage before it's too late."

"All right, but I'm driving."

Annalise nodded. "Probably for the best."

# CHAPTER NINE

We reached the edge of the forest closest to the center of the pentagram and found a place to park the SUV where it wouldn't stick out like a sore thumb. We'd passed the section where the FBI techs still swarmed the area. Annalise cocked her head and listened to their chatter. It sounded like they hadn't found much, and that was frustrating to them. Annalise's ability to listen in on their conversations from several miles away was astounding.

She held the portable GPS and, using the coordinates she'd plugged in, began hiking to the approximate center.

"As long as we stay in this vicinity, I won't get in trouble. If they don't see me checking things out, Gary can't yell at me and extend the suspension," Annalise stated as if that was the most reasonable conclusion. "I wish I could get closer. I might be able to see the path he took when he ran away. Considering I know I hit him, I'd probably be able to find some blood."

"I suppose I could hike to that area and check it out, but I'm hesitant to leave you all alone in case you freak out again. My vision isn't as keen as yours, but I can focus enough to spot blood."

"That's a brilliant idea," Annalise exclaimed. She offered me the handheld GPS after changing the coordinates. Pulling evidence bags and an extra set of gloves from her pocket, she handed me the supply.

"You planned this all along," I challenged. "That's why you told me to put on bike shorts with the side pockets."

Annalise smiled. "You might want to remove that oversized T-shirt. You can keep your sports bra on. That fits snugly enough against your body for your invisible woman act to work. I'm fine. I'm getting a lot better at focusing and blocking out any extraneous stimuli. Besides, you'll feel me if I get into any trouble."

"I suppose so," I reluctantly agreed. Glancing at the portable GPS, I shrieked, "It's four miles away."

"Let's hope you have super speed, too. You haven't tested that yet, have you?"

I was never a sports-minded person, but I absolutely hated running. This was the primary reason I never joined Annalise on her long-distance trots around my neighborhood. It was also my flimsy justification for not examining that possibility more closely during the testing phase of my powers.

"No, I haven't," I grumbled.

"What kind of scientist are you?" she teased.

"Apparently, a shitty one," I griped. "You know I hate you right now," I said as I pulled the T-shirt over my head.

Annalise chuckled. "No, you don't. By the way, looking very sexy in that sports bra."

Before Annalise could see me turn bright red, I concentrated on becoming invisible and began my trek, using the portable GPS to guide me. Sure enough, I moved quickly through the forest. Add super speed to my list of powers. Rookie move that I hadn't tested this before now. I should have known based on how quickly I'd reached Annalise after feeling her adrenaline surge.

I slowed my pace, approaching the location where The Hunter had shot me. Almost on reflex, I looked at the exact spot where I'd landed after being shot, and then I saw it. Either my enhanced vision helped me detect the blood-spattered leaves and pine needles, or my blood hadn't remained invisible after all. I couldn't let the FBI find damning proof of my presence in the woods. I quickly gathered the evidence and stuffed it into my pocket, then continued to search the area in case I missed anything.

Every time I looked at the handheld GPS floating in the air, it reminded me I needed to stash the portable GPS in a safe location before I got too close to the swarm of FBI agents. Approximately a quarter mile from the buzz of activity, I slowed and looked around for a place to hide the GPS. I needed a marker I would remember. Narrowing my eyes, I found the perfect spot. A gnarled tree trunk had a distinctive shape that I knew I couldn't miss. Hastily brushing aside dead leaves and needles, I placed the GPS navigator and blood evidence I'd gathered earlier at the tree's base and covered it with the surrounding brush.

As I closed the distance between myself and the techs, I scanned the area, looking for The Hunter's blood. Forget the old saying about the impossibility of finding a needle in a haystack. I chuckled to myself as I thought finding a specific pine needle in a forest was far more challenging—a pine needle with blood, to be exact. It wasn't nearly as easy as locating the blood I'd left behind because I wasn't sure of the precise location of The Hunter when Annalise had shot him. Then there was the possibility that whatever blood I found might be Carmen's.

I was so busy looking for evidence that I hadn't noticed how close I was to the activity, or that I was no longer invisible. My joy at finding the sprinkles of blood had me hyper-focused on collecting the sample and looking for more.

"Tamara?"

I startled when I heard my name and looked up. About fifty yards away, a forensic tech I'd worked with several years ago stood blinking. I looked down at my body and gasped.

"Why are you out here? Is there another body? Nobody told me that," Karen said.

"Um, no, I was out for a run," I meekly answered. It was the first thing that came to mind.

Karen furrowed her brow. "In the forest? Barefoot?"

*Crap.*

Doug, an FBI agent assigned to the task force, clomped into the clearing and scowled. I didn't know him well, but from what Annalise said about him, I felt a sense of panic. He was a first-class asshole who seemed to box Annalise out of nearly every major investigation. The fact that someone had insisted they add Annalise to the task force really chapped his hide.

"Annalise was sidelined, so she sent you, didn't she?" Doug snarled. "You tell her to stay the fuck away from my investigation."

Now he was pissing me off. "Your investigation?" I crossed my arms against my chest, partly as an act of defiance but also as a way to cover up since I felt so exposed. "I wasn't aware this was a solo investigation. Last I heard, there was a task force that Annalise is a part of."

"Not anymore. They suspended her." He pointed at me. "A little underdressed to join the party."

"Not that it's any of your business, but I was out for a run."

"I seriously doubt that. And what's with the sports bra? You honestly want me to buy that you're some kind of elite tri-athlete, training in your sports bra and bike shorts? Way to oversell the ruse, but you forgot your running shoes. I don't believe that foregoing shoes puts you in some kind of stealth mode."

*Well, this intermittent invisibility is rather inconvenient.*

"Go to hell, Doug. I don't need to justify my actions to you or anyone else. Just remember, the next time you want my expertise on a case, it might take longer than expected. It's important to be thorough, you know."

Doug began to laugh. "Not you, doc. You care too much to delay submitting your report."

"Maybe not, but I could insist on presenting my findings to Annalise and only Annalise. Don't test me, Doug. I'm not in the mood," I threatened.

"Just get the hell out of my crime scene before your actions cause more trouble for your precious Annalise. Fucking dykes," he mumbled. "You may be the sweetheart forensic pathologist the FBI exalts for their expertise with skin, but Annalise is nothing special."

I turned away, waving my hand in the air. "See you later, Doug. Good luck finding any usable evidence. Too bad the FBI is too shortsighted to use Annalise. I guess you've forgotten that she was the one who located his next dump site. She saved that woman and could easily help you narrow the search parameters," I called while walking away. "Maybe you don't want to catch him after all," I taunted.

As soon as I'd cleared myself from his line of vision, I sucked in air and calmed my nerves. I concentrated on becoming invisible again, to no avail. *Hmm, maybe there is a time limit on the effects of the fruit.* This was a new wrinkle I hadn't considered. Before I lost my newly discovered super speed, I retrieved the handheld GPS and blood evidence, accessed the coordinates for where Annalise was searching, and hightailed it back to her.

†

I didn't want to startle Annalise, so when I got close to the spot on the tiny screen, I slowed to a fast walk. I was still panting when I reached her. She was crouched over some sort of solid metal door, cleverly hidden in a dense part of the forest.

"I found something!" she exclaimed. "I'm glad you're back. What happened? I felt your momentary panic. I almost went after you, but without the portable GPS, I wasn't sure which way to go. Everything looks so similar. We need a second GPS."

"Apparently, invisibility has an expiration date. And it isn't like the grocery items in a store where they stamp a date, but in reality, you have a lot more time before it goes bad. Your pal, Dougy, read me the riot act."

"Interesting. He's an incompetent dicknob. I hope you held your ground with him. How did you make it there and back so quickly?"

I grinned. "Well, it was kind of hard to do in my sports bra. That was embarrassing. But, fun fact, I have super speed. Fortunately, that hasn't stopped working."

"Good. I was just about to break these padlocks. You take one, and I'll take the other." Annalise yanked on the padlock she was closest to while I donned a pair of gloves, squatted down, and pulled on the other.

"This is going to send him in a tizzy. You know that, right?"

"I'm counting on it." Annalise lifted the heavy steel door and peered inside. "It's an old bomb shelter. Super creepy. There doesn't appear to be too much down there. There are several bottles of water. I'm going down to retrieve them. We can analyze the contents, and maybe we'll get lucky and find a few prints." She handed me her flashlight. "Will you shine this down while I gather the evidence?" Annalise started climbing down the built-in rungs of a makeshift ladder.

"Hey, I forgot to tell you that before I became visible, I found what I hope is The Hunter's blood. It could also be Carmen's, but it wasn't mine because I'd already gathered and removed any evidence of my presence in the forest. I managed to collect it in an evidence bag, shove it in my pocket, and hide it with the portable GPS, before Karen caught me. Then Doug had to swagger over and make his presence known. I know you haven't wanted to give up on this case, but have you thought about how to get this new evidence to your colleagues without compromising the investigation and decreasing our chances of a conviction when we catch this guy?"

Annalise looked up into the flashlight that was revealing an eerie glow on her face. The tiny wrinkle on her forehead appeared. "I haven't gotten that far. You haven't been suspended, so you could collect the evidence and testify honestly."

"I'm their skin expert. That would be atypical."

"You're still part of the forensics team," she argued.

"I think we need to call this in. It's more important for us not to compromise the investigation. I know you don't really care who gets the credit," I reasoned.

"Yeah, I only care about catching this guy. Okay. Damn the consequences. If I lose my job, so be it." Annalise stopped her climb into the black hole, reversing direction as she ascended to the top.

"I'll do it," I blurted. "They pretty much let me do whatever I want because they need my expertise. I won't get in trouble. Go back to the car, and I'll meet you there." I removed the bag of leaves and pine needles with my blood from my bulging pocket and handed it to Annalise. "Take this and stay hidden until I'm finished. Who else is on the task force that you trust more than Doug?"

"Reese. You can call Reese. I trust her. She'll figure I was involved but won't say anything." Annalise reached the top and hopped out.

"You sure? Isn't she still pissed at you?" I asked.

Annalise had been in a relatively short-lived thing with the fellow agent. She wouldn't tell me what had happened exactly between the two, but every time Reese came to our department, she would glare at me.

"She's over it."

"I wouldn't be so sure of that. She obviously hates me, and I believe that's an extension of her unresolved feelings toward you."

Annalise cringed. "Sorry about that. She's still the one I trust most, and she wants to catch this guy as much as I do."

"All right. But if Reese makes a single derogatory comment about you and your possible involvement in this, I'm going to let her have it."

Annalise chuckled. "Oh, so now you're my fierce protector. I think your powers are going to your head," she joked.

Puffing out my chest, I declared, "I held my own with Doug. I think I can handle Reese."

† 

Once Annalise began her trek to the car, I made the call to Reese. To state she was surprised to hear from me was an understatement. But to her credit, she agreed to meet me at the coordinates I provided without alerting the rest of the team.

"Was that Annalise's car I saw partially hidden?" Reese asked.

"Um, yeah. Hers is a better off-road vehicle." Not an outright lie.

Reese narrowed her eyes. "Where is she? Why didn't she call?"

"I'd prefer not to answer that question," I responded. "All you need to know is that this finding results from following a hunch. Take it as a compliment that I called you instead of Dougy."

Reese shook her head. "That buffoon. He couldn't find his ass with both hands." Reese crouched and fingered the broken locks with her gloved hands. "You going to tell me how these locks were broken?"

I shook my head. "Nope."

"Am I going to find either yours or Annalise's fingerprints?" she asked.

I help up my gloved hands. "Negative."

Reese chuckled. "No wonder Annalise is enamored with you." She eyed my sparse clothing, and only then did I remember I hadn't put my oversized T-shirt back on.

Wanting to put her on a fresh track, I reached into the side pocket of my bike shorts and pulled out the evidence bag. "It's slightly smashed but contains the blood-smattered leaves I found close to where your techs are combing the area. It was approximately five hundred feet from most of the activity. There might be more if you widen the search parameters. I'm sure Annalise told you she got a piece of him, but it could also be the surviving victim's blood since she had a pretty deep cut."

Reese nodded and accepted the bag. "How do you know that about our victim? Never mind. I don't want to know." She pointed to the hole. "So, what's down there?"

"Bottles of water. It's possible there's something more, but I suspect you might want to get a tech team to comb every inch of that prison."

"You're sure it's where he keeps his victims until he's ready to hunt them?" she asked.

"I'd bet my house on it," I said more forcefully than intended. "Can I go now?"

Reese smiled. "Yeah, get the hell out of here and tell Annalise I said hello. Oh, and thank her for me, too."

On the way back to the car, I looked for my discarded T-shirt. When I finally found it, I plucked it from the ground and pulled it over my head. Annalise must have heard the crunching of the leaves underneath my not so careful trek to her SUV.

Emerging from the brush, she asked, "How did it go?"

"Reese says hello and thanks," I repeated. "Can I ask you something?"

"Sure."

"Why disturb his lair?"

Annalise chuckled. "You sound like he's Dracula or something. His lair?"

"Well, what else would you call it?" I responded.

"Um, holding pen," she answered.

"Oh, right. That makes sense. Won't breaking the locks change his routine? He won't have a place to take them anymore."

"Exactly. The guy is meticulous and organized. This is the second time his pattern has been disturbed. First, he wasn't able to complete the ritual, and then his next victim escaped. Now, we've disturbed his holding pen. That's got to unsettle him. He'll make more mistakes, and we'll be there when he does."

"Or he'll develop a brand-new pattern, and we'll have to start all over," I countered.

"Nope. Putting the bastard off his game will work to our advantage. We're close. I can feel it," Annalise insisted.

"So, what's your next step?" I asked.

"We need to do some research on his hunting grounds. I want to determine how much of the forest was ever privately owned, and if there is any portion that is still private land.

This guy knows this part of the forest. That isn't a coincidence."

Annalise didn't give herself enough credit. She might not be a science expert, but she had one of the keenest minds I'd ever known. Sometimes, I believed she deliberately underplayed her intelligence.

"You know, if you let your superiors in on your thinking, they'd give you a wide berth to do your thing. Why do you always hold your cards so close to the vest?"

Annalise shrugged. "I guess I'm not a very good team player."

"Or they've vastly underestimated your talents."

## CHAPTER TEN

On the way home, my stomach growled so loudly it sounded like we'd picked up a hitchhiking bear. I stifled a laugh at that visual. I realized we hadn't had dinner yet, and it was late. This quest had become an obsession, tied haphazardly into a messy package with the discovery of the alien seeds. Although I kept referring to the seeds and flowers as alien, I knew I'd probably never receive definitive confirmation of that. But what else could it be? Were we specifically chosen because we could handle the responsibility? It reminded me of the saying, with great power comes great responsibility. Although Voltaire first coined the phrase, Marvel comics popularized it with the Spider-Man comic.

"Feed me, Seymour, feed me," I joked, parroting the line from *Little Shop of Horrors*.

Annalise laughed. "I'm really glad those flowers of yours didn't turn into man-eating plants. What are you in the mood for?"

"Sushi?"

"All right. Call ahead, and hopefully, they'll have it ready when we swing by. Is raw fish good for brain power?"

I laughed. "Why? Have we decided the best way to spend a Saturday night is to engage in a night of mental gymnastics? Never mind, I know the answer. You can't help yourself, can you? Once you start tracking a killer, you don't stop. And yes, fatty fish tops the list of foods that support healthy brain function. However, research suggests that taking a break can help a person focus on a complex problem. It's called an incubation period. I suggest we do that tonight."

"I'm sorry. I'm being a shitty friend, dragging you into all of this. The weekend is the only time you have to recharge, and I'm totally ruining it for you. I've been dominating your free time."

"No more than usual, but I suppose I could use a break from death and dismemberment," I noted.

I could almost feel Annalise quiet herself and attempt to block whatever emotion had surfaced before she answered. "I need a social life. And so do you. I could start dating again and give you the break you so desperately need. You should do the same, Tamara. How long has it been since you've had a proper date?"

A hint of panic emerged from deep within my core. Dating for Annalise was sporadic at best. However, whenever she would jump on the dating bandwagon, she'd practically disappear from my life, or at least it felt like that. None of her relationships, if you could categorize them as that, lasted very long. Reese was her longest at three months. It had been the longest three months of my life. We still spent time together, but it wasn't the same.

"I wasn't saying I need a break from you. Of course, if you want to start dating again, I understand, but I'm not sure dating is my thing. You know that. A release of endorphins can occur without the need to become involved," I reasoned.

Annalise shook her head. "You mean a one-night stand. That doesn't work for me. I want all the messy complications of a real relationship. Love, passion, disagreements, maybe even jealousy, anger and irritation. We aren't robots, Annalise."

"Then why don't your relationships ever last?" The words spilled from my mouth before I had a chance to censor them. The pang I felt was unmistakable. I'd hurt Annalise deeply with my question. It was the last thing I wanted to do. "I'm sorry."

"I think I'll just drop you at home after we pick up dinner and then head back to my place."

"I said I'm sorry." My protest was weak at best, but I didn't know what else to say.

"I know you are. An incubation period is not the worst thing, you know."

†

Over the next week, Annalise and I spoke only once. I tried calling on Sunday, but she didn't return my calls. Forensics is like its own incubator of gossip. By Monday, everyone had learned of Annalise's suspension and kept asking if I knew what happened. The chatter was at nearly frenzied levels with all the evidence collected at the bomb shelter. On Wednesday, Reese called me personally to let me know the evidence had definitively tied many of his victims to the cement prison, but they'd learned nothing more about the killer's identity. The DNA in the blood sample did not match any known person in our databases, nor was it from the surviving victim.

Reese's phone call was a subtle message to relay the information to Annalise. Pride was never something I'd fallen victim to, so the minute I got off the phone with Reese, I called Annalise. It hadn't mattered that she'd ignored my previous attempts to reach out to her.

I listened to Annalise's voice, telling the caller to leave a message. "Hey, I know you're still pissed at me, but I have some news about the case. Call me as soon as you get this message." I pushed the button to end the call and sighed.

A couple of minutes later, my cell rang. I didn't even listen for the second ring before answering. "Annalise?"

"Yeah. I'm not pissed," she blurted. "I told you I just need to incubate a little. Incubation is the process of development. I looked up the definition, and that seemed to fit best. It seems I've been stuck for so long. I need time to think, which I hope will lead to personal development. You've got to give me that time. But that doesn't mean I've let go of this case. Change and growth are slow. I'm still prone to obsession." A sad chuckle escaped. "So, tell me what they've discovered from the evidence we collected and found."

I filled her in on everything I'd heard and what Reese relayed to me. Desperately needing to keep the conversation going, even if it was about the case and nothing personal, I asked, "Have you learned anything about land ownership?"

"Still working on it."

"I miss hanging out," I admitted.

I could almost hear the smile in her voice. "I miss you, too. A little more time. That's all I need."

"Okay. Promise me you'll call if you plan on taking another trek into the forest or decide to follow up on whatever lead you find after researching the land. I'm also learning more about the fruit, and I'd love to tell you all about it. I can't talk to anyone else, and Einstein isn't the best conversationalist."

"I'll call you when I'm ready to talk. By the way, you don't need to worry about the evidence of your presence in the woods. I took care of it." Annalise ended the call, and I felt a wave of despair.

My blood being found in the woods was the least of my concerns. I hadn't even given the evidence bag a second thought after I'd handed it to Annalise.

Fortunately, emotional telepathy appeared to be another side effect that diminished over time. I wasn't receiving any powerful messages from Einstein or Annalise. I theorized this was because neither had continued to consume the fruit or come in contact with the healing properties from the flower petals. Our connection depended on all three of us ingesting the alien fruit or handling the plant.

†

What other choice did I have? I gave Annalise the time she requested. The only thing I could do was immerse myself in work. Without Annalise, I could only continue researching the effects of the alien fruit on my body chemistry.

I kept meticulous notes and found that while the effects diminished over time, to the point of losing my ability to turn myself invisible, my body was developing a sort of reverse tolerance. After two weeks, I'd gained sixty-two additional minutes of invisibility upon demand after consuming one piece of fruit. I thought of the old adage, an apple a day keeps the doctor away. In this case, approximately one alien fruit per day kept my powers at fully functioning levels. By my calculations, I could build up whatever chemical in the fruit allowed me to disappear at will by almost twenty-seven hours every year. That wasn't a lot of additional time. Thus, if I wanted to maintain the physical enhancements to my body, I would need to build a greenhouse and have the fruit available year-round. It was a good thing I wasn't the type of person to tire easily of a particular food. Quite the opposite. I could eat the same thing every day and not at all be bothered by a lack of variety.

It was late Sunday evening, and I was in my lab, analyzing my latest sample of blood, when I heard the key slide into the lock on my front door. *Annalise.* My heart rate increased in anticipation. I waited for her to come to me. She'd said she would call, but this was so much better.

Her tall form appeared in the doorway, and a shy smile formed on her face. She had dark circles under her eyes and seemed almost gaunt, but I was delighted to note that none of her scars had returned. At least the miracle gel from the plant did not require reapplication to continue providing benefits to the skin. That tracked with the powerful self-healing properties of the plants, which did not appear to diminish over time. It was only invisibility, super-strength, enhanced vision and hearing, that seemed to fade, unless I topped myself off, a bit like adding gas to my tank.

"Hi," she whispered as she inched her way closer to me.

I wasn't really a big hugger. In fact, the only person I ever hugged was Annalise. Not even my mother or father received that honor except on special occasions. But today, I had the insane need to touch Annalise. Before I recognized what I was doing, I had moved in her direction. We were inches from one another, and almost as if we were at an impasse, neither one closed the final distance. I had to break the gridlock. Similar to how oxygen is essential to sustain life, I knew if I was going to survive, I needed Annalise in my life.

"Please don't stay away that long ever again. I don't think I'll survive the absence." It was the most honest thing I'd ever said to her. I reached out and pulled her into an embrace. We stayed in one another's arms for much longer than I was usually comfortable with, but it seemed like our connection was far too fragile to interrupt.

Once we broke apart, Annalise remained inches away. We were so close, I almost thought she would kiss me. To my utter surprise, I wanted her to. Instead, she laid her forehead against mine, sighed, then moved away, grabbed my hand, and led me out of the lab. "Let's talk. Really talk. I need to tell you some things."

I blinked. "Okay. You know you can tell me anything."

"Maybe. But given our different perspectives on life, you may not exactly appreciate what I have to share with you."

I let her lead me to the couch in my main living area, and we sat side by side. I wasn't sure why this question popped out. It wasn't like we'd been talking about anything remotely related to what I asked, but it came tumbling out of my mouth without regard to internal analysis.

"Why did you and Reese split up? It seemed like you two were doing really well. Clearly, there was sexual attraction and compatibility. You both had a lot in common. That's good for a potential mate, isn't it?"

Annalise burst out in laughter. "Where did that come from?"

I turned to face Annalise. "She said something to me that I've had a hard time processing. I suspect those endorphins you call love are still very strong within her. I wonder if she believes I was the reason you two are not together anymore."

Annalise wrinkled her nose. "Why would you say that?"

"She mentioned something about you being enamored with me, suggesting that you have feelings for me. I sensed that did not at all please her."

Annalise seemed to squirm a little before answering, "I had hoped to sort of ease into this—"

"Oh, you and Reese are a thing again, and you're trying to find a way to tell me that we can't hang out anymore. Jealousy is a normal emotion for most people."

Annalise pushed her hand through her short hair. "Goddess, you are such an impossible person to say this to."

My brow wrinkled as I responded, "I don't understand."

"Of course you don't. Love isn't in your vocabulary, but it's in mine," Annalise insisted.

"I understand now. Annalise, just because I don't believe in love doesn't mean I want you to give up on your beliefs. You should pursue whatever makes you happy. If you think you love Reese, you should go for it. I'd never stand in the way of your happiness." Even as I said these words, a sourness developed in the pit of my stomach.

Annalise shook her head. "I'm not in love with Reese. We split because I'm in love with *you*. Honestly, she figured it out before I did. What I've been struggling with these past two weeks is how to tell you and then how to proceed.

Eventually, I decided it was better to be candid and see where the chips fell. If friendship is all we'll ever have, I guess I'm good with that. The alternative is much worse."

"I don't know what to say. This is a lot to process. I only know one thing: I can't imagine a satisfying life that doesn't include you in it."

A sad smile formed before Annalise responded, "Me either, Tamara. It might take some time to get back to our normal, but I'm convinced we'll get there."

I didn't enjoy seeing Annalise hurt and maybe a little lost. One thing I was good at was research. There were a lot of unknowns in the universe, and nearly every culture recognized love. Perhaps my view of love wasn't as solid as I thought. Too bad I didn't have access to equipment that would measure the changes in my brain when I thought about Annalise and what it might be like to lose her.

"It seems like I'm the one who may need some time," I answered.

"Okay. Fair enough. I'll leave you to it."

"No, no, I don't mean you should leave. I'd like it if you stayed. I just meant that I need time to do some research on love and process what you've said."

"Of course you do." Annalise chuckled. "In the meantime, how about you take a break, and we do something mind-numbing like binge on old *Star Trek* episodes? Absolutely no talk about alien plants or psycho killers."

"Which *Star Trek*?" I asked.

"Your choice. By the way, I'm guessing you haven't had dinner yet, have you?"

"I'll call in an order. Thai okay?"

"Perfect," she answered with a smile.

"I think I'm in the mood for *Discovery*."

"Okay, I'll cue it up," she answered.

And just like that, we were back to normal, or as normal as we could get after Annalise's declaration. There was plenty of time for me to fill her in on my research and for her to tell me what she'd been up to for the past two weeks.

## CHAPTER ELEVEN

I'd fooled myself into believing the world had righted itself, and Annalise and I had returned to our normal. Instead, we created a new normal. One I didn't particularly care for.

I think she wanted to ease us both into the new normal. Naively believing everything was business as usual, I left work on time, hoping that since Annalise was still on suspension, she would be at my house waiting for me. I wanted to catch up and tell her all about my findings regarding the alien fruit. By silent agreement, we had avoided talking about the missing two weeks and how we'd occupied our time, preferring to drown ourselves in drivel.

However, when I returned and searched the house, starting in the guest room, I found all her extra clothes, electric toothbrush, and other personal items were gone. Over the years, she'd accumulated quite a stash, leaving more and more of herself in my home. It wasn't like we lived together, but for all intents and purposes, Annalise had moved out. It felt dangerously close to a breakup.

Most animals are capable of adapting. Survival of the fittest and all that. And humans are the most adept at adjusting to a changing environment. As if dealing with a festering wound, Annalise had lanced the swollen infection, and feelings oozed out. My feelings. But like an accomplished medical professional, I wiped those away, sanitized and stitched up the wound.

In a panic, I grabbed my cell phone and was about to call Annalise. I needed to know what the hell was going on. Before I pushed the button, my phone rang.

"Hello."

"Dr. Childs? It's Reese."

My heart pounded loudly in my chest. "Is Annalise okay?"

I could hear the confusion in her voice. "Annalise? Yeah, I presume so. Um, we have a new body. This one is different, but we believe it's the Hunter."

"Why?"

"Same spot as where he hunted the woman who got away. You'll see. Can you get here soon and take a look? We'd like your perspective since you've been consulting on the case. Can you find the location, or do you need someone to meet you?"

"No need. I can find it. Just for clarity, you know I'm going to call Annalise and tell her about this," I stated.

"She knows. Annalise was the one who suggested we call you."

"Is she back on the case?" I asked.

"Not officially, no. But Gary knows I've been keeping her up to date. It was only fair after the two of you led us to the most promising evidence we've collected so far on the case. Doug made a big stink about it, but Gary told him to shut the fuck up, or he'd take him off the case."

"Good, I'll be there as soon as I can."

Apparently, the Hunter was as adept at change as we were. We'd taken his holding pen, and instead of putting him off his game, he altered his hunting pattern.

†

I could see the rotating blue and red lights on the line of police vehicles that marked the spot from a distance away even without my enhanced vision. It was still a short trek into the forest where several of the task force, forensic techs, and local police milled about. The flash from a camera recording every detail of the body The Hunter gruesomely had displayed for all to see, quickly brought my eyes to the major attraction.

"Careful where you walk," Reese announced. "We believe we found all the traps, but we can't be a hundred percent sure of that. Unfortunately, it was necessary to set them all off to get a closer look. Weighing the safety of our people against the possible loss of evidence was a call I took personal responsibility for." She glanced over at Doug, piercing him with a warning gaze.

The last thing I needed was a front-seat view of my body's miraculous healing abilities. Scanning the area, I found a large branch, relatively free of leaves. Using it as a sort of cane, much like a blind person, I tapped a path to the body. I'd seen a lot of disgusting things in my time, but this rattled me. It didn't take long for me to declare he had been alive while each trap snapped shut on all four limbs.

I pointed to his left leg. "He stepped in that one first. Fell on the ground. And before he was able to pry it open to free himself, his left hand activated the second trap. I suspect that once The Hunter had incapacitated his victim, he forced activation of two additional traps." Crouching next to the body, I lifted the victim's head to view the wound on his neck. "The cause of death is most likely a clean slice across his throat. Perhaps he wanted to put him out of his misery and couldn't risk attracting attention with a bullet to the head. We'll know more after we transport the body back to the lab. He seems to have evolved again, or he was interrupted. All body parts are intact."

Reese nodded. "Poor bastard didn't stand a chance. There were over fifty traps carefully placed in concentric circles hidden in the brush. It didn't matter which direction he ran. The victim was going to step into one of them. And since The Hunter is known to drug his victims, he was likely still groggy from whatever The Hunter gave him. No missing persons report over the last couple of days, either. As soon as we identify the victim, we'll know more about when he went missing. If he went missing," Reese added.

I nodded. "Why did you call me in? The Hunter didn't skin him this time? I'm sure Dr. Warren could have provided you with the same assessment."

Reese shrugged. "You're more thorough. I'll walk you back to your car after you're done."

Part of me wanted to encourage Annalise and Reese to make another go of it. Reese was intelligent, insightful, and clearly had been interested in Annalise, even before the miracle gel had removed all evidence of scarring. Plus, she was attractive in that conventional manner. Tall, blonde, sky-blue eyes, and full lips. Her facial features came together nicely. She enjoyed sports, including running. They were perfect for one another. But the other part of me, that I was starting to realize existed, desperately wanted Annalise to stay far away from Reese. It was like that part was in some kind of stasis, ready to emerge with only the slightest provocation.

Before I climbed into my car, Reese announced, "I'll send all the photos to your cell phone. If you choose to share them with Annalise, I don't need to know about it. Oh, and one more thing. Dr. Warren is already back at the lab and ready to perform the autopsy. Obviously, he hasn't made an initial determination of the time of death yet. When he completes the autopsy, I'll send you his report. You can head home now."

I didn't know if Annalise was waiting for my call, but that was the first thing I would do when I returned. As it turns out, I didn't have to contact Annalise because she was waiting in my driveway. I felt a pang of sadness that she hadn't used her key and simply gone inside.

†

When we both were inside my house, ignoring the huge elephant in the room, Annalise started right in on the case.

"So, he's escalating and changing his pattern. Leslie would have called me if someone, within the parameters I told her to look for, went missing."

"Didn't Reese already fill you in?" I tried to keep the edge out of my voice, but maybe I hadn't succeeded.

Annalise arched her eyebrow. "Are you angry? I thought you'd want to be involved?"

I wasn't about to pussyfoot around. "Why did you remove your clothes and things from the guest bedroom?"

"Can we talk about that later? There's a serial killer out there, and he's getting bolder. It took time for him to set those traps. A lot of time. Anyone could have seen him."

"I'm aware of that, but no, we cannot talk about that later." This time, I knew my tone was decidedly frosty. As frosty as I ever got. Normally, I was even keeled. It would be hard to detect any emotion from my words or tone of voice.

Annalise sighed, made a beeline to the couch, and sat as if she were about to get blasted with a phaser. Which, if those existed, and I had one in my hand, she would. On the stun setting of course. Still, I was that angry.

"Honestly, I don't want another two weeks with minimal contact again. So, can we talk without saying hurtful things to one another?"

I swallowed the emotion that had unwittingly erupted. On the verge of tears, I choked back my initial response and decided on probably the most honest thing I could ever admit to. "You hurt me."

"How? We aren't together, Tamara. It's not like I'm moving out after a breakup. I've accepted I'll always be in your friend zone, so I figured I needed to start acting like a friend, not a love-sick puppy, pretending that we're the next best thing to living together as a couple."

"We didn't even talk about it. I like that you keep your stuff here, spend the night, and consider this your second home. I don't want that to change. You said we'd get back to our normal, but you yanked the rug out. The bare floor is cold and lonely. It feels awful."

"I can't be your consolation prize or substitute for love. Maybe you don't believe in love, but I do. I get that you need order, and maybe you love me in your own special way, but to me, it isn't a spike in brain chemicals designed to make you feel good."

"Oh." What could I say in response to that? The room closed in on me, and I did the only thing I could do to stifle my burgeoning feelings. I abruptly changed the subject. "I learned a few things about the alien fruit over these past two weeks. It should help if I'm going to go incognito to the suspected location of the Hunter's next kill."

"You will do no such thing," Annalise angrily responded. "We don't even know when he'll strike next. It could be tomorrow or two years from now. The predictive model advantage is gone. He isn't holding them for several days before a hunt anymore. The only pattern he's held onto is killing them the day before their birthdays. We need an algorithm to identify possible victims before he strikes."

"Narrow the parameters," I suggested.

"How?"

"First, confirm where each of his past victims lived. That should give you his geographic hunting ground. Research any other commonalities. Then look at every person who is about to turn thirty-one in the next month."

"That's still likely to be hundreds of possible victims," Annalise lamented.

"It's a start. And if you can narrow the geographic region, that should limit the possibilities. Find another common factor, and maybe you'll get a manageable number."

Annalise nodded. "Are we okay?"

I paused before answering, "Not yet, but I hope we'll get there. Will you help me build a greenhouse?"

Annalise laughed. "Yeah, I've got a lot of time on my hands right now, but where did that come from?"

"If I don't keep eating the alien fruit, I lose my powers. The only silver lining is that the time span is increasing."

"What time span?" she asked.

"I've gained sixty-two additional minutes since I learned the powers fade after approximately twenty-four hours. However, at the rate of 4.43 minutes per day, it will take me almost thirty years to gain enough time to reduce my needed consumption to once per month. I need an ample year-round supply. That's where the greenhouse comes into play. Fortunately, the fruits aren't difficult to grow."

"Well, okay then. Might I suggest purchasing a kit?"

"I already did the research. The materials will be here tomorrow. Will you spend the night and be here tomorrow to accept delivery? I'd originally planned to take the day off, but now that we have a new body, I feel the need to help Dr. Warren. I *am* the skin expert. He may miss something. There are clothes you didn't remove that were part of the laundry. I put them in your drawers. I set out an extra toothbrush in your bathroom."

The hesitation in Annalise's voice was painfully obvious. "Sure. But I can't slip into old habits. This is a one-time thing, Tamara."

"Thank you."

## CHAPTER TWELVE

Annalise was true to her word. She settled into the guest bedroom and even made coffee for me in the morning. However, when I returned home, the large package with the greenhouse materials sat on the right side of the empty garage—the spot where Annalise normally parked her SUV. At least Einstein was happy to see me as he wove in and out of my legs and meowed.

"Yes, I know, Einstein, I miss her too. How about some chicken?"

Hoping to entice Annalise to spend more time with me, I brought home Dr. Warren's preliminary findings, along with my assessment and several notes and photos Reese had forwarded to my personal cell phone. The level of disappointment I felt at not finding Annalise's SUV in its spot was off the charts. The only cause for a glimmer of hope was that the toothbrush remained on the guest bathroom counter, and I found the clothes she wore yesterday in the hamper. I smiled. *Baby steps.*

After feeding Einstein, I picked up my phone and called Annalise. She answered on the second ring, and I blurted, "I have files for you to review. Reese sent me notes and pictures, too. I forgot to tell you that last night."

"Okay, I'll be right over. Leslie's been working on narrowing the parameters, but we need to give her more if we even have a prayer of predicting who his next victim will be. Give me twenty minutes. Have you eaten yet?"

"No. I just got home."

"I'll swing by the deli and pick up something. Turkey sandwich okay with you?"

"Yes, thanks."

While I waited, I tossed her dirty clothes from the hamper into the wash and considered why I was acting so irrationally. Sure, I wasn't comfortable with change, and Annalise had altered the parameters of our relationship, but it was more than that. I started to consider how I might be taking advantage of our friendship. I often missed cues, so I was undoubtedly being insensitive to Annalise's feelings. There was the tiniest possibility I was also not being honest with myself. If I was completely truthful, I was attracted to Annalise. I'd always thought Annalise was pleasing to look at despite her scars. But if I admitted that to Annalise, she might believe it was only because the alien gel had literally rubbed them away.

Whenever I had a complicated problem to work out, I would conduct an experiment to test my hypothesis and come to a conclusion. Annalise would definitely hate how I intended to approach this particular enigma. This needed a two-pronged question. Could Annalise and I enter into a sexual relationship without destroying our fondness for one another? Would sex with Annalise be better than with a relative stranger because I was familiar with her and enjoyed her company?

I wasn't a virgin. I'd had sex before and found it quite enjoyable, a pleasurable way to release endorphins. Normally, I'd wait to seek a willing partner for an evening until Annalise was in one of her short-lived relationships. I'd never told Annalise that was how I occupied my time when she was spending her nights with a temporary girlfriend because I suspected she would disapprove. For reasons beyond my comprehension, I didn't want Annalise to think poorly of me, so I kept this part of my life to myself.

The knock on the door interrupted my thoughts. When I answered, it threw me into what others would describe as an emotional tizzy. Annalise stood on my doorstep, shifting awkwardly on her feet. She'd never knocked on my door before. Annalise had her own key. She could enter whenever she wanted and often did. Thus, my plans to propose a trial were completely derailed. Of course, I hadn't intended to present my aim to look at this scientifically. That would only hurt Annalise, and I recognized that.

Annalise lifted the paper bag in her hand. "I brought dinner. Um, are you going to invite me in?"

"Why did you knock? You never knock," I stated, completely perplexed by this recent development. "You're still my best friend, aren't you?"

Something in my outward expression must have caused Annalise a great deal of pain. Or maybe it was my pain reflected back to me when I felt the warmth of my tears slowly travel down my cheeks.

Annalise dropped the bag and gathered me in her arms as I cried softly against her broad chest. "Oh, Tamara, I don't know what I'm doing. I don't know how to act around you anymore. I can't decide what hurts more, creating distance or pulling you close and never letting go," she confessed.

Separating just enough for me to look her in the eye, I stated, "I vote for the latter. Why can't we just go back to the way things were? Was it so horrible?"

"Horrible, no. Untenable, yes. Don't you know you can't recreate the past? The only logical thing is to move forward, even if that means in an entirely new direction that seems bumpy at first but eventually levels off." She let go of me and stepped inside, closing the door behind her, then slumping against it as if she needed something solid to lean on.

I didn't believe I had a better opportunity to present my plan. I was starting to have hope that all was not lost between Annalise and me. "I have a proposal to help move us forward. I've been thinking we should have sex."

Annalise's eyes widened. "What? No. That's not what I was angling for when I, uh, made my declaration…"

"You confessed to being in love with me, and your notion of love involves a relationship that includes sex. We have a friendship that doesn't include sex, so adding that component meets your requirements. I like sex. Perhaps having sex with you will be better than my past experiences? I'd like to find out if that is an accurate theory. I find you attractive. I always have. You are exactly my type. So, what do you think of my solution to our impasse?" I asked.

Annalise shook her head. "I'm still stuck on past experiences. Since when have you had sex?"

"I am *not* a robot, Annalise. Sex is a basic human need," I argued. "Do you suppose we can finish talking about this in the living room?"

"Okay." Annalise picked up the bag she'd dropped and followed me inside, taking her normal spot on the couch, before continuing. "For as long as I've known you, you've never dated, except that one time with Stacey."

"I suppose that depends on one's definition of a date. Over the course of our friendship, whenever you had a girlfriend, that offered me the opportunity to explore. I'm not saying you ignored me, but you had your date nights, and I had mine. I've preferred sex without strings. But lately, I've wondered if I've been missing out on something."

Annalise tilted her head and stared at me as if I were a strange new being she'd yet to figure out. "Okay, this is news to me. You never said a word. I always told you about my dates. It hardly seems fair for you to have kept this information to yourself. I feel like I don't even know you," Annalise stated with pain in her voice. "What else have you kept from me?"

"Nothing. It hardly seemed important to share. None of my fleeting partners were possible mates, or even persons I wanted to spend additional time with. Honestly, Annalise, lately, I've been so confused. I might be very wrong about love. What I can say with the utmost certainty is that if I ever choose a life partner, it would be you. Despite our differences, we seem compatible. The only area I am not sure about regarding compatibility is sex, which is why I think we should sleep together."

Annalise leaned back and rested her head on the couch before popping back up and turning to look me directly in the eye. "I'm not saying no, but I might need a minute to, oh, I don't know, get my bearings again. You have completely thrown me for a loop. One or both of us could really get hurt. Probably more likely me."

"I don't think that's entirely accurate. I've been very sad these last few weeks. Too bad I don't believe in a higher power, or I would have been praying nonstop for you to stop being angry with me."

"I was never angry with you, Tamara. Goddess, help me, but I'm still madly in love with you—despite the level of aggravation and confusion I sometimes feel whenever I'm inside your orbit. And for the record, I do believe in a higher power, who I've been calling upon quite frequently."

I smiled. "I know you do. One of our many differences. We shouldn't be compatible at all with one another, but we are. My life would be shades of black and white without you in it, and what a pity that would be if my world lacked color."

"Are you turning into a closet romantic?" Annalise teased.

"Maybe that alien fruit has changed more of my chemistry than I thought," I theorized out loud.

"In that case, I'm going to continue sending positive thoughts to the universe because they appear to be working."

"Since I've eaten the fruit, I've had an almost overwhelming need to kiss you, and I believe, based on watching movies and reading those light and fluffy romance novels you gave to me, I've experienced a twinge of jealousy."

Annalise burst out laughing. "Oh, please, tell me the next time you feel jealous. I'd like to mark that down."

"This is all rather disconcerting to me," I confessed with considerable exasperation.

Annalise pulled me into her arms and stroked my back. "I know it is, Tamara. I'm not going anywhere."

"Will you stay the night again? After we look over the files and have dinner," I added. Then, I had an almost crazy notion, but it felt right, so I blurted it out. "Maybe stay with me in my room. I think I would like to snuggle with you. Whenever we do that, I feel comforted."

"I should probably say no, but I won't." Annalise smiled, and I relaxed.

"Can I have my dinner now?"

"Pushy. Yes, as long as you share your notes, files, and pictures while we eat. It *is* why I came over."

†

We had to be missing a critical piece of information that might help us narrow down the potential list of subjects. Annalise kept staring at the photos and notes, believing something would rise to the surface.

Pulling her hand through her short hair, she grumbled. "Argh, this is impossible. There's nothing more here."

I picked up each file and read through the interviews with family members. A distinct pattern began to emerge. Flipping through the pages quickly, I blurted, "They're all locals. Born and raised here. And all of them were outstanding athletes in high school."

"Same high school?" Annalise asked.

"No, but he's picking victims who are a challenge to him. Physically fit, former stars in their respective schools for sports that require strength and stamina."

"That's got to narrow down the potential pool." Annalise glanced at her watch. "Shit. It's too late to phone Leslie tonight. We should call it a night, and I'll ask her to rerun the data. I'm not sure how we'll capture this latest revelation. How do you think he's finding former athletes? Do you think he went to school at the same time as his victims?"

"Not all of them. Maybe the first victim?" I theorized. "He could have been the catalyst. A bully who picked on kids that didn't quite fit in."

"How does killing them one day before their birthdays fit in?" Annalise asked.

I shook my head. "It's hard getting inside the head of a killer. He doesn't want them to reach a milestone. The first victim was forty, right? That's an important birthday. I don't know about you, but the birthdays generally recognized as milestones are sweet sixteen, twenty-one, and forty. Maybe something happened to him at age sixteen or twenty-one. If that's the case, he could be a long way away from stopping."

"But isn't his star almost complete?" Annalise wondered.

"It is, but something tells me he isn't done. He'll start a new pattern for the dumps, which probably won't make sense with only a few data points to look at."

"Fuck. Is this asshole angling for the most prolific serial killer of all time? Any other insights you might have?"

I shrugged. "I already mentioned that removing their heads might show remorse because he didn't want to see them as people. He changed his hunting method, but not the fact that he didn't want to look his victim in the eye. The guy was face down. It's possible someone took him hunting at sixteen or twenty-one, and that left a lasting impression on him."

Annalise grabbed her chin in thought. "Hmm. That's as good a theory as any. It's more than the profilers have come up with. His pattern only changed after we took away his holding pen. The Hunter couldn't very well reduce him to a piece of meat because his hands and feet were in the traps. This is all theory right now until we catch the sick bastard. Do you think he planned his first kill, or was the bomb shelter another adaptation?"

"Good question. We should look over the forensic evidence collected from the shelter. As I recall, that evidence tied many of his victims to the shelter, but not all of them. Want to bet the first guy who was about to turn forty was not included in that list? Look for a connection to that victim," I suggested.

Once again, Annalise failed to maintain her distance in the excitement and grabbed me, smashing her lips against mine. "What would I do without that brilliant mind of yours? Thank you, Tamara."

"Oh, um, you're welcome."

My shell-shocked response must have registered with Annalise, because she quickly apologized. "Fuck, I'm sorry, Tamara. I shouldn't have done that."

It was now or never. I leaned in, stroked the side of Annalise's face, which was now scar-free, and brought my lips to hers slowly, with deliberation. This was not a spontaneous action. I could sense the hesitation as we connected. Still, it didn't take long for Annalise to surrender to the glorious sensation of my lips tentatively exploring, seeking entrance with my tongue. We might not be compatible sexually. I hadn't tested that out yet. But we sure were meant for kissing one another.

I sighed once our lips broke apart. "That was nice. I'd like to do that again."

Annalise chuckled. "Whoa. Slow your roll. You keep saying things like that, and I'm not sure how much self-control I'll have when I hold you tonight. You said snuggle only. Which, for the record, is not a word I would have ever imagined might come out of your mouth."

"I know, right? It's got to be those alien fruits. They're turning me into…I don't know what."

"You're still you. I wouldn't worry too much. Just think of yourself as Tamara Childs version two point oh. I quite like this new version." Annalise grabbed my hand and pulled me to a standing position. "I think it's time we got some sleep."

While Annalise brushed her teeth with the toothbrush she left in the guest bath, I gathered the wet clothes from the washing machine and tossed them into the dryer, adding the lavender dryer sheets she loved. I wanted her to have fresh clothes to change into, even if they were the clothes she wore only two days ago. Then, I completed my nightly ritual before climbing into bed. Annalise initially appeared shy as she approached the bed with what I could only perceive as trepidation. However, as soon as she slipped underneath the covers, her arms wrapped around my body, offering me a cocoon of comfort. It didn't take long for me to fall asleep.

## CHAPTER THIRTEEN

---

Unless I'd pulled an all-nighter, it never mattered how late I remained awake. After so many years, my body taught me to wake before six. When my eyes opened, I registered Annalise's long arm draped over my stomach as she spooned against me. I felt her soft breath against my neck. Not wanting to wake her, I lay there for several minutes, enjoying the closeness of another person in my bed, wrapped around me like a piece of bacon on a scallop. All the previous times I had sex with another person I'd never fallen asleep with them. Not that Annalise and I had been intimate, except for the kiss I had initiated.

Sometime during the night, Einstein had found a corner at the end of the bed, and I wondered if he'd slept with Annalise whenever she stayed in the guest bedroom. Probably. He looked quite content sleeping inches away from Annalise's feet.

I tried to move Annalise's arm without disturbing her, but that failed. As soon as we separated, her eyes opened, and she murmured, "Morning." She sat up and propped herself against the headboard. "Just give me a few minutes to wake up, and I'll make coffee. Want me to pop a bagel in the toaster for you?"

I smiled. It was so like Annalise to take charge and care for me. She didn't even give it a second thought. No matter what happened between us, Annalise's first instinct was to care for me. I suspected she would make dinner for me every night if she'd been a better cook. Instead, we often relied on takeout.

Einstein's eyes blinked open, and he crawled next to Annalise. As if this was their morning ritual, she began to rub his ears.

"Thanks. Um, will you be here when I get home tonight?" I tossed off the covers and slipped my feet into the slippers next to my bed.

Annalise offered a gentle smile. "I will. Maybe Leslie will have done her thing and given me a reasonable number of possible victims to follow up on."

Opening my closet, I pulled out a dress shirt and pair of pants, laying them on the bed, while I continued to talk to Annalise about the case. "Don't you think we should loop Reese in now? Let the task force handle it. They have the resources to follow up. Have you forgotten you're still on suspension? If Gary finds out you're working on the case without authorization, you could lose your job."

"Don't care. It's more important to catch this guy before he strikes again. But I do trust Reese, so I suppose we could bring her up to speed on your theories," Annalise conceded, and gave Einstein one more pat before finally emerging from the bed.

"Reese has been remarkably cooperative. She still cares for you. I don't know how I feel about that." I frowned as I retrieved my pantyhose and bra from the dresser drawer.

Annalise laughed. "I really am liking the new Tamara. It's called jealousy. I know that is foreign to you, but trust me, that's how you're feeling." She leaned against the wall and smirked.

"You can't possibly know that," I argued. "If you want clean clothes to change into, yours are in the dryer from the other night when you stayed to help out with the greenhouse delivery."

Annalise pointed at my face. "My gut never lies. It's all in the non-verbals, darling. A person's face doesn't exactly turn green, but there are telltale signs, like that pinched look you got when you noted what you perceived as Reese still having feelings for me. I could argue the same thing, that you couldn't possibly know that."

"Ha. Exactly! What you've often described as a gut feeling is actually a finely tuned ability to pick up on micro-expressions and other clues obtained through your five senses. Research suggests that some individuals are better at this than others," I concluded before stomping into the master bath and shutting the door, effectively ending our familiar debate.

†

I barely got inside my house that evening when Annalise approached.

"Finally, you're home. Something's been bothering me about this case."

"Okay." I walked into the kitchen and followed my daily ritual, placing my keys in the space in my junk drawer where they belonged, then setting my bag on the counter.

Annalise followed me to the kitchen and leaned against the counter. "How has he managed to incapacitate all of his victims without a single person seeing anything?"

"Well, these aren't exactly random targets, so it can't be a crime of opportunity," I explained. "He stalks them, learns their patterns ahead of time, and finds the right moment to drug them. Until recently, he had the luxury of nabbing them several days before he set up the hunt. We've interrupted that, so he has to really track their habits now."

"That's what I thought, too," Annalise answered excitedly. "In fact, I believe he might have every single one of his victims pre-selected, and he's been tracking all of them for a long time. That's a lot of victims to keep track of."

"Can you give me a minute to change?" I walked into my bedroom so I could get into more comfortable clothes.

"Sure, sure, sorry. I was just excited to bounce ideas off your big brain."

She followed me into my bedroom. I didn't have a single thought about removing my work clothes, pantyhose, and bra before grabbing a T-shirt and shorts to change into. We'd seen each other naked thousands of times before and thought nothing of it.

"Do you think he has help?" I asked.

Annalise coughed and turned away, but not before I caught a flush to her face. Apparently, now that she had confessed her feelings, the entire ball game had changed. She managed to croak out a response while keeping her face pointed in the opposite direction.

"There's no indication of a second killer. Some of them may have made it easier on him. I hate this trend that you have to post every second of your day on social media. It makes it so much easier on criminals," she grumbled. "They've all been popular former athletes. I should ask Leslie to comb their social media pages. Find out which of his past victims felt the need to share everything."

Tossing my work clothes into the hamper, I stepped into the shorts and quickly pulled the T-shirt over my head. "Has my semi-nakedness bothered you?" I teased.

"I didn't trust myself not to stare, lest you get the wrong idea," she answered, gaining some of her usual mischievousness.

I chuckled. "Oh, I don't know, maybe it would be the right idea," I bantered, then took a step closer.

"The new you *is* going to be the death of me. I'm not sure if I can devote the energy needed to whatever this is," she waved her hand between us, "and catching a deranged killer."

I smiled. "Whatever you say. You may want to concentrate on potential victims. If Leslie has limited time, especially since she's doing a favor for you, that might be a better use of her time. Don't forget to loop Reese in on this," I reminded. "I think the potential victims have a right to know if some maniac is stalking them."

"Can we finish talking about this in the living room?" she asked.

"Bedroom making you uncomfortable?" I teased.

"Yes, yes, it is." She scurried from the bedroom, and I followed.

Taking a seat on the couch, Annalise continued. "I agree they should get a warning. Reese has the list that Leslie prepared for us. Doug, of course, is skeptical. And he's convinced the rest of the team it's a waste of time. He argued that because the victims didn't attend the same high school, we'd be going down a rabbit hole that would take us on the wrong path and expend valuable resources needed to catch the guy. Plus, approaching anyone on the list might unnecessarily scare them and cause bad press if any of this leaked to the public. That's all Gary needed to hear. He's so afraid of how we're being perceived. The coverage on this has been brutal."

"So, what do you want to do? Every night he doesn't strike is a gift, but that won't last forever."

"My gut is leading me to one guy on the list. His birthday is the closest date. I did my own research, and he's a bit of a douche. Still very fit. In fact, the guy practically lives at the gym when he isn't making house calls. He's a personal trainer. I'm pretty sure he's sleeping with a different woman every night. Reese offered to help by joining a stakeout, but she has limited time. I thought we might tail this guy tonight. Leslie got hold of his schedule. First up is a famous YouTuber, named Gemma. He has his weekly appointment with her tonight."

"Why can't I do the stakeout with you? I'd be an incredible asset. With my ability to turn invisible, he'd never see me," I insisted. "I could even follow him inside and provide some level of protection. You never know. Maybe the guy is so sneaky that he breaks into their homes and waits for them. You can't rule that out."

Annalise laughed. "You just don't want Reese and I to do a stakeout together."

"No, that's not it," I argued. "I'm only thinking logically. I could take a leave of absence for unspecified personal reasons and work with you until this guy is caught. Come on. You have to admit that makes perfect sense. We'd make a great team. You could eat some more fruit and bulk up like you're on steroids without the nasty side effects. There's only one thing we need to decide."

"What's that?" Annalise shot me a curious look.

"Who will be the main superhero, and who is the sidekick?" I asked.

"You'll be the sidekick, of course. I'm the law enforcement professional here. Plus, I'm taller and bigger than you."

"Since when have law enforcement professionals been superheroes? As I recall, there are a fair number of scientists, nerds, and rich folks. No FBI agents. The Flash was a scientist in the Criminal and Forensic Science Division, and Dick Grayson was a cop. Flash was no sidekick, but Robin was. I rest my case."

"This is a ridiculous debate while a serial killer is still on the loose," Annalise deflected.

"So does that mean I can join you in your stakeout?"

"Sure, why not? I'll call Reese to ask her to do more work on the other potential victims."

Before we left for the stakeout, I made a call to my supervisor. She wasn't the kind of person to push for details, so that definitely worked in my favor. I can't say she was pleased with my request, but she knew it was a choice between letting me have the time or losing me altogether. She wisely chose the former. It wasn't arrogance on my part to recognize I was the best in my specialty. It was merely a well-established fact.

†

Annalise scanned the area, looking for a place to park that would be inconspicuous. I didn't believe we'd find anywhere that wouldn't shine a neon light on us after five minutes.

"Fancy neighborhood. I don't think your SUV is going to blend in," I remarked. "It would be ironic if someone called the cops on us."

"Shit, you're right. Who knew that YouTubers hawking different shades of lipstick made this much money? Gemma is really making bank off her videos. Ideas?"

"Sorry, fresh out," I answered. "Even if we had a dog to walk, which we don't, I don't believe that would provide adequate cover. We'd still have to park the SUV somewhere visible. Wait. How about you go to that park a couple of miles away? I'll make myself invisible and check things out. Hopefully, I'll be able to determine his next stop, then I'll come get you."

"I'm not sure I like that plan. We were supposed to be on this stakeout together," Annalise practically whined.

I chuckled. "Aw, come on, be a good sidekick," I teased.

Annalise scowled. "I really wish my body chemistry was different. A human glow stick is not at all impressive. At least I have super strength."

"And other sensory enhancements. Don't forget those bonus side effects," I added before concentrating enough to turn invisible. I'd already removed all of my jewelry and anything else that would bring attention to me. Unfortunately, an earpiece to remain in communication was out. No matter how tiny it might be, something floating in the air was bound to draw attention. Emotional telepathy wasn't as good as the ability to communicate in words and sentences.

"That's still so freaky," Annalise noted when the car door opened, even though she couldn't see me. "Be careful."

"Don't be a worrywart. You'll feel me if something goes wrong."

I was going to have to get used to going barefoot. Although the pavement was relatively smooth, I felt a small pebble grind into the bottom of my foot occasionally. At least it wasn't as rough as the forest floor with all the needles and stickers. The discomfort never lasted long, though. Even if whatever I stepped on broke the skin, my self-healing would kick in quickly.

After checking the windows facing the street, I made my way to the back of the property, listening intently. I estimated the property sat on at least three acres and backed up against the forest. While concentrating on the music, laughter, and subdued voices inside the house, I almost missed the slight disturbance in the copse of trees. Out of the corner of my eye, I saw the outline of a man crouching in the brush. I could just make out his binoculars.

The sliding glass doors opened. A man and woman stepped outside and followed a path to the hot tub, carrying a bottle and two glasses. At this point, I noticed the hot tub cover carefully propped against one side, and I could hear the jets bubbling away. Not that the woman's property was a voyeur's dream, but carefully placed trees and bushes surrounding three sides nearly gave the hot tub a wall of privacy.

Giggling, the woman dropped her robe and stepped into the bubbling water, beckoning the man, who disrobed quickly after setting the bottle and glasses on a small table beside the tub. My focus turned to the man several hundred yards away as he silently moved toward the hot tub. He was still a fair distance from the couple. I had a decision to make. Should I try to take him out, and then call for reinforcements? Or interrupt him and then find a way to follow? If I took him out, how would I explain that? Maybe it wasn't the best decision, but I ran toward the couple and didn't bother keeping quiet. Disturbing as many trees and bushes as I could, I focused my attention on the area surrounding the hot tub. It worked like a charm. Startled by the disruption, the couple broke apart from their amorous embrace. The man squinted in the dark, looking for the source. He stood quickly and hopped out of the tub, grabbing his robe.

"Someone's out here. I'm going to catch the little bastard. Call 911. That'll be the last time someone thinks they can stalk you and get a picture," the man shouted.

I continued to make a racket as I moved toward the man crouched beside a large tree. I assume he decided to cut his losses as he moved quickly but silently away from the man who had now become the hunter versus the prey.

It was possible the man was some slimebag paparazzi, but I wasn't willing to take the chance. Once he reached the forest, he tossed aside the branches hiding his ATV and hopped on board, quickly starting the engine. I had another decision to make. I could try to climb on the back, use my super speed to follow him, or memorize the tag and have Annalise or Reese follow up.

Feeling a surge of emotion, I thought of Annalise and how pissed she would be if I jumped onto the back of the ATV with nothing to hold on to and then fell off or tried to follow without her backup. My adrenaline surge, or whatever spike of emotions I was emitting, had reached Annalise. It was like a boomerang blast of panics—so much for the benefits of emotional telepathy. We really needed to get a handle on this particular superpower. So, I opted for the third option, saving the fight for another day.

I kept repeating the numbers and letters on the tag until I felt like I had seared them into my memory. I imagined a humorous visual of the tag tattooed on my brain, and the only way to retrieve the evidence was with an autopsy. Forensic humor, I suppose.

Shaking those thoughts away, I watched the stalker peel out. The man in the robe was still a fair distance away. I heard him curse loudly.

"Fucking leeches."

This time, I made my way back to the road quietly and used my super speed to reach the park in record time. I startled Annalise when I slipped inside before concentrating on turning visible again, then shouted, "Go, go, we need to leave right now." Opening the glove compartment, I searched for a pen and any scrap of paper.

"What the hell, Tamara?" Annalise replied while peeling out.

"Shush. I need to write down the tag before I forget."

"The tag?" Annalise asked.

"Yeah, to the ATV," I answered.

"Um, I'm going to need a little more information than that. What happened? I felt a surge of something."

I heard a siren in the distance and waved my hand in the air to shut her up. I couldn't risk any distraction until I wrote down the tag. Finally, I found a pen and grabbed her discovery pass. I didn't have time to do a thorough search for a blank piece of paper. After I scribbled the tag number on her discovery parking permit, I explained.

"I don't know if the guy who took off on the ATV was The Hunter or an opportunistic paparazzi. It kind of sounded like Gemma might have enough of a following to make her a celebrity worthy of compromising pictures." I lifted the discovery pass in the air. "Reese can run a check on this, and we can learn more about our mystery guy."

"Or I can have Leslie run a check," Annalise countered. "A warrant for DNA or his home might be difficult to obtain without evidence. Judges can be a bit persnickety about a possible violation of rights. I'm not sure how I'll explain how you happened upon this tag. It might be a dead end if the guy is a slimy paparazzi. I could teach you how to pick a lock so you can sneak into his home."

"I'm always up for learning new skills. Good plan, sidekick."

Annalise growled. "Quit referring to me as your sidekick."

## CHAPTER FOURTEEN

On the way back to my place, Annalise's cell phone rang. Reese's name flashed on the screen of her car, and Annalise gave me the side eye.

"Answer it," I directed.

Annalise pushed the button on the steering wheel to accept the call. "What's up, Reese?"

"Please tell me you weren't poking around in that dipshit Gemma's backyard because Bryce Hardgrove is playing hide the salami with her."

"Nope, not me. Why?" Annalise adopted her most innocent tone.

"What did you do? I know Leslie's been doing some work for you," Reese challenged. "She gave me the list of names. Bryce's birthday is a couple of days away. They called the cops, thinking there was a stalker. I can't protect you if you're trespassing on someone's property. Do you want to lose your job?" Reese sounded exasperated.

"I swear to you. I wasn't trespassing." Annalise winked at me. "I'll admit I had an inkling The Hunter's next victim would be Bryce and might have been on a stake-out, which is completely legit," Annalise quickly added. "It's a free country. Whatever I choose to do with my free time while on suspension is my business. Bryce Hardgrove might be a douche of epic proportions, but he doesn't deserve whatever The Hunter has planned for him. I'm not saying I was on the property, but I have solid information suggesting it's highly likely The Hunter was there. You need to convince the higher-ups to provide Bryce with a protection detail until his birthday. That will at least take him out of play."

"Anything else you'd like to share with me?" Reese asked. "Or maybe you'd like to add your two cents, Tamara."

I placed my hand over my mouth to keep from laughing too loudly and whispered, "Busted. Um, no, nothing to add."

"Just promise me that when you have something important to share, you'll call," Reese pleaded.

"You'll be the first to know," Annalise assured her. "Get that protection detail in place, or you *will* have another body to deal with. I'll be in touch."

"Wait. I heard Tamara took a personal leave. Everything okay?" It warmed my heart to hear genuine concern in Reese's voice. Jealousy set aside, I was starting to admire this woman.

"Wow! The grapevine works quickly," I noted. "I'm fine. Thank you for asking. I'd rather not go into detail with someone I don't know very well. Even I recognize that sharing personal details of one's life with an acquaintance doesn't follow social convention."

"Just be careful. I suspect you're helping Annalise. I'd hate for us to lose a top-notch forensic scientist. You watch your step, too, Annalise," she cautioned.

"Thanks, Reese. I'll call when I have something for you to follow up on. I don't need or want the recognition. The accolades can go to you. It's just important that we catch this guy before he strikes again." Annalise ended the call and briefly turned to me. "I think there's a piece of information you failed to share with me. Did Bryce call the police?"

I shook my head. "No, he directed Gemma to make the call. That's why I told you we needed to leave quickly. I didn't think it would be a good look if they found you anywhere near Gemma's house."

Annalise sighed. "I suppose that isn't the worst thing to happen tonight. Why did they call the police, anyway? Despite us forcing him to adopt new patterns, The Hunter doesn't strike me as someone careless or sloppy. How did they even know he was there?"

"I might have made enough noise to alert them. On purpose," I amended.

"Why?"

"I had to make a split-second decision. I believed the better option was to rattle Bryce, disrupt the intruder's plans and then follow him. Since I was the more prudent choice to trespass, coming up with a reasonable explanation for what I was doing on private property after taking him out seemed an additional complication."

"Okay. That makes sense. Once we have the owner of the ATV, we'll know more. My gut says he's not paparazzi."

"Are you going to call Leslie tonight?" I asked.

"No. I'm going to let things settle a little. I'll call first thing tomorrow morning. I don't know how I'm going to keep Leslie from sharing the information with Reese, though. If the FBI pays the owner a visit and starts asking questions, that will spook him. My gut says that'll just make our killer run. Retreat to deep underground. I think he has survival training, or at the very least, can get lost in the woods. When confronting him, we better be prepared to arrest him, not go on a fishing expedition."

"Let's hope the guy works the day shift, so I can snoop around while he's at work. All I need is an address," I stated. "Should we swing by your place so you can pick up a change of clothes?"

Annalise chuckled. "And why do I need a change of clothes?"

"We've got to put a plan in place tonight. I suspect anything I find won't be admissible in court, considering I will have obtained evidence illegally. It could take well into the evening to devise a viable plan for how to get the FBI involved without spooking The Hunter or getting you into more trouble than you already are."

"I'm never going to win an argument with you, am I?"

"Nope, but I still think of you as my trusty sidekick. If you lose your job, we can start our own business. You know, be like Queen Latifah in *The Equalizer*. We love that show. I'll be Robin, Reese can be our Dante. You can be Melodie, and Leslie can be the female version of Harry. But in our version, Dante and Robin don't fall in love. And Harry and Melodie aren't married." I left the rest unspoken, but I hoped the implication was clear.

Annalise laughed. "That's the craziest thing I've ever heard come out of your mouth."

"Is it, though? A superhero crime-fighting team!" I exclaimed. "If we were a television show, I'd watch it. We're simply improving on the existing *Equalizer* series by adding the superhero element."

"Don't be too hasty. We haven't even solved our first case yet."

"Oh, ye of little faith. We will. You have your gut to guide you. I have facts and confidence."

†

I thought I might get more pushback from Annalise on spending her third night in a row at my house, but apparently, I was learning the art of persuasion. Or maybe I was evolving in ways that allowed a slow and steady progress toward something I hadn't seriously considered before Annalise's brave confession. It didn't really matter why. I was just delighted that the awkwardness seemed to dissipate with every hour we worked together to catch The Hunter.

We were close. Both of us could feel it. Once we obtained the address, the rest would fall into place. Looking at the situation from every possible angle, we landed on a plan. It was simple, really. Using the anonymous hotline, we would feed Reese all the information we learned.

By silent agreement, Annalise followed me into my bedroom without me having to repeat my embarrassing request. I folded myself into her arms like it was a normal occurrence, and we did this every night.

"Big day tomorrow." She kissed my forehead. "Get some sleep."

"Do you think we'll ever have sex?" I blurted as I turned to face her. "You stated you needed a minute to get your bearings. I know that's just an expression, but it's been over twenty-four hours."

"Um, well, we've been a little busy, you know. Tracking a serial killer and all," she answered.

"So, you haven't thought at all about having sex?"

Annalise sighed. "That's not exactly what I was saying. Can we talk about this after we catch the bad guy?"

"For someone who is supposed to be in touch with their emotions, you sure have a hard time expressing them," I stated.

"Excuse me? Sex is not an emotion. Yes, I believe making love is inextricably tied to emotion, but…"

"Maybe you're just a prude," I concluded. "I already admitted to my willingness to concede that sex combined with a fondness for a person makes sense. That's why I asked if you'd thought more about us having sex. You keep dodging the question. So, the only logical conclusion is that you're overly concerned with propriety or decorum. I know a lot of women who talk about sex with their friends. Why haven't we ever done that?"

Annalise propped herself against the headboard and sighed. "All right. Cards on the table. I think about making love with you all the time. Sleeping beside you has tested every ounce of willpower I possess. Happy now?"

"I'd be happier if we were having sex."

"Then what? Experiment concluded. You'll jot down your findings in your little book and present them to whom? Is the scientific community just dying to read all about it? After, we'll go back to being good friends without the benefits. No harm, no foul," Annalise spat out through gritted teeth.

"You're angry. Even without our emotional connection, I'd know that. You always grind your teeth when you're mad. Why are you mad? All these emotions are so hard to understand. I don't think we'd go back to being just friends. Would you want that? Because I sure wouldn't. Annalise, I've been trying to tell you how I feel, but I don't know how. I thought maybe I could show you if we had sex."

Annalise smashed her lips against mine. I suppose this is what a person might refer to as a passionate kiss. Surprised by her action, it took me a beat to respond, but then I was all in. I could honestly say this was the second-best kiss of my life. The first was when I had surprised Annalise and kissed her. I wondered if that meant that I preferred being in control.

Soon, Annalise was lifting my sleep shirt over my head. She kissed my neck and made her way to my breasts, licking and sucking. Pausing, she asked, "This okay?"

"Mmhm," I answered as my body lifted, meeting the movement of her hips against mine. The rocking motion generated a very pleasurable feeling whenever she connected with my core, but it wasn't enough. I either wanted to feel her skin against mine, or some other direct touch. I didn't really have a preference—fingers, tongue, bare pubis, or toy against my clit—any of those options would do.

As if I had spoken the words out loud, Annalise stopped the worship of my breasts and her grinding to remove her shirt. The removal of her briefs and my shorts quickly followed. Our combined excitement seemed to bounce around like inside an echo chamber, gathering speed and velocity. Our emotions were feeding off one another, almost as if we were in a frenzy. For a split second, I wondered how safe this was and worked to slow the pace.

"I think we need to calm ourselves before the intensity causes harm."

"Oh, shit. Have I hurt you?"

I chuckled. "No, no, far from it. It's just this effect from the fruit is untested. Not that I want to reduce this wonderful feeling to an experiment. Slow is good, too."

Annalise grinned. "Yes, slow is good. Some of my best orgasms are after a whole lot of teasing. See, I'm not a prude. I can talk about sex without withering away with embarrassment."

Annalise straddled me, and this time, when our lips met, the kiss was slow. Languorous. She took her time to explore my lips, mapping every contour of my mouth, both inside and out. Right then and there, I decided that this was another area in which we were perfectly compatible. Kissing Annalise was fast turning into my favorite thing to do. I tried not to wonder too much about how Annalise came to be such a skilled lover. Her long, slender fingers found their way to where I needed the physical connection to complement the emotional one that felt like a pulsating organism taking on a life of its own.

Through what was probably unattractive panting, I finally cried out after she brought me to the edge and kept me there for what felt like an eternity. Instead of listening for her release, I felt it. A simultaneous orgasm wasn't something I had ever experienced before. I wasn't sure if this was because we were perfectly attuned to one another's body, or if Annalise was skilled and experienced in the art of lovemaking. Neither of us had directed the other in any way. No actual words were spoken until I said her name at the height of the most powerful orgasm of my life.

"We climaxed together," I said in awe.

Annalise continued to caress me, allowing my body to relax and enjoy the aftermath of our experience. "Yes, we did. You may not be able to recognize it yet, but that's the result of two people in love coming together for the first time. I'm enjoying the hell out of what the alien fruit has done. I love you. And now I know you love me too."

Annalise made the declaration with such confidence that it was hard to dispute her claim. I didn't say anything. I professed zero assertions of love, but I did tighten my hold and smiled, feeling a kind of bliss that was foreign to me. If this was love, I was all for it.

"Best sleep aid on the market," Annalise teased. She kissed my forehead again and repeated, "Get some sleep."

I remained tangled in her embrace as my eyes closed, and I succumbed to a deep and restful sleep.

## CHAPTER FIFTEEN

I woke to the heavenly smell of coffee. Glancing at the clock, I couldn't believe I had slept so late. It was nearly seven. I jumped from the bed and threw on the clothes I'd tossed over the side.

Annalise was at the stove, flipping over a pancake. I smiled because I remembered when she had insisted I purchase the Snoqualmie Falls pancake mix because she'd argued it was the best mix in the world. Her mother used to make pancakes, and it was the one meal Annalise made with precision. We often had pancakes for breakfast on the weekends.

Once I settled on the stool, Annalise turned around and said, "Morning, sleepyhead. I was going to bring breakfast to you, but it seems I didn't get the chance to surprise you."

"The coffee woke me up."

"Have you called Leslie?" I wasn't ready to talk about the previous evening just yet. Discussing the case put us on safe ground.

"No, I thought I'd give her a break. I'll call around eight." Annalise pivoted, removed the last pancake from the grill, and added it to an empty plate with one of the alien fruits split in half. She opened the oven, pulled out the stack she had warming inside, and added two more pancakes to the plate. Pushing the plate in front of me, she directed, "Eat, while they're still hot. I figured you needed to top off, so I picked an alien fruit for you." The bottle of syrup and butter were already on the counter, along with eating utensils.

"Thanks. Yes, I was planning on eating a piece of alien fruit. I've gotten in the habit of having one each morning. Mmm, the pancakes look great as always. I can never seem to get that perfect golden hue. Mine are either undercooked or burned beyond salvation. Aren't you going to have some?"

"Yup. Let me bring you your coffee first." After Annalise prepared my coffee, she set it next to me and grabbed her cup that sat next to the stove. I guessed she'd already consumed at least half a cup while cooking. Before she joined me at the counter, she leaned over and kissed my cheek. "Thank you for last night. I don't know where we go from here, but I'll always treasure that moment with you."

I guessed we were going to talk about it. Whether I was ready to or not. "Annalise," I began.

"Don't worry. I'm not going to force you to have a lengthy discussion on how you're feeling right at this moment. I know you need time to absorb everything."

I smiled. She knew me so well. But the one thing I could give her was an assurance that it meant as much to me as it did to her, no matter how confused I still felt regarding the depth of my feelings for Annalise and how that had evolved. Evolution was good, wasn't it? A species only survived as a result of evolution. Everyone needed to adapt and grow as a result of a changing environment. Relationships couldn't be too different from that.

"I want you to know that last night meant as much to me as it did to you. The only way I can engage in a robust discussion about last night will undoubtedly come across as far too scientific and clinical for you. So, I recognize the necessity of not traveling that dangerous road."

Annalise chuckled. "Yes, let's not do that. Besides, actions speak louder than words. Rightio." She cleared her throat. "I wanted to make sure you were properly fueled. When we get the information we need from Leslie, we'll need to jump into a different kind of action. Hopefully, whoever owns that ATV is working, and we can check out where he lives."

†

After breakfast, Annalise decided it was time to call Leslie before she got busy with requests from other agents, including those on the task force. I listened as Annalise spoke with Leslie who must have told her to stay on the line since tracking an address and gathering preliminary information on the person tied to the tag would be a quick search.

Annalise frowned as she listened to Leslie. "You sure?" She pressed the button activating the phone's speaker so I could hear what Leslie was saying.

"Yeah. Jacob Tompkins died this past year in a freak accident. He wasn't exactly old, but he wasn't young, either," Leslie said. "Certainly a lot older than the profile for The Hunter."

"Hmm. What did it say in his obituary?" Annalise asked.

"He didn't have one. Do you want me to do some more digging?" Leslie asked.

"Yes, please. I'd like to know if he's survived by anyone. Wife? Kids? Also, send me whatever you can dig up regarding his accident. I'd still like his last known address."

"You're going to loop Reese in at some point, right?"

"Yeah, yeah, as soon as I have anything worth following up on," Annalise assured her. "You are the best Leslie. I owe you."

"You've been saying that for years, but I never seem to reap the benefits. One of these days, you're going to get me in hot water with you know who. Then where will we be? Although, it wouldn't be the worst thing to happen. I'll finally be away from a job that causes frequent nightmares. I swear Doug gets some kind of perverse pleasure in showing me crime scene photos. Like I really need to see that shit to do my job. For the record, I don't." Leslie ended her rant.

"That's why I'm your favorite. I'm very careful with the information I give to you. I know how it affects you delicate sorts."

"Do not call me a delicate sort for wanting to avoid pictorial evidence of how depraved a person can become. Most normal people would react in the same manner," Leslie countered. "When they reinstate you, I better find a dutch apple pie from my favorite bakery sitting on my desk."

"Done. I'll buy out the entire bakery if it keeps me in your good graces. Thanks, Leslie."

Once Annalise ended her call with Leslie, she turned to me and asked, "So, what do you think?"

"Freak accident is a red flag," I noted. "It could be The Hunter's first kill before he established a pattern. I'd need more details. I could probably get my hands on the coroner's report and take another look. Coroners sometimes miss things that medical examiners don't. Even with easy access to the FBI office in their backyard."

"That was my first thought, too. If we're lucky, he's related to the man who died. If not, we could be right back at square one. I still think it's worth checking out the dead guy's last known address." Annalise grinned. "Are you up for a road trip?"

"Sure am. I need to shower and change into something that will allow me to turn invisible. Once we get there, I'll scope out the place in incognito mode. We should collect more data before proceeding."

"Absolutely. Where would we be without data?" Annalise teased.

†

Traveling the rural route that led us along the edge of the forest, I noticed civilization becoming increasingly less populated. Finally, the GPS noted we would be on roads that were no longer marked, and we would have to use the visuals on the screen to direct us.

I pointed to a gravel road lined with trees. "I think you're supposed to turn here."

"Perfect place for a psycho killer. I'm having a hard time believing an old man would drag a wife and kids out here. Maybe he was some kind of recluse," Annalise theorized.

"Or, the perfect man to groom a serial killer," I deadpanned. "In case this is the killer's place, we should probably park the car and go on foot. The map shows it's just at the end of this road."

"I bet he had a hard time getting mail or deliveries way out here." Annalise found a small clearing to pull into, large enough for her SUV.

"His property butts up against the national forest. That can't be a coincidence," she noted.

I shuddered. Although I'd always loved the forest and the beauty of nature, there was a creepiness about this place when I focused my enhanced vision on the end of the road and caught a glimpse of the house. It looked run down, but something caught my eye that seemed out of place.

Annalise appeared to hesitate and was reaching for the door handle when her phone rang, startling both of us. Selecting the button to answer the call, she immediately put the call on speaker.

"Hey, Leslie. What do you have for me?"

"Jacob Tompkins did have a wife, but she died a long time ago. Sounds like foul play was suspected, but the police didn't have enough to make an arrest. His wife's sister was convinced that he beat her to death. Apparently, she'd had numerous prior 'accidents' landing her in the emergency room with broken ribs and other injuries consistent with domestic abuse. He claimed she fell down a cliff and broke her neck. Guess how he died?"

"Broken neck after taking a tumble down a cliff," Annalise answered. "Maybe that's why they didn't investigate his death too closely. Probably thought it was poetic justice, and the bastard got what he deserved,"

Annalise mumbled. "What else? I can almost hear the excitement in your voice."

"He had a son, Benjamin Tompkins," Leslie reported. "Social services paid the father numerous visits because the kid missed a lot of school. Benjamin was in the same graduating class as your first victim."

"Bingo. The coincidences are stacking up. Does he work?" Annalise asked.

"He does, but I suspect he does that from home. So, proceed with caution with whatever you're planning. He's a computer consultant. After landing in a bit of trouble by hacking into the wrong places, he caught the attention of a very large security firm. They're mercenaries for hire, but untouchable so far by the government because they provide needed services to augment our military."

"Shit. I hate the smart ones. Okay, thanks, Leslie. Feel free to fill Reese in on what you dug up. Pie coming your way as soon as we catch this bastard."

"One more thing. I don't know if it's important or not, but I looked up his picture in the yearbook, and Benjamin doesn't look like the kind of kid who would have anything to do with guns. There was only one picture I could find. I suspect he was picked on quite a bit, though. Coke-bottle glasses. Definitely overweight with bad skin. He looks like the type who would have spent his free time behind a computer, playing games. Hardly the outdoorsy type."

"Did you find any recent pictures of him? Maybe he's bulked up since high school," Annalise suggested.

"Hard to tell from DMV photos, but, yeah, it's possible," Leslie paused, and I could hear clicking in the background. "Oh yeah, I just pulled up his license. And it says he's six-four. So, if he did lose his baby fat and started working out, he'd be formidable. I'll continue to do some more digging. If I learn anything else that might help, I'll let you know."

"Any chance you can look into his finances? Maybe find whatever he's been purchasing over the last year. We need something that will allow us to serve a search warrant on this property."

"You got it."

Annalise reached for the door handle again, but I laid my hand across her stomach to hold her back. While she was talking to Leslie, I had scanned the area, noting that what was out of place was no sign of his own personal security, which undoubtedly included cameras.

"Wait. He probably has cameras around the perimeter of his place. Let me check it out first."

"All right. Be careful," Annalise cautioned. "Remember, he likes to hide bear traps under piles of leaves and debris."

As I cautiously made my way along the gravel road, I noted a sign declaring, "Trespassers will be shot without warning." I focused my eyes on every detail of the road, looking for anything that would suggest there was a safe path to the house. Finally, I found tire tracks leading to the back of the property and a well-worn path to a side door. The ATV was either hidden, or if I was especially lucky, he was off somewhere doing whatever serial killers do to prepare for their next kill.

The path was far from the shortest course, snaking around a more direct route. I caught a glimpse of wire hidden among dead leaves to the left of the path. The wire ran through the more obvious path to the door. *Clever.*

When I reached the door without setting off any of his booby traps, I sighed with relief. Placing my ear against the wood, I concentrated on listening to anything that might suggest someone was home. Hearing nothing, I tried the doorknob. I figured with my super strength I could break it open if necessary. To my surprise, it wasn't locked. I suppose he figured he had enough precautions around his place that he didn't find it necessary to lock his door. Too bad he hadn't counted on an invisible woman paying him a visit.

The odor of death and decay hit me the minute I stepped inside. I resisted the urge to leave as the overwhelming smell invaded my senses. It felt like the house itself was dying. However, contradictions abounded inside the house. While the inside wasn't any better than the outside regarding its state of disrepair, there was a sense of organization I hadn't expected to find. Dingy walls surrounded a space filled with old furniture, worn-down wood floors, and dated carpet. Despite how drab the inside appeared, it was meticulously clean and free of clutter. The kitchen, while functional and spotless, had appliances that looked to be at least forty years old. Nothing was on any of the counters. The walls were filled with deer heads and other game—a literal museum of death.

I made my way through the old house until I found a room full of monitors and fancy computers. There was the wall of pictures, complete with details on each person with neat white labels, where they worked, places they frequented, friends, and family. Detailed schedules for some of the victims were arranged next to each grouping of photos. Candid shots populated the wall. The wall was so precisely organized, that I wondered if he'd measured the distance between each photo and the label beneath. This guy was compulsive.

I recognized several from the files Annalise had brought home, but there were at least fifteen more I didn't recognize. Several looked like they were still in their teens. This guy was not done. Not by a long shot.

I continued my perusal of the room, attempting to commit to memory each photo so that I could help identify every potential victim. I wished I had my phone with me to take pictures, but becoming invisible required me to relinquish anything made of hard metals.

After leaving the room, I discovered another room containing a wall of rifles. Someone had stacked bear traps along with other trapping paraphernalia neatly in one corner of the room. Dead animal skins littered another corner, along with stacks of antlers. Several bows and arrows hung on the opposite wall from the guns, with the final wall dedicated to his human trophies. Heads, hands, and feet hung on the wall in various degrees of decomposition. It appeared as though he'd tried to preserve his human trophies like deer heads without success. Then I noticed the eyes, every single one was carefully sewn shut. Clearly, he hadn't wanted to look into the dead eyes of his victims. Everything was hung with the same obsessive precision. I gagged. I'd seen enough. This was our guy.

Suddenly, I felt a sense of panic, a split second before I heard the loud motor. I listened as a door slammed open. A large man entered the room where I stood, nearly frozen. Yup, Tompkins had definitely bulked up since high school. He couldn't see me, but he could certainly feel me. At the last moment, I dodged away. I could hear him rooting around, while I cautiously retraced my steps. Once I made it to the gravel road, I sprinted away, ignoring the pain on the bottom of my feet. I could hear the crunching of the gravel underneath my feet along with the beating of my heart, but I didn't stop until I reached Annalise's SUV.

Flinging open the passenger side door, I yelled, "Time to go."

"No shit," Annalise responded.

Once my door had closed, Annalise peeled out, barreling down the gravel road, fishtailing all the way. I kept turning my head to look behind us. I didn't see him following, and that gave me a small sense of calm, but I didn't take a breath of relief until we made it to the main road and then got lost in traffic. It was a darn good thing that Annalise's SUV was a popular model and color.

As soon as I felt we were safe enough to talk, I announced, "He's definitely The Hunter."

# CHAPTER SIXTEEN

While Annalise drove, I called Reese. We both feared that if the FBI didn't execute a search warrant pronto, we'd lose our chance of catching him. In addition to what I referred to as his stalking room and hunting-trophy room, I'd seen equipment and gear worthy of a survivalist. I suspected he'd be just as comfortable living in the woods as in a house.

Once Reese answered, I hurried to update her. "Reese, whatever magic you can perform to get a search warrant on 3467 RR 65 should be a top priority. It's at the end of a gravel road, tucked away in the trees and adjacent to the forest. There is ample evidence inside the house to convict the guy. Proceed with caution, though. He's got the entire place wired with booby traps."

I wondered what the profiler would make of the two very different sides to his personality. What had turned a shy computer genius into a killing machine? I was about to describe in detail what I found in the house, when Reese interrupted.

"Please don't give me any details on how you know that," Reese answered. "Plausible deniability. I'll see what I can do. I'm at the high school right now, talking to any of the teachers or staff here who might remember Benjamin Tompkins. So far, the only person who remembers him and has any relevant information, is the school counselor. He started as the guidance counselor. Apparently, the kid opened up about his abusive father, who would take him hunting every year for his birthday. The father incessantly berated him. Called him a pathetic sissy who would never be a man until he bagged his first kill."

"Well, that fits. Bring a very big forensic team to collect evidence. You're going to need it," I relayed. "Unfortunately, we might have spooked him. There's a distinct possibility he'll take to the woods."

"La la la la la. No details," Reese chastised.

"Just one more thing. Make sure they're all veterans and not at all squeamish. I've seen a lot of gruesome scenes, and I almost lost my breakfast."

"Perfect. I'll be sure to loop Doug in on this," Reese declared. "I quite enjoy watching him turn that delightful shade of green. I better get the ball rolling. Annalise, do you want me to see if I can convince Gary to end the suspension? He's getting a lot of pressure for results, so it's been all hands on deck, and the guy they brought in to replace you on the task force is worse than Doug."

"I'd appreciate that, but don't get yourself in hot water," Annalise cautioned. "I sure hope you catch this guy at home, but let me know as soon as you attempt to serve the warrant."

"The place smells like death, Reese," I noted. "That should give you probable cause to bust inside."

"Thanks. I've got to go and get the ball rolling." Reese ended the call.

Annalise glanced over at me. "Want to tell me what has you so rattled? What exactly did you find inside?"

"I don't think taxidermy is a skill he's mastered," I quipped.

"Taxidermy? What the hell, Tamara?"

"Sorry. Bad joke. He mounted his trophies on a wall. In addition to human taxidermy being illegal, historically, it's never been successful. Even *Bodies: The Exhibition,* which utilized the controversial process of plastination to preserve human body parts, never had a complete taxidermied head. That didn't stop Tompkins from trying," I explained.

"Ew."

"Yeah. It was extremely gruesome. He had an entire room dedicated to hunting, including his trophies displayed on one wall. Tompkins has devoted two other walls to the tools of his trade—rifles and shotguns on one wall, bows and arrows on an adjacent wall. He also has what I'm calling his stalker room. An entire wall contains pictures and details on all his past victims, as well as future victims. Some were obviously in their teens. He isn't done. Not by a long shot. I'm afraid that by the time they try to serve the warrant, he'll be long gone."

"Then why did you tell me to go? We need to double back and do whatever it takes to stop him," Annalise insisted.

"I wasn't willing to test out our healing capabilities. Shotguns make a real mess of human tissue. I couldn't risk your life." I laid my hand over hers. "We'll find him."

"Fuck." Annalise slammed her left hand on the steering wheel. "I sure hope so."

"Have faith. We keep interrupting him. That's got him off his game. He'll make more errors, and when he does, we'll get him," I insisted. "He's compulsive. Which means he won't be able to stop. He isn't going to choose new victims because too much time has gone into his selections. That provides us an advantage. The best thing to do right now is to wait for Reese to call. She'll get you back on the task force. At least now we have a name and a physical description of the killer."

"True. That's more than we had two weeks ago." Annalise's shoulders relaxed. "I'd like to take another look at the map. Maybe if he does disappear into the forest, we can narrow the search to the areas he seems more comfortable with. As I recall, it's still an enormous area, but at least it's a place to start. Public panic over this guy is at an all-time high. I imagine Gary would be inclined to authorize a grid search if he decides to flee."

"FBI agents tromping through the woods isn't exactly hard to avoid. But an invisible woman is not something he'll expect. My hearing, vision, and strength are all superhuman; maybe I have enhanced smell, too. I haven't really tested that out."

Annalise chuckled. "Are you saying you might be a human hound dog?"

I shrugged. "You never know. So many mysteries with our alien fruit. I could be like the shapeshifters in those paranormal novels you love. Don't they have those same gifts along with an ability to heal when shifting?"

Annalise smiled. "Where did my analytical scientist go? You have changed if you're seriously discussing shapeshifters with me."

"I never said the books didn't present interesting phenomena to consider. How is that any different from my fascination with science fiction and superheros?"

Annalise crinkled her nose. "True. Good point."

†

On the way home, we picked up sandwiches from the deli. As Annalise stared at the map, I pondered a way to test my sense of smell. Of course, Annalise had a unique odor that I believed I would recognize and distinguish from other smells. The forest was full of scents. How might I isolate one above others? I needed to start out small.

"Do you think Reese would be willing to donate one of her T-shirts? A dirty one," I added before unwrapping the sandwich we'd picked up from the deli. The pancakes were long gone. Stalking a serial killer sure expended a lot of energy.

Annalise lifted her head to look at me, her face a mask of confusion. "What? Why would you want one of Reese's dirty T-shirts?"

"I need to conduct a basic smell test," I stated.

Annalise laughed. "Of course you do. But I don't think your ability to pick out my smell versus Reese's will prove anything. I could do that in my sleep. I know exactly what you smell like. I've had your smell burned into my memory since we were young."

"Could you find my T-shirt if I hid it in the woods?" I countered as I took a big bite of my sandwich.

Annalise grinned. "Maybe."

"Liar," I said around a mouthful of food.

"I think if we asked Reese for a dirty T-shirt, she'd think we finally lost our last marbles, and she'll wonder why in the world she's following up on any lead we provide her." Annalise unwrapped her own sandwich and took a much smaller bite. Maybe she wasn't as hungry because other than that small spike of adrenaline I had felt when Tompkins came home, she'd remained in the car while I had to witness his house of horrors.

"I don't suppose you'd be willing to nick one from her?" I suggested.

"And how do you propose I do that? We're only barely becoming friends again. It's not like she invites me over for drinks. Besides, even if she did, you'd be okay with that?"

I considered her question. Normally, I wasn't one for subterfuge, preferring complete honesty. "I suppose not, even for the advancement of science. It wouldn't be right for you to charm your way into an invite in order to steal one of her T-shirts."

Annalise chuckled. "I meant, wouldn't going there tweak that new jealousy bug you've developed? But, yeah, dishonesty isn't your thing, either."

"I believe I know you well enough to feel secure about us. You don't view sex in the same manner as I do. Plus, you believe in monogamy. I don't think you're capable of having sex with two women at the same time."

Annalise had just taken a bite of her sandwich and chewed quickly before responding. "Us? I had hopes, but I wasn't sure what was going on in that brilliant mind of yours. As for monogamy, you know my views, but since I'm only recently discovering things about you I never knew, I sure would like your perspective on the topic."

"What do you mean you're only recently discovering things about me? You know me better than anyone."

"Um, your little sexcapades," Annalise noted with a grin. "Monogamy," she prompted.

"Well, if you must know, until recently I didn't believe monogamy made sense. From a purely anthropological perspective, it's a cultural phenomenon versus a natural one. Humans generally have stronger natural urges for sexual exploration than just being in a romantic relationship. In the animal kingdom, monogamy is rare unless there is an evolutionary requirement."

"I'm going to latch onto two words you said in the long-involved explanation: 'until recently.' Does this mean your views have changed?"

I paused before responding. *Had my views changed?* A lot of things had changed within me. After having sex with Annalise, I honestly didn't see the need to seek out other women to meet my sexual needs. In the past, I'd only done that when Annalise was in a relationship with another person and spending less time with me. Plus, I always had my trusty vibrator as a backup.

"You're taking an awfully long time to answer," Annalise said with a frown.

"Sorry, I was considering my answer carefully before responding. You are quite a talented sexual partner. I don't see the need to explore others, as I believe you will be able to meet all my sexual needs. I also have several toys to help spice things up, should we fall into a slump."

Annalise chuckled. "So many things to unpack with your answer, but I'll take it. I suppose that's as close as I'm going to get to a commitment from you that you aren't planning on sleeping with anyone else, and that we are, in fact, in a relationship. All your future exploration will need to be with me," she said possessively.

"Well, yes, isn't that what I just said?"

All the talk of sex and the way Annalise was looking at me must have had an impact. I had a sudden urge to remove all of Annalise's clothing and make her scream my name. I hadn't even finished eating before I grabbed Annalise's hand, pulled her to her feet, and led her to my bedroom.

Annalise shot me her cocky grin. "Guess you want some more of my talented tongue and fingers, huh?"

"Shush. I believe it's my turn to demonstrate my skill."

"I look forward to that," she replied.

# CHAPTER SEVENTEEN

---

We'd gotten sidetracked with discussions of testing my sense of smell, redefining our relationship, and engaging in spirited sex. Annalise was the first woman I'd had sex with more than once. We had completely ignored the case. Annalise hadn't looked at the map or asked about any additional details from my exploration of Tompkin's home. As we lay on the bed, attempting to catch our breath, I heard Annalise's phone ring from the other room.

"Your cell is ringing," I stated.

Annalise turned to face me. "Damn, I'm sorry, but I really should answer it. Maybe Reese is calling with an update."

"No apology necessary. We got sidetracked earlier, but I believe it's important to refocus our energies on the case now."

Annalise tossed aside the covers and walked naked into the living room as I followed her. By the time she reached her phone, it had stopped ringing. She pressed the button to listen to the voice message and played it on speaker so I could listen as well.

"Hey Annalise, it's Reese. We have the search warrant and are heading to the address right now. Gary figured out where some of the information necessary for the warrant came from. Sorry about that. But the good news is that he agreed that having you officially back on the task force would be better than keeping you away. We have a SWAT team, just in case. I'll bring an extra vest for you. If you get this message in time, meet us at the address."

Annalise hit the button to return Reese's call. "Hey Reese. Thanks for whatever you said to Gary to convince him to reinstate me. We're on our way." Annalise glanced at me, and I nodded, already heading to my bedroom to dress.

I wasn't sure if I had a heightened sense of smell or not, but we reeked of sex. I wondered if Annalise or others would pick up on the clues. We didn't have time to shower, so I just hoped it wouldn't be an issue once we showed up at Tompkin's address.

We arrived on the scene thirty minutes later, just in time to join the rest of the team. Annalise jumped out of the car and approached Reese, who glanced in my direction. She remained separate from the rest of the team that had gathered a fair distance from the house.

"Tamara should stay back until we clear the house, just in case he starts shooting," Reese directed. I watched her stare at Annalise's smooth skin where her scar used to be. I could sense she wanted to say something, ask about her face, but instead she remained oddly silent.

I scanned the area and noted the ATV wasn't parked anywhere near the house. "I doubt he's still here," I argued. "No ATV. Do you need me to show you a path to the house without setting off his booby traps?"

Reese squinted at me. "I think we'll be able to figure it out. The SWAT team are professionals."

"Tell them to avoid the front door," I advised.

Reese pressed the button on her radio. "Stay clear of the front door. Traps likely surround that area."

"There's an indirect worn path that leads to a side door and tire tracks from the ATV to the back of the property. They need to stay on those paths and go single file. Any other pattern of approach is going to get someone injured or killed," I stated with authority.

Reese's radio crackled. "Wires located. Unable to proceed until the traps are cleared."

Reese sighed and pressed the button again. "I have someone here who can lead the team through the traps."

Gary's unmistakable voice blared through the radio. "Fine. Have Annalise gear up and approach."

"It isn't Annalise. It's Dr. Childs," Reese admitted as she cringed in expectation of the inevitable blowup.

"Oh, for fuck's sake," Gary yelled. "Why doesn't that surprise me?"

I heard his shoes crunching on the gravel road before I saw a very pissed-off Gary approach. "I sure hope that however you came by this information is not going to come back to bite us." I opened my mouth to respond, but Gary held his hand up. "No, nope, do not say a word. Come on, lead the way."

Gary gruffly introduced me to the SWAT team, who looked at me with more than a little curiosity. Doug glared at me, and if possible, his expression grew even more feral as Reese and Annalise strolled up to the group.

I pointed to the ATV tire tracks in the dirt. "Follow these tracks, single file, please."

The lead man nodded, and the team proceeded to move along the tracks to the back of the property. He stopped where the tracks ended and scanned the area before turning around, pointing to the start of the path, and asking, "This roundabout well-worn path to the side door is the safe route?"

I nodded. I didn't think The Hunter had enough time to set any triggers on the door, but I couldn't be sure of that. "Be careful before entering."

The man banged on the door and announced, "FBI. We have a warrant to search the property."

When no response came, the team stepped back as a battering ram busted open the door. I sighed in relief when no explosion followed. I wasn't sure what type of traps he'd set on the perimeter of his home. It didn't seem like he was an explosives expert, but what did I know? Later, a different team was tasked with removing anything that might impede the work of the forensic techs. They found that he'd engineered a few ingenious spring-loaded bows and shotguns, hidden in the brush and trees surrounding the house, in addition to his favored hidden bear traps.

†

The forensics team was on standby, and as soon as the SWAT team cleared the house, Gary was on the phone calling in the special team that would clear the outside of the home, making it safe for the science geeks to do their job. It was well into the evening before we were allowed inside. Since I was the foremost skin expert, Gary reluctantly allowed me to be part of the forensic team. I'd already seen the trophies hanging from the walls, but I was finally allowed to inspect them more thoroughly and give my expert opinion.

After I'd conducted my preliminary analysis and instructed the intern to transport the remains with care to the lab, I exited the home and saw Reese and Annalise in an animated discussion. I caught the tail end of what looked like a very interesting interchange. I'd almost forgotten about Annalise's miraculous healing.

Reese pushed up the sleeve of Annalise's long-sleeved T-shirt. "And I suppose that's the result of plastic surgery as well? Want to explain how there is zero evidence of skin grafts? I may not know everything about you, Annalise, but I can tell when you're lying."

"All right. I applied this special gel I got from Tamara," Annalise admitted. "You know how brilliant she is, and a skin expert as well."

It wasn't technically a lie. Merely suggesting I'd developed this gel was simply leading Reese to a different conclusion than reality. I was proud of Annalise's quick thinking.

Reese pulled Annalise into a hug. "I know you've never really hidden your scars, but I could tell they still bothered you. I'm so happy for you. Is Annalise going to market this miracle gel she invented? She'd make a mint."

I ignored the hug, tamping down that uncomfortable twinge of jealousy I couldn't seem to avoid. "I'm still conducting tests. It's far from market readiness. Annalise jumped the gun. She shouldn't have used herself as a guinea pig. I'd appreciate it if you wouldn't say anything to anyone.

I could get in trouble for not going through the proper channels to obtain FDA approval. While cosmetics do not require FDA approval, anything intended to affect the structure or function of the body, such as skin, is considered a drug or medical device. That's why anti-aging creams that increase the production of collagen require FDA approval," I explained.

"I promise not to say anything. Hey, I'm happy for you. For both of you. You're together, right?"

Annalise turned an adorable shade of red. "How did you know?"

"You reek of sex, my friend. It's about time. I knew I never stood a chance with you. It's fine. Really. I'm over us," Reese assured Annalise, but I could see a small amount of sadness in her eyes. She turned to me and said, "I guess you have a bit of work to do on the remains, while Annalise and the rest of the task force figure out where we can find this guy. You suggested he'd hide in the forest. Any chance you and Annalise have that narrowed down for us?"

"Not enough to make a big difference. Do we have access to dogs?" Annalise asked.

"Gary is working on gathering all available resources to track this guy. The high-profile nature of the case means he'll get whatever he's asking for. I think we're going to work in two-person teams. It'll be dark soon, but time is of the essence, since it appears as though he has a huge head start. I was going to join the search crew. Not much else to do here now that the forensics team has taken over. While Tamara does her thing at the lab, do you want to be the other half of my team?"

"Um, sure." Annalise turned to me. "Will you call me when you're done at the lab?"

"Aw, new love," Reese teased.

I nodded. "It could take a while. There's a lot to process."

# CHAPTER EIGHTEEN

I'm not exactly proud of the way I interacted with Reggie, my assistant, whom I'd called in to help me process the remains. Other forensic scientists in the lab were busy with the multitude of samples collected and left the skin to us. I was in a particularly foul mood because I wanted to be in the forest searching for Tompkins. With Annalise! But instead, she was teamed up with Reese. It wasn't jealousy, I argued to myself, but practicality. I didn't understand how they couldn't see the logic in my assessment that it would be nearly impossible to catch him. To be fair, I hadn't exactly expressed my opinion on the matter, but surely Annalise would have come to the same conclusion.

Day or night, it wouldn't make a bit of difference. With hundreds of police officers and FBI agents combing the forest with dogs, he'd hear them coming a mile away. Tompkins was far too intelligent and knowledgeable about the forest to allow himself to be captured. No, our best chance was for me to track him down while invisible.

Reggie interrupted my internal assessment of the situation. "You seem distracted, Dr. T. Are you worried about Annalise? You shouldn't worry. She'll find him. I'm glad they lifted her suspension. I didn't think that was the right thing to do. Is that why you took a leave? Were you acting in solidarity?"

I glanced in Reggie's direction and asked a question that was completely out of character for me. "Do you think Reese is more capable of tracking down this killer than I am?"

"Um," Reggie stuttered. "I think the forensics team and the FBI agents play very different roles. We're important in helping to achieve conviction once the agents find the guy."

Technically, Reggie was correct about that, but she didn't have all the facts, and I couldn't let her know about my abilities. So, I decided the question I had really wanted to ask that she could weigh in on was something I'd never considered asking anyone. But that didn't stop me from blurting it out.

"Is Reese more attractive than me? Objectively speaking, by societal standards," I added.

Stumbling over her words, Reggie replied, "No, Dr. T. You're what most people would classify as hot. But, if I may speak freely…"

I motioned for her to continue.

"Well, um, you're kind of intimidating. So, even if you weren't our superior, we wouldn't dream of asking you out. Plus, everyone knows you don't date."

"I'm dating Annalise now. I'm sorry, Reggie. I know you were interested in her."

Reggie choked on her words. "You are?" she asked in surprise. "Since when?"

"Oh, it's very recent. I wouldn't expect you to have known this."

"Okay, wow. I guess I can see it. The way that Annalise looks at you. It was pretty obvious how she felt. I suppose I just thought you were asexual or something and that it would never work between the two of you. She's like fire, and you're like ice." Reggie slapped her hand over her mouth. "Sorry, Dr. T. I didn't mean it like it must have come out."

I wasn't offended by what Reggie said, but I was confused. "Why would you think I was asexual? I like sex."

"You do? You don't really talk about your life outside of this lab. I know you and Annalise have been friends for years, but that's the only personal thing I know about you. I'm not suggesting that you're a terrible boss or anything. I've learned so much from you, and I'm very grateful to be working with you."

"Thank you. You've come a long way, Reggie. You'll make a fine forensic anthropologist once you complete your doctorate. Your honesty is appreciated. Perhaps we should return to the remains so that we can leave at a reasonable hour. I'm sure you have better things to do with your time than spend every minute of it at this lab."

Reggie grinned. "So, how's the sex with Annalise? I bet it's amazing. She seems like she knows her way around a woman's body."

"The remains, Reggie. Let's get back to doing our job." I smiled to take the sting out of my response.

Reggie laughed but returned to examining a hand. I'd unleashed a monster by showing a side of myself to Reggie that I didn't know I possessed.

✝

When I returned home, I found Annalise napping on my couch. She looked so peaceful that I almost left her alone, but a lock of hair had flopped over one eye, and I couldn't resist pushing it back against her forehead. Her eyes fluttered open.

"You're back. Long night, huh? Why didn't you call?"

"I wasn't sure if you'd still be looking for Tompkins, but if you weren't at home when I returned, I was going to call and see where you were. Are they still combing the forest for any sign of him?" I asked.

"Yeah, but nothing so far. Not that I expected success. With everyone clomping through the forest and the dogs barking, he's found a cozy spot to hide and wait us out. The dogs found a trail, then lost it." Annalise sounded frustrated. "My enhanced senses haven't even helped me with so many echo trails to follow."

"I could have told you that your chances of catching him were minimal."

"We had to try. They're going to fly drones today in the hope of catching a glimpse of him. I agreed to go back out there with Reese after I've gotten a few hours of sleep. I was practically sleepwalking. So was Reese. We figured we weren't at our best and needed rest before giving it another go."

"Will you let me know if you're able to narrow the search to a particular area? I'm planning to go out tonight while it's dark. He won't be able to see me. That should give us an advantage. I'm going to find this guy, and when I do, you'll be the first person I call."

"I don't know how I feel about you going out there on your own," Annalise said.

"Then come with me. But stay in the car while I do my thing. It won't do any good if you come into the forest with me. That takes away the element of surprise."

"Hey, I almost forgot. I got you a present."

"A present? Don't you think it's inappropriate to go shopping for a present while a serial killer is still on the loose? I'm not sure how I feel about courting rituals at this particular moment."

Annalise shot me her cocky half-grin. "Courting rituals? Sometimes, Tamara, I think you traveled directly from the nineteenth century. You're going to love this gift, trust me." She emerged from the couch and walked to the kitchen, where an evidence bag with a shirt lay on the counter. "I liberated this piece of evidence after the dogs got a good sniff. You wanted to do a sniff test. Well, I got you something much better than one of Reese's dirty T-shirts. I figured if you do have the same sense of smell as a dog," she held up the bag, "this should help."

I clapped my hands together like a child opening a birthday present. "I love your gift." I snatched the evidence bag from Annalise.

"You can open it and sniff, but you probably shouldn't handle it. I still need to ensure it ends up in the evidence locker. Not that we need his shirt for anything. It's not critical to the case because we have a mountain of evidence tying him to each victim."

"Can I wait until this evening before opening the bag? I don't want to conduct the test too early. I need to have his scent seared into my brain before going on the hunt tonight."

"You really think it's possible for you to catch his scent?"

I nodded. "I do. If I don't control it, scents, like sounds, are overpowering. I noticed that when I entered Tompkin's home."

"I'm not so sure that was the reason the odor was overpowering. The minute I walked into the house, I gagged, too. I think most of the team detected the odor of death and decay," Annalise explained as she leaned against the counter.

"Maybe. But in my line of work, you get desensitized to strong odors. I've been noticing various odors that, prior to consuming the alien fruit, did not at all register in my olfactory receptors. I knew you wanted to have sex before we actually did. I could smell your arousal."

"Again, not that hard to notice. I was practically squatting and leaving my scent in every corner of this house," Annalise quipped. "It wasn't all that easy to control my desire for you."

"Now that I understand the effects of the alien fruit, it makes more sense to me. I hate to admit that I didn't pull together the facts quickly enough prior to that first night, or we might have had sex much sooner."

"I don't quite know how to react to that declaration. Should I be thanking the alien fruit for being a kind of love potion designed to awaken your latent feelings?" Annalise teased.

"Perhaps."

## CHAPTER NINETEEN

---

After three days, we were still no closer to catching Tompkins. I felt as though the missed opportunities were taunting me. Annalise continued to burn the candle at both ends, and I knew she couldn't keep up the pace for much longer. She wouldn't like it, but I decided the only logical solution was to sneak out of bed and go on a solo hunt for the killer. I couldn't be sure, but on the previous evening, I thought I had caught his scent in a particularly dense area of the forest surrounding a maze of caves that he could have easily hidden in. I would start my search there.

I'd almost made it out of the bedroom, dressed and ready to go, when Annalise flopped over and opened her eyes. "What do you think you're doing, Missy?"

I patted the deep side pocket on the bike shorts I'd found at a local sporting goods store. "These bike shorts are perfect.

172

I can carry a cell phone and remain invisible. I'll call you when I've caught him. I think I know where to look."

"Not without me." Annalise sat up and rubbed her eyes. "I'll nap in the car, but I'm coming with."

"Annalise," I began reasonably, "it doesn't make sense for you to operate effectively and efficiently with minimal sleep. Sleep deprivation increases your chances for a major misstep."

"I know my limits, and I haven't reached them. This is one argument you're not going to win. If you believe so strongly that I'm unable to be an effective partner tonight, then we'll take a night off and return to the forest tomorrow."

She had me cornered, and she knew it. "Bring your pillow and a blanket. It'll be more comfortable for you."

Annalise grinned and hopped from the bed with surprising enthusiasm. "I felt your excitement, or maybe it was adrenaline. That's what woke me up, you know. You believe you're going to find him tonight, don't you?"

I nodded. "I caught his scent in that area of the forest where the caves are. It makes perfect sense he would hide there. Those caves are vast."

Annalise dressed quickly. Before we left, I harvested two fruits for us to eat on the way to our destination. I wanted to make sure I was at full strength. Losing invisibility at the wrong time might prove deadly. I wasn't willing to take any chances on that. Besides, it seemed like my enhanced senses were at their peak shortly after I consumed the alien fruit.

†

Annalise found a place to park close to the section of forest I wanted to search. It would still be a short hike to the caves. At least I now had neoprene booties that would provide minimal protection to my feet. I opened the evidence bag with Tompkin's shirt inside and inhaled his scent, not that I could completely forget the noxious odor. I imagined that because he'd spent so much time around death and decay, his shirt reeked of it, along with a uniquely powerful musky scent.

As soon as I'd turned invisible, Annalise remarked, "Looking good, or rather the opposite, I can't even see your phone."

"Yeah, all I need is tight-fitting clothes with built-in pockets, and I can carry small items. I grabbed a few zip ties just in case I need to subdue him before you arrive." I touched the other side pocket, reassuring myself that they were still there.

"Goddess, that is still so freaky—to hear you but not see you."

I opened the door and stepped outside. Before shutting the door, I said, "Wish me luck."

"You got it. Find this guy so we can end this."

After about an hour, I reached the edge of the location where I'd last detected his scent. It was still present, but perhaps slightly less prevalent. Stepping carefully around downed trees with their own odor of decay, I found a barely noticeable footprint. Inhaling the air, I tried to separate each smell, isolating the one I needed to follow. It seemed stronger as I pushed the branches and prickly plants aside to reveal a rock formation completely hidden behind the dense foliage. Brushing against a patch of stinging nettles, I forced myself not to cry out in discomfort. I knew that in a matter of seconds, I would no longer feel the irritating bite of hundreds of tiny hair-like thorns. Thank goodness for my body's ability to push the invaders from my skin and heal the inevitable red blotches.

A surge of adrenaline hit when his unmistakable odor seemed to cling to each plant I passed on my way to the mouth of the cave. I was careful to navigate once inside, stopping every few feet to use all of my senses in an effort to detect Tompkins. Cocking my head to the side, I thought I heard the crackle of a fire. He must have found a large enough space to avoid the possibility of smoke inhalation. Since this cave was enormous, that probably wasn't a huge impediment.

It was easier to proceed inside the cave without making a sound. The neoprene, while marginally slippery, was relatively silent against the rock. Finally, I saw the wisps of smoke pirouetting into darkness, twirling upward as if they meant to escape their prison, before dissipating, leaving nothing behind. The glowing red embers almost looked inviting until I saw the man hovering over the flames like a demon calling on evil spirits.

He raised his head, and he scanned the area, almost as if he detected an unknown presence. He grabbed his rifle and continued to stare into the relative darkness. I wondered how acute his senses were, and if he detected someone else was inside the cave with him. I halted my progress, feeling my heart beat rapidly in my chest. Then I remembered, no way could he see me. I looked down, making sure I was still invisible.

Throwing caution to the wind, I ran full speed ahead, leaping over the small fire and tackling him to the ground. I jumped aside, ready to grab his rifle, and if necessary, whack him over the head.

"Oompf. What the hell?" he called out. He whipped his head around, lifting the rifle and waving it around, desperately searching for his invisible enemy. I didn't have fighting skills, but I was freakishly strong. That was something I needed to correct, pronto. What good was having superhuman abilities if I couldn't fight my way out of a paper bag?

I grabbed the first thing I could get my hands on and broke off a stalagmite, swinging it like a bat, connecting with his head. He slumped to the ground, and I checked his neck for a pulse. I sighed in relief when I noted the steady beat. I didn't want to kill him but feared I had, only pulling back on my strength at the last minute.

He groaned and began to sit up before I had the good sense to kick his gun away. I crawled behind him and not so gently yanked his arms behind his back before pushing him face down against the hard rock. With my knee against his back, I managed to retrieve my zip ties and secured his wrists. I might have pulled them a bit too tight as I heard him cry out in pain, or maybe I'd pulled back his arms a bit too enthusiastically.

Lifting his body with ease, I returned him to a sitting position as he tried unsuccessfully to kick out at his unknown assailant.

"Why can't I see you?"

I decided he didn't deserve a response. Let him believe he'd gone a little crazy. Ironically, I suspected he had, but quite some time ago. The FBI profiler indicated The Hunter may have experienced a kind of psychotic break, instigated by a specific event yet to be determined.

Clamping down on his legs, I struggled to fasten the remaining zip ties to secure them. Perhaps another well-placed smack on the head would subdue him enough to ensure his capture. Not holding back this time, I balled my hand into a tight fist and struck him in the face. I heard the satisfying crunch and shook my hand out. The surprise sucker punch was enough to still his movement, enough for me to immobilize his legs. Already, I could feel the bones in my hand begin to mend. Learning how to punch was added to my list of skills I needed to develop.

Satisfied that Tompkins wasn't going anywhere, I moved quickly to the mouth of the cave to make my call.

Annalise answered on the first ring. "You okay? I felt a spike of adrenaline."

"We got him. But, I'm relatively confident that I broke his nose. He might have a goose egg on his head, too."

Annalise chuckled. "I guess he resisted arrest."

"Not that I'm a huge proponent of providing false statements, but I think we need to get our stories straight before taking him in. I'll come to the car, and we can discuss the best approach while we hike back to the cave." I began walking through the forest, retracing my steps to the car.

"As long as we don't make a habit of this, I believe the ends justify the means," Annalise agreed. "Broke his nose, huh? What did you use? A branch? A rock?"

"My fist. But the goose egg was the result of a well-placed strike with a stalagmite. I may join a softball team," I bragged.

"Now that, I would most definitely want to see. Maybe you should consider a second career as a boxer," she teased.

"It's on my list to becoming a proper superhero. Will you teach me to fight? I lack the proper form and knowledge to be successful." I continued at a brisk pace. I was eager to reunite with Annalise now that the nightmare was almost over.

Annalise broke out in a fit of laughter. "The fact that I know how serious you are about this makes it all the more hilarious. I'm picturing you in a fighting stance right now. Do me a favor and drop a pin with your location."

"Okay." I fumbled with my phone and dropped the pin for Annalise. Suddenly, I had a bad feeling. I hadn't removed his belongings, nor had I considered how he might use the sharp rocks to remove the zip ties. "Annalise, I've got to go."

"Wait."

It was the last thing I heard before stuffing my phone in my pocket and doubling back to where I'd left Tompkins.

When I reached the spot where I'd left him, I scanned the area and finally saw him attempting to use one of the stalagmites on the hard plastic. I suspected he was scraping his wrists and hands as much as connecting in the right spot to free himself. Somehow, he'd already freed his legs. He was starting to be a real pain in the ass.

I wasn't one to make assumptions on hard science, but I had to make an educated guess on how much force it would take to knock him out but not kill him. Then I remembered the vagus nerve. Yup, that should do it. A little pinch there and lights out. This time, I'd toss the freak over my shoulders and carry him all the way to the car if I had to. I was cursing myself for using zip ties instead of handcuffs.

†

I'd taken a circuitous route to the cave, but this time, carrying a man over two hundred pounds firefighter style, I looked for the most direct path to the car. I was going at a healthy clip but didn't get very far when Tompkins began to squirm. Tossing him on the forest floor, I decided to take a break. He was starting to be a total pain in my ass. We were still a fair distance from the car, but I doubted he'd find much of anything to use to release his restraints. I was not very gentle when I reapplied several more zip ties.

Remaining perfectly quiet, I heard Annalise crashing through the forest well before I saw her. A light bobbed in the air from what I assumed was a flashlight. Skidding to a stop, she lifted her gun and announced, "FBI. Hands in the air where I can see them."

Tompkins scoffed. "I don't know what the fuck is going on, but if you take a closer look you'll see I can't exactly follow your orders. I'm the victim here. Something is out there. I…I…can't explain it…"

Annalise smirked. "Even with that smashed-in nose, I'd recognize you. Mr. Tompkins you've made it to the list of the top ten most wanted. My backup should be here any minute. Benjamin Tompkins, you're under arrest for the murder of…" Annalise recounted the list of his victims and read him his rights while he sat there docilely, mumbling almost incoherently like the madman he was.

*Oh, now he decides to cooperate.* I wondered if he figured the enemy he could see was better than the one he couldn't. Annalise removed the zip ties on his wrist and replaced them with handcuffs.

She gave a gentle push and said, "Let's go. This way to your future, Mr. Tompkins."

I heard the distant whine of a siren and figured that Annalise had everything under control, so as silently as possible, I made my way back to the car to wait for her. By the time I arrived at Annalise's SUV, Reese had pulled her car next to Annalise's. She frowned as she emerged from the car, shining a light into the dark forest. I crept closer to her to make out what she was grumbling.

"Damn cowgirl. Has to go off half-cocked all the time. All she had to do was call if she had a lead, and I would have come with her," Reese mumbled before pulling her phone from her pocket. "Okay, I'm at your vehicle. Where are you?" She paused before answering, "You sure?"

Reese kept mumbling, and I had to contain the laughter that threatened to bubble from inside. Finally, I saw Annalise's flashlight a split second before Reese stopped her pacing and approached Annalise and Tompkins.

Annalise pushed Tomkins and said, "He's all yours. I've already read him his rights. I can follow you back."

Tompkins continued to mumble incoherently about an invisible monster, which thankfully, Reese ignored.

"It doesn't look like you needed the backup. Why call me, and why should I take him instead of you?" Reese narrowed her eyes and focused on Tompkins, who looked like he'd been in a barroom brawl. She had the good sense to lead him to her car and settle him into the back seat before addressing Annalise again. "What the fuck happened? He looks like you beat on him."

"Not me." Technically true. I grinned while I listened to Annalise explain, leaving out a few pertinent details. "Why do you think I want you to take him in? I just had my car cleaned. Do you know how hard it is to get blood out?"

"Very funny." Reese sighed. "If you want me to back up your report, I'm going to need a few more details."

"All right. At approximately 10:05, I received a call with the location where I would find Tompkins. He was already subdued when I found him. I cut off the zip ties, cuffed him, and read him his rights. All by the book," Annalise added. Also, all technically true. Annalise was a master at providing just enough details without sharing any inconvenient facts that would be difficult to explain.

"So, you're telling me someone else beat and trussed him up for you like a Thanksgiving turkey ready to go in the oven?" Reese asked with a touch of disbelief.

"I doubt he beat himself up," Annalise quipped.

"And you have no idea who this concerned citizen might be? I notice you didn't say it was an anonymous caller."

Annalise shrugged. "I've provided you with all the information you need to know."

"Shit. I hope this does not come back to bite either one of us," Reese grumbled.

"Doubtful. All anyone is going to care about is that we got him," Annalise argued.

"I suppose you don't have any idea why Tompkins sounds like a crazy homeless person. Invisible monsters, that's a new one. What did he do? Revert to childhood where monsters hovered in his closet and under his bed?"

Annalise lifted one eyebrow. "How many sane people do you know that would mount human heads, hands, and feet to their wall? We should leave that to the profilers to figure out. They're going to have a field day with him. My theory is that he's had a full psychotic break. Maybe the dude is schizophrenic. Honestly, I don't give a shit as long as he remains behind bars for the rest of his life."

"Great. Maybe it's all an act. It wouldn't be the first time someone pulled the insanity defense," Reese groused as she pivoted and climbed into her car. Rolling down her window, she said, "See you back at the office."

After she pulled away and I couldn't see her car anymore, I concentrated on shimmering back into view.

"Heard all that, didn't you?" Annalise asked.

"Mmhm. Nicely done. I don't think she bought everything, but I also don't believe she'll make a fuss."

## CHAPTER TWENTY

Annalise dropped me off at home before heading to the office. I didn't know if she was uncharacteristically quiet on the way home because exhaustion was finally kicking in, or if she had something else on her mind. I was experiencing my own change in energy. After the adrenaline high of the past couple of hours, I was content to listen to the radio and relax.

Annalise kept the car running in my driveway and turned to me as my hand reached for the door. "We make a good team, don't we?"

"The best," I answered.

"But I don't know if I can continue to lie to Reese," Annalise said, with a hint of sadness in her voice. "She's been nothing but supportive to both of us."

I nodded. "I understand. Does that mean we won't be forming our own private eye business?" I replied half-jokingly.

"I'm an FBI agent, and you're the foremost forensic expert in all things related to skin. We can't go around playing superhero."

"Why not?" I challenged. "Lots of superheroes have alternate identities."

"Comic books? Come on, Tamara. You can't be serious."

Making an awkward attempt at a joke, I teased, "Is this about you being the sidekick? Fine, I'll be the sidekick, but it doesn't really make sense since you can't turn invisible."

"I'm not kidding, Tamara. I don't see how this is going to work. And yet, I also don't see you stopping anytime soon. It's like you have a taste for crime-fighting now. I get it. It's a rush when you catch a killer. This is a real conundrum for me. Add the fact that we just started a relationship, and I don't have a clue where that's going. Well, you get the picture. I'm feeling slightly overwhelmed right now."

I touched her arm. "We'll figure it out. Together," I added. "You have to know how much I want things to work out between us." Telling her I loved her was on the tip of my tongue, but I couldn't quite get the words out. Maybe I should have taken the plunge. It seemed like she needed something from me at that moment. I hoped that what I'd said was enough.

Annalise smiled. "Good to know. Get some rest. I'm sure I have a lot of paperwork waiting for me. I'll come back as soon as possible, but it could be several hours."

†

By the time Annalise returned, I'd fallen asleep on the couch. I'd always been a light sleeper, but I was especially so right before my normal time to wake. Sitting up, I pulled the blanket against myself and smiled as Annalise approached. As if it were the most normal thing in the world, she greeted me with a kiss, but it lacked any fire. I looked at her face, finally noticing the exhaustion. She had to be running on fumes.

I stood and took her hand. "To the bed, now," I ordered.

A crooked smile appeared on her face. "Is that an invitation?" The question came out in her usual teasing manner, but it definitely lacked the necessary oomph. "The heart is willing, but the body, not so much," she teased. "What a shit show that was, processing Tompkins."

"I definitely want to follow up on that statement, but I really think you need to settle in for a long-deserved rest. Gary better have given you the next two days off because I believe that's the minimum time you deserve to re-energize."

"Oh, I've got that time off and a whole lot more," Annalise cryptically revealed.

"That bastard suspended you again?" I didn't typically let anger take over, but lately, emotions seemed to take off running without my permission. I was furious for probably the first time in my life.

"Settle down Caucasian She-Hulk. You look ready to tear someone apart. Where's my mild-mannered scientist? Perhaps you need to conduct emotion tests after consuming that fruit," she teased. "I thought you said I need to nap first and explain later."

I concentrated on slowing my heart to calm myself while taking several deep breaths. "Sorry. You're right. I can wait patiently for the full story. Let me just say one thing. If you need me to fess up to assaulting Tompkins, I will. What's the worst that can happen?"

Annalise ran her skeptical eyes up and down my body. "Right. Like they would believe that. Even if you claimed to have recently discovered the benefits of strength training and exercise, a five-foot-two woman weighing just over a hundred pounds taking down a two-hundred-and-fifty-pound man defies logic. It's fine. I'm sure it'll all blow over. Even the apparently crazy Tompkins did not validate their theory that I went rogue, tortured, and beat him before following protocol to arrest him." Annalise sighed. "I suppose it didn't help that I was evasive about the call I received. Typically, my reports contain more detail. I couldn't bring myself to outright lie. Gary presumes I won't make a solid witness when they bring this to trial. That makes him extremely angry. Ironically, he believes I was lying about the phone call, but he can't figure out exactly what occurred. I have to meet with Merrill later today. She's the prosecutor assigned to this case. Unfortunately, Gary is correct. Any defense attorney with a lick of sense will ask pointed questions about this mysterious call. They might even subpoena phone records."

I grinned. "Good thing I had sense enough to purchase a burner phone."

"You what? Why would you do that?"

"I suppose I've given a little more thought to this idea of an alternate identity, and cell phones are entirely too traceable. It was a somewhat rash purchase, I know, totally out of character, but I have to admit this superhero business has been exciting. I got caught up in the possibilities."

Annalise began laughing so hard she snorted. "You continually surprise me. So, are you proposing that I should be your Lois Lane? The only person to know your real identity? I think I'm more offended by that than the role of sidekick. Although, come to think of it, Lois Lane was far less deceitful than Superman."

"Well, you're going to have to get comfortable lying. Because if there is any chance Tompkins might get off by exploiting weak testimony, all this would have been for naught," I insisted. "Deceit for the greater good is always justified."

"Not too sure now about the Tamara Childs two point oh. You sound like a completely different person advocating for dishonesty, but I'm far too tired to continue this discussion. Soon, I'll enter the punchy stage."

"I believe you're already there, comparing yourself to Lois Lane and me to Superman," I quipped.

I led Annalise to my bed and settled next to her, managing to get a few hours of sleep before slipping from the bed. I jotted a few ideas down for arguments to Annalise on how we might seriously continue this journey to fight crime and ensure justice was served. I was pleased when Annalise failed to stir for twelve straight hours. She'd be pissed to learn I answered her phone and informed Gary, in no uncertain terms, that she would not be meeting with Merrill today. I was convinced Annalise would get over it. Love had a way of making difficult problems less gnarly. Everyone would learn quickly that this five-foot-two woman was a force to be reckoned with.

†

I was in the process of finalizing my arguments when Annalise stumbled into the living room, wiping the sleep from her eyes.

"Fuck. I missed my meeting," she exclaimed after noting the time. "Why didn't you wake me?"

"Because I answered your phone and told Gary you'd call him tomorrow to reschedule."

"I bet that went over well."

"Not particularly, but I handled it. He's an ass."

Annalise groaned. "I know you think you're helping, but you're not."

I waved her over. "Come. Sit. I've created a list of items for you to consider."

Annalise joined me on the couch. "This, I've got to hear."

"One, the effects of the alien fruit are a dangerous secret. In the wrong hands, it could be disastrous. Wouldn't you agree?"

"Yes," Annalise answered reluctantly.

"Two, every possible consideration should be entertained to ensure the secret never gets out. It's basic logic to conclude that telling a falsehood is a legitimate choice for the greater good."

"That is not fair using logic on an issue of morality," Annalise insisted.

"I have more. Shall I continue?"

Annalise twirled her hand, gesturing for me to continue. "Why not? I know you won't stop until you've outlined everything on that list of yours." She pointed to my tablet that I was reading from.

"During interrogations, isn't a legitimate tactic telling falsehoods? I believe you call that deception. Potato, potahto."

"Oh, you're really not playing fair. The fact of the matter is that the legitimate technique of using guilt-presumptive questions during interrogations is specifically authorized by the 1969 Supreme Court case, Frazier v. Cupp."

"Mmhm, the Reid Technique," I answered.

"I doubt you'll find a court case authorizing a law enforcement professional to lie under oath," she argued.

"I call that selective reasoning, but I will grant you a point for the counterargument. What if there were a way to testify without committing perjury?"

Annalise narrowed her eyes. "What do you propose?"

"Three words. Police Informant Privilege."

Annalise smiled. "I can't believe you've found a way to thread the needle. I need to stop underestimating your powers of persuasion. Okay, let me get this straight. You're proposing I justify lying to my boss and Reese because of the legitimacy of the Reid Technique so that I can consider you a confidential informant and exercise the Police Informant Privilege."

"Yes!" I answered excitedly. "And furthermore, I believe you should, from this point forward, consider me a confidential informant. We still have work to do, and that should make it a lot easier on your moral compass."

## CHAPTER TWENTY-ONE

It took Annalise and me several days to return to normalcy regarding our sleeping schedules. In all honesty, it was much longer and more painful for Annalise to get comfortable with her own version of the Reid Technique. She tried evasiveness at first, but when Reese and her supervisor pushed, she was forced to tell half-truths and what I classified as little white lies for the greater good.

When Gary admonished Annalise for protecting a rogue vigilante because she wouldn't give up her source, Annalise insisted she wasn't there to witness any assault. Thus, she could not confirm or deny whether the person she was protecting as a confidential source was responsible for Tompkins' injuries. Since Tompkins was not specific about his identification of the unknown assailant, that shored up her argument for protecting the source. She insisted it was critical if the FBI wanted more intel in the future. I was so proud of her. Even with the threat of losing her job, Annalise did not budge.

Annalise settled on the couch, placed a piece of pizza onto her plate, and relayed her most recent conversation with Gary. "He threatened to suspend me again, even after Merrill said she could work with what I planned to do on the stand. She almost sounded excited to try this novel idea. The dicknob just doesn't like when he's not one hundred percent in control."

"I'm so proud of you. Do you feel any better about lying to Reese?"

"Not really," Annalise admitted. "She doesn't understand why I'm not more forthcoming with her. I think it hurts her. Reese believes I don't trust her. Finally, I told her I made a promise that I simply could not break, and I wouldn't be a very honorable person if I didn't keep my word. Thankfully, she's dropped it, but there is irreparable damage to our friendship. That's the hardest thing to swallow. Goddess help me, but I'm becoming more comfortable with the lies."

Caressing the side of her face, I soothed, "I doubt that very much. I appreciate how difficult this is for you, and I'm sorry for that."

"No, I get it. We blundered onto something that the world is not ready for."

"Sometimes, I wonder if it was really a good thing we stumbled on that strange glowing pod," I confessed. "But then I remember that a monster is safely behind bars because of it. Makes me believe we were the ones destined to find the alien fruit. So, I've made a decision."

Annalise arched her eyebrow. "Uh oh. I know that look."

"I've decided to leave the FBI," I blurted. "I can work as an independent consultant, but only on cases that interest me.

I'll need the free time to pursue cases that are not restricted to this area. I'll offer my services to the Behavioral Analysis Unit. They approached me last year, and I said no at the time, because—"

"You're serious. I thought you were joking about becoming the real-life version of *The Equalizer*. That's just crazy talk. What about us?"

One look at Annalise's face told me I hadn't fully considered her feelings. Then I felt her distress. Love and relationships were so new to me. The nuances evaded my logical thought processes. I needed to understand what was behind Annalise's reaction.

"I'm confused. Why are you upset?"

Annalise sighed. "Never mind. Become The Invisible Woman. Fly all over the damn country and do your thing. I'm sure we'll find a spare moment here and there to have sex whenever you have an itch that needs scratching. Or maybe you'll find a way to have your needs met elsewhere." She grabbed the pizza getting cold on her plate and viciously ripped off a chunk with her teeth, chewing with vigor.

"I hoped you might consider joining the BAU," I responded. "They have an opening, and I know for a fact you've garnered their interest. Everyone knows you're the agent responsible for capturing The Hunter."

Annalise set her cold pizza back on the plate. "So, you've mapped out my whole life, have you? What if I'm happy working at this FBI office?"

"Are you?" I asked. "Wouldn't you like having colleagues with a higher level of skill? And a supervisor who appreciates you? I'm not saying that Reese isn't good, but Doug and Gary are perfect examples of the Peter Principle."

Finally, that elicited a chuckle out of Annalise. "The Peter Principle, really?"

"Well, yeah, they've both certainly risen to an epic level of incompetence."

Annalise's brow furrowed, and she asked, "When did the BAU approach you? You never told me about that. Why?"

I shrugged. "Last year. I didn't think it was important to share since I wasn't going to accept their offer."

"Why not?" Annalise asked.

"Because of you, silly. It meant I wouldn't get to spend as much time with you, and I missed you enough whenever you dated someone. I didn't want to make it worse by taking a job that would take me away from you even more."

"But you're considering doing just that right now," she argued.

"It's time for a change. For both of us," I implored. "If I'm finally ready to take the leap, not just with my career, but love, shouldn't you at least consider it? Will you please mull over a conversation with Erica Channing, the head of the BAU? She asked about you, you know?"

Annalise grinned. "You're just full of surprises, aren't you? Yeah, I guess I can talk with her. But can you keep those surprises to a minimum in the future? I don't expect you to share everything that's going on in that big brain of yours, but perhaps you might consider telling me the big things."

I was confused again. "I'm literally sharing with you right now."

"Timing, Tamara, is everything. I meant revealing those juicy tidbits sooner rather than later. It would have been nice to know you spoke with the head of the BAU, and that you'd considered a job with them."

"Oh, I suppose these are the important topics a person discusses with their partner," I admitted. "You'll have to give me a little grace. I'm new at this relationship thing."

"It's also the kind of thing you could have shared with your best friend, too."

"Yes, I imagine that's accurate as well. But at the time of the offer, it didn't seem important because I wasn't planning on accepting it. Now, our circumstances have changed. I believe this is the right time. As you stated before, timing is everything," I countered.

"When will I ever learn?" Annalise teased as she shook her head. "Never get into an argument with a person governed by logic."

"Not completely governed by logic. As much as I find emotions inconvenient, they have played a more prominent role in my life these past few weeks. So, have I convinced you to speak with Erica?"

Annalise smiled. "Yes. I'd do just about anything for you."

†

I was busy wrapping things up with my position. Who knew I had so many colleagues who had evolved into friends? Apparently, they'd gotten used to my way of doing things and my sometimes brusk manner.

Annalise had her own challenges as she wrestled with leaving a place where she felt comfortable and settled. Despite her issues with her supervisor and a few agents like Doug, she'd always been close with most of her colleagues. And she'd garnered their respect with her easygoing manner. She had the capability of turning on a dime, one moment joking and teasing with her colleagues, and the next minute hyper-focused on tracking a killer. I admired that about her. She kept procrastinating, and I wondered if she would ever take the plunge and connect with Erica. I was starting to get nervous, and that was so unlike me. But I forced myself to let Annalise do whatever was best for her on her timeline, not mine. I had to believe it would all work out the way I envisioned it would.

The turning point arrived about a week later. I could tell right away something was wrong, even without our strange connection. Annalise was rarely in a foul mood. So, when she tossed her keys on the counter and headed straight for the refrigerator to grab a beer before greeting me, I knew something was up. I incorrectly assumed she had finally contacted the BAU, and the conversation didn't go well.

After she plopped on the couch and drank nearly a quarter of her beer, I took her hand and attempted to comfort her. "It's okay, Annalise. We'll figure it out. I'll stay here and fight local crime. Maybe they'll let me consult remotely."

"What are you talking about?" she barked.

Annalise rarely raised her voice to me. I was so shocked I dropped her hand and scooted away from her, severely wounded by her tone.

"Damn, I'm so sorry, Tamara. I didn't mean to bite your head off. I just got some very disturbing news today."

"Okay, will you talk to me and tell me what happened?"

"Tompkins hired a high-powered attorney. I have no idea where he got the money. He has an almost perfect record. I consider most defense attorneys, snakes, but this guy is a bloody python." Annalise took another long pull from her beer.

"So, you think there's a possibility he'll actually get Tompkins off?" I asked. "I thought that people who prevail on an insanity defense often spend more time confined than if they'd taken their chances on a prison sentence."

"He's not arguing insanity. The attorney filed a motion to suppress all the evidence collected at his home because of an improperly obtained search warrant. He's claiming the search warrant was not based on reliable information." Annalise slammed the empty bottle on my coffee table.

"What happens if the attorney wins on this motion?"

Annalise frowned. "Our case goes up in smoke."

"But you have his DNA that matches the blood collected in the forest. And one of his victims lived. You have a witness. Surely, that's enough to convict, even without the evidence in his home."

"Yeah, about that. The woman we rescued was so traumatized she wasn't able to identify him in a line-up. It was dark, Tompkins had drugged her, and he wore a mask. The voice identification didn't work either. Even under the best of circumstances, eyewitnesses are unreliable. And to add insult to injury, Tompkins is claiming that I shot an innocent man who just happened to be in the forest at the same time. He's suing the FBI, and that puts me directly in the crosshairs again. They'll probably bring in the Office of Professional Responsibility just to cover their asses. The only thing that went our way was the judge denied bail, and he's still locked up."

A red-hot rage bubbled from inside me. I'd never experienced such anger. I wasn't even sure I was capable of that amount of wrath, but clearly, I was. "I'm not going to let Tompkins get away with this."

"And just what do you propose?"

"Can you imagine how unsettling it might be to hear and feel an invisible force taunting you, day and night?" I proposed. "By the time I'm done with him, he'll beg for a plea deal that keeps him locked up for life in exchange for taking the death penalty off the table."

"You're serious," Annalise remarked with a touch of incredulity. "How in the hell do you think you'll be able to do that? He's still behind bars, you know. You can't actually want to break into his cell?"

"I'll figure it out. I have to."

Although I'd expressed a great deal of bravado, I had no clue how I would manage to get him alone and begin my assault. I almost wished they'd let him out on bail with an ankle monitor.

"I hope I'm worrying for nothing. Defense attorneys often argue to suppress evidence without success. I suppose it's a wait-and-see situation until the judge rules. I just despise being under scrutiny yet again. This asshole has caused me more aggravation than any other perpetrator I've ever dealt with. At least now, I'm ready to take the plunge and make that call to the BAU. Unfortunately, they may no longer be interested after learning that a formal investigation was launched, and I'm at the center of that intense scrutiny."

"They're only doing that to cover their asses. It's all for appearance. Anyone who saw the inside of his house of horrors knows we have the right guy," I argued.

"Won't matter if this all blows up in our faces. They'll need a scapegoat, and that's me."

"I won't let that happen," I insisted. "What good is it to have all these powers if I can't help the person I love?"

"Will you please wait until the judge rules before becoming Casper the unfriendly ghost?" Annalise's eyes widened. "Wait, did you just say what I think you said?"

"What?"

"You admitted to loving me." Annalise grinned.

I paused to consider my spontaneous outburst. "Yes, I suppose I did, and I believe I do. Although, my declaration could simply be a turn of phrase. You know, a familiar expression."

Annalise chuckled. "I know what turn of phrase means. Was it?"

"No."

Annalise grabbed me and pulled me into an enthusiastic embrace, kissing me like it might be the last opportunity to do so. "Right, I didn't think so either, but I wanted you to acknowledge it for the record."

"But I wasn't under oath," I teased. "Perhaps I was implementing the Reid Technique."

"To what purpose?" Annalise inquired.

"For sex, of course. To ensure continued satisfying orgasms."

Annalise grabbed my hand and pulled me to my feet. "I guess that's my cue then…"

## CHAPTER TWENTY-TWO

Over the next week, I visited the county lock-up just to get the lay of the land. I'd turned into a woman of action. There was no way I wanted to simply wait for the judge to rule on the attorney's flurry of motions. I needed to study the patterns and routines. I was looking for any opening or opportunity to get Tompkins alone. It seemed rec time was my only chance. The county jail was a dreary place, almost the exact opposite of the forest where Tompkins felt so at ease. Cement was the prevailing material used, including in the small area where prisoners were taken for daily recreation. The guards looked almost bored as they watched over the prisoners who milled about, smoking cigarettes, lifting weights, or playing basketball on the dingy court. The net had seen better days. Little effort was made to spruce up the area.

Tompkins made it easy for me to get to him. He remained set apart from the rest of the prisoners. I wasn't sure if word had gotten around that he was the infamous Hunter or if he lacked any skill in interacting with other individuals.

Walking silently beside him as he strolled on the perimeter of the large yard, I began my assault. I bumped against him, making physical contact, and whispered, "Your attorney is selling you out. He wants to make a name for himself at your expense. There isn't a chance in hell he'll prevail on any of his motions. You're going to get the needle. I'll bet he hasn't even presented the plea deal to you. And even if by some miracle you get out, I'll be waiting for you. If you think a broken nose was bad…" I let the threat linger in the air.

Tompkins grabbed his ears, hoping to shut out my taunts. When that didn't work, he flailed his arms, trying to connect with his invisible foe. But I dodged his attempts.

"Get away from me, devil woman. You're not real," he muttered.

"I'm not?" I taunted. "Then who smashed in your face and trussed you up like the animal you are? I'm the hunter now, and you're my prey."

"Leave me alone. What do you want from me?" he screamed.

I almost felt sorry for Tompkins when some of the other prisoners began to mutter taunts, with the most common being, "Crazy mother fucker." A few shared their basic knowledge of his deeds.

One of the guards strolled over and asked, "What the hell's your problem, Tompkins? If you continue acting up, we're going to have to cut short your time in the yard."

After the guard strolled away, I pressed, "Yeah, keep acting up, Tompkins. Maybe that will help with an insanity defense, because that's the only chance you have to avoid the death penalty."

"Shut up, shut up, shut up," Tompkins screamed.

The guard approached again and barked impatiently, "That's it. I'm revoking your outside privileges." He grabbed Tompkins by the arm, and I slipped away, following both men back inside.

The rest of the prisoners in the yard clapped and continued their taunts. After following the guard and Tompkins back inside, I looked for my opportunity to leave the premises. But I planned on returning the next day to continue my assault.

It took only two days for Tompkins to request to see his attorney. I was determined to find a way into that room, hoping for a free moment to chirp in Tompkin's ear again. I knew it wasn't ethical what I was doing and what I planned to do, but I couldn't allow this monster to go free.

I wasn't lying about the plea deal. Annalise had told me that Merrill had presented the deal, hoping to avoid a long, drawn-out trial. In reality, neither side had the winning hand. The case was toast if Tompkin's attorney lost his motion to suppress the evidence collected in his home. On the other hand, if the attorney prevailed on his motion, the case was weak at best, and the chances of an acquittal were high despite the high-profile nature of the case. The only sliver of hope was the distasteful notion of letting a serial killer go free. Someone had leaked bits and pieces of what the police had found in his home. The press was having a field day with the gory details. It would be nearly impossible to find a jury that hadn't heard a single thing about the case. Ignoring the sensational nature of those reports would be difficult, regardless of any potential jury instructions provided to the twelve unlucky men and women.

There was a fifty-fifty chance the judge would favor the prosecution. He had a reputation for being a fair and thoughtful judge. It all depended on what evidence Reese and Leslie had found to present to the judge who had issued the warrant. Annalise had informed me they had gone to a sympathetic judge, but judges rarely second-guessed another's decision unless an obviously wrong decision was rendered.

†

I sat at my breakfast counter with a cup of coffee, planning my latest assault on Tompkins. Based on the empirical evidence before me, including Tompkins' increasing distress and demand to see his attorney today, I knew I was close. Annalise was less than thrilled with my plan. She felt I might get caught inside a room or somewhere I'd have difficulty freeing myself from. But I kept reassuring her I'd already thoroughly cased the joint prior to beginning my assault on his sanity.

While I was deep in thought, Annalise snuck up behind me and draped her arms around my stomach, kissing the back of my neck. I leaned into her touch.

"You're up early," she said.

"Mmhm. Tompkins is meeting with his attorney today. I want to be there for that."

"Eavesdropping on a confidential conversation. That's not very sporting of you," Annalise teased before heading straight for the coffeepot to pour herself a cup.

"You know I hate sports," I quipped. "I think ethics went out the window a long time ago. Incessant taunting from an invisible woman isn't exactly playing fair, but I'm okay with that. Are you?"

"Getting there," Annalise replied. "Honestly, it's probably not very flattering for me to admit this, but I'm more concerned about your ability to slip in and out of places without incident. I've resolved my internal struggle with the ethical implications of our actions." After she'd fixed her coffee, she took a seat next to me.

"My actions," I corrected. "You've only danced on the edges by driving me places. Speaking of which, want to drop me off again a half a mile away? I can find my way to your office on my own. You still haven't called Erica. Why?"

Annalise shifted uncomfortably on the stool, then sipped her coffee, presumably giving her ample time to respond. "I hoped to see how this all shakes out. Either I'll be in a better position to present my credentials to Erica, or I'll be out of a job, and working as an independent investigator might be my only option. You may have an unrealistic view of the kinds of jobs an independent investigator is hired for. I don't. It isn't like Hollywood. It's mostly spying on unfaithful spouses, and that does not at all appeal to me."

"I have faith that our reputation for solving crimes and tracking the most notorious criminals will generate the type of business we're both interested in, even if you don't secure a position with the BAU, which I very much doubt," I argued.

"Okay, I'll admit, I'm a little scared that things will change too much, and I won't be able to adapt."

I stood and turned her stool so that I could shimmy between her legs. Wrapping my arms around her neck, I kissed her.

"If I can adjust to my newfound emotions, I've no doubt all this change will be a piece of cake for you. By the way, when is your meeting with OPR?"

Annalise lost the smile I'd put on her face after the kiss. "Today. I'm definitely not looking forward to that."

"What time?"

"This afternoon. So, I have the entire morning to ruminate and get my story straight. Lying does not come easy for me."

"Just stick to what you've already written. Like in court, only answer the questions asked. Avoid adding extraneous details. That's what always trips a person up."

Annalise chuckled. "Since when did you become so proficient at lying?"

I shrugged. "I did a little research. Do you know they've actually studied this? Apparently, good liars keep their lies clear and simple, tell a plausible story, are vague about the details, and weave the truth within a lie. I suggest you employ those tactics. Also, don't avoid eye contact, keep calm, and manage your facial expressions."

"Oh, is that all?" Annalise teased.

I stroked both her arms in an effort to assure her. "Even if they think you're lying, they can't prove anything. Whatever happened to that 'blue wall of silence?' Doesn't that also apply to the FBI?"

"Doesn't apply to OPR. The Office of Professional Responsibility generally has a big stick up their ass. Ironically, I've always admired them. And I've never adhered to that 'blue wall of silence.' Corrupt law enforcement officers give all of us a bad name."

"You're not corrupt," I insisted. "There are shades of gray. It's not like you planted evidence to make the case. Coloring outside the lines is hardly cause for concern. I prefer not to think of myself as a vigilante. We're more like collaborators."

"There are lines I won't cross. Not even if I lose my job and become an independent investigator."

"I know that, and I agree. While I might want to smash in Tompkins' face again, I won't. I only broke his nose because I needed to subdue him. I'll do better in the future. Excessive force shouldn't be necessary, but it's not like I have a lot of practice at this," I explained.

Annalise grinned and kissed the tip of my nose. "You're adorable. I wish I'd been there to see it, but then again, I wouldn't be able to actually see you. Watching your tiny self beat up an over six-foot man would have been quite entertaining."

"See, it'll be easy to lie about what happened. No one would ever believe that a five-foot-two invisible woman beat up Tompkins."

Annalise grimaced. "That's what I'm afraid of. It's far more likely I'm the one responsible for breaking his nose."

"Yeah, but even Tompkins isn't claiming that."

"No, but he and his lawyer are insisting I shot an innocent man who happened to be in the forest at the same time as The Hunter."

"Surely, that story won't fly with the OPR. Not after finding all the corroborating evidence in his home." I reluctantly disengaged from Annalise. "I need to jump in the shower. The meeting with the lawyer is at nine."

"All right. I'll shower after you. We don't have time to shower together?" Annalise waggled her brows at me.

"No, we do not."

†

As luck would have it, the guard brought Tompkins into the room and secured his hands before his attorney arrived. I wasn't sure how much time I had with Tompkins, so the minute the guard left to retrieve his attorney, I began my attack.

"It's time to ask your attorney about the plea deal on the table," I whispered in his ear.

Tompkins pulled on his cuff hands, struggling in the chair, and screamed, "Shut up, shut up, shut up."

"I'll never leave you alone. Not unless you do the right thing. Take the deal," I coaxed.

When I heard the door, I melted into the corner and watched as the guard released Tompkins' hands and reminded him, "The camera is on, and this room is being monitored."

The attorney nodded, and the guard left the room. His expression oozed irritation. "What did you need to see me about. I've submitted the motions. There isn't anything more to discuss until the judge rules on them."

"Why didn't you tell me about the plea deal?"

"How did you hear about that? I'll have that prosecutor debarred if he spoke with you."

Tompkins shook his head. "It was the she-devil. The one who attacked me."

"The FBI agent who arrested you?"

"No, no, I told you. I can't see her. She's going to haunt me if I don't take the deal. She told me you were selling me out, trying to make a name for yourself. I'm going to get the needle."

"I already have a stellar reputation. I don't need your case for that," the attorney spat out. "Maybe we should pivot and offer an insanity defense. I can easily sell that."

"I'm not insane," Tompkins screamed. "I want the deal." He pushed from his chair and lunged at his attorney, who quickly scrambled away. The guard burst into the room and reattached Tompkins' hands to the cuffs on the table.

The attorney threw his hands in the air. "Fine. I'm done with you." He turned to the guard. "We're finished. You can take him back to his cell."

Tompkins kept muttering, "I'm not crazy. She's real."

Following the attorney, I slipped from the room. My job was complete. I couldn't wait to tell Annalise all about it. Finally, some good news, and we could celebrate. I was so jubilant about my success that I almost didn't make it out of the building. It was tricky following someone without touching them but maintaining enough proximity to make it through open doors. At one point, the attorney turned his head, presumably sensing there was someone close behind.

He shook his head and muttered, "Now he's got me believing in invisible demons."

I stifled a chuckle that threatened to escape. But then again, haunting this attorney might be a bonus, so I let my dampened laughter out. He spun around again, and I barely had enough time to dodge his briefcase.

So much for getting cocky. I wouldn't chance that again.

I couldn't wait to go to Annalise's office and give her the good news. Hopefully, that would shift the focus off of her with the successful resolution to The Hunter case. *All's well that ends well, as John Heywood would say.* I almost chuckled out loud, revealing myself as I remembered when Annalise and I had debated the origin of that saying. I gave her credit for knowing the title of the Shakespeare play, which was the exact wording of the original proverb. However, I insisted that John Heywood was an extremely underrated historical figure when you considered that nearly thirty famous quotes could be attributed to him. They included "out of sight, out of mind" and "two heads are better than one." I had pulled out my copy of *The Proverbs of John Heywood* as proof.

Annalise wasn't too happy when I proved her wrong and called me a show-off. I would miss our debates if the nature of our relationship changed too much. I wondered if she would as well. My changing views on the concept of love remained a little disconcerting to me.

It was still early, so I strolled to the park and enjoyed sitting on a bench before picking up lunch for Annalise and me. I hoped that the good news would be enough of a catalyst for the very change she was so afraid of. I believed in her skills, and I knew for a fact that the BAU did as well.

# CHAPTER TWENTY-THREE

Once I found my way to Annalise's favorite deli within walking distance of the FBI offices, I slipped into their public restroom and made myself visible again. I ordered her favorite sandwich and one for me, even though the sandwiches were huge and could easily be shared. Then, I added four different side salads, chips, and cookies. Everything looked so good, and I was starved since I'd skipped breakfast. The security control at the office always seemed overkill to me, but I supposed that lately it was necessary with all the divisive politics.

Reese saw me before I made it to Annalise's office. She studied my outfit and asked, "Out for a run? I didn't know you were a runner."

"I'm not," I answered without filling in any details regarding why I was dressed in a tight-fitting workout outfit.

"Heard you left forensics. I suppose now you're a woman of leisure. I see you brought lunch. Annalise must love how you spoil her."

"She deserves it. But I won't always be a woman of leisure. I decided to go out on my own and become an independent consultant to the BAU. It provides me with the flexibility of working on cases that I'm interested in versus every garden variety homicide. I wanted to catch Annalise before her meeting this afternoon."

"Yeah, that's crap. I met with OPR and confirmed that Tompkins ranted about an invisible monster and never once claimed that Annalise beat on him. I also reiterated that with all the evidence found at Tompkin's home, he was not an innocent man shot in the forest because he was in the wrong place at the wrong time. In my humble opinion, the shot was clean, even though I wasn't there when Annalise tagged him. Something big is happening, though. Merrill barreled into Gary's office a few minutes ago."

"Oh?" I worked hard to keep my face impassive.

My focus on Reese shifted when Gary's door popped open, and he called out, "Reese, can you come into my office? And grab Annalise, please."

"Shit," Reese muttered. "They better not be dropping the charges against Tompkins."

I used every ounce of effort I had to keep from smiling because I already knew why they were being called in.

"Can I wait in Annalise's office?" I asked. "Sounds like she's being called into a meeting."

Reese nodded. "Sure, but I don't know how long we'll be."

"That's okay. Woman of leisure, remember? She's got to eat, right?"

I followed Reese to Annalise's office. Two quick knocks, and Reese opened the door. Annalise looked up, her face a mask of confusion, when she saw both of us hovering outside her door.

"What's going on?" Annalise asked.

"Gary asked me to get you. Merrill looked like she was on a mission when she marched into Gary's office ten minutes ago," Reese answered.

"Now what? I'm resigning if Merrill tells us she's dropping the case," Annalise barked.

"I'll join you," Reese stated.

I shook my head. "For two accomplished FBI agents, you sure jump to conclusions quickly. I suggest gathering the facts before going off half-cocked."

Reese grinned. "She has a point. Leave it to Tamara to be the voice of reason."

Annalise glanced at the bags in my hand. "Will you wait here? Whatever news they have to share, hopefully the meeting won't last long. Looks like you brought enough for all three of us."

"Not exactly, but I suppose there is enough food. I might have gone a little overboard ordering for you."

"Sold. Thanks, Tamara," Reese declared.

I made myself comfortable in her office and resisted the urge to nibble on one of the side salads. Surely, it wouldn't take long for Merrill to share that Tompkins had accepted a plea deal. Would Annalise even need to keep her meeting with OPR?

†

I lost my fight to keep from breaking into the food and was happily munching on a bag of chips when Reese and Annalise strolled into the office with enormous smiles on their faces. I couldn't admit to Reese that I already knew the reason for their apparent good mood.

After quickly chewing the chip I'd just placed in my mouth, I said, "I guess you jumped to conclusions before. You should remember that in the future."

"How do you know that?" Reese asked.

"You two aren't the only ones who can read facial expressions and body language. So, what happened? Can you share that with me?" I asked, keeping up pretenses.

Annalise shrugged. "Merrill didn't specifically direct us to keep this under wraps. Tompkins took her plea deal. Life without parole."

"What does that mean for the internal investigation? Do you still have to meet with OPR this afternoon?" I asked.

Annalise frowned. "Unfortunately, yes. Once they're involved, there is no stopping an investigation. I understand. I'd probably have the same questions if the shoe was on the other foot. It doesn't matter. I'm not giving up my confidential informant. If I didn't share that information with you, Reese, I'm certainly not going to reveal the name to them."

Reese narrowed her eyes and studied me. I suspected she was trying to determine if I was the confidential informant and how it was even possible for me to best Tompkins. David versus Goliath came to mind, but that was mythology, not real life.

"You know, I still haven't forgiven you for that," Reese noted. "If I didn't know any better, I'd think it was Tamara because who else would you go out of your way to protect so fiercely?"

Annalise chuckled nervously. "Yeah, right. Because Tamara is such a fierce Amazon warrior. Just look at her."

I worried that Reese would pick up on Annalise's nervous laughter, so I changed the subject. "Let's eat. As you can see, I didn't have a lot of willpower to wait. Although I did manage to save the sandwiches, salads, and cookies. Maybe we can go out for drinks to celebrate tonight. You up for that, Reese?"

"Sure, why not?"

†

O'Malley's was your typical bar. One that often catered to law enforcement and the agents at the FBI. The dark wood chosen for the long bar that took up nearly half the space inside reflected the limited light. Annalise had always preferred this bar. I wondered if that was because a person's features were never clearly visible. I couldn't speak to why it was a favorite for most of the other agents other than its proximity to their office.

Beer wasn't exactly my drink of choice, but when in Rome, as the old saying goes. I offered to get us a pitcher of beer, and by the time I returned, I caught the end of their conversation.

"Why didn't you tell me you were planning on leaving?" Reese asked, a hint of disappointment in her voice. "Who else am I going to commiserate with?"

"It wasn't a sure thing," Annalise answered. "With the way the Tompkins case was going, I didn't believe I had a

213

snowball's chance in hell. I only decided today, and I'm telling you now."

I set down the pitcher of beer with the glasses and arched an eyebrow. "Something you forgot to share with me?"

"Sorry. I was going to talk to you tonight," Annalise confessed. "After I met with the OPR, I took the plunge and called. They asked when I could start and seemed quite desperate to have me begin as soon as possible, so I gave my notice today."

Reese picked up the pitcher of beer and poured three glasses. She leaned back in her chair. "Guess I'm not the only person you're keeping secrets from. I suppose I don't feel so bad anymore. I still hate the fact that you're leaving, though."

I was starting to appreciate Reese more and more. Despite my previous irrational feelings, my emotions were settling regarding Annalise and Reese's apparently close relationship. I saw it for what it was—two colleagues who respected one another.

"You should apply to the BAU, too," I blurted.

Annalise grinned. "Tamara's right. We made a great team. Both our talents are being wasted in this office."

"Hey, what about me?" I interjected in a teasing tone. "I believe my contributions were critical."

Reese narrowed her eyes, turning her focus on me. "Why do I get the impression that you were far more involved than either of you are willing to admit?"

Annalise picked up her glass and lifted it into the air. "How about a toast to celebrate getting another psycho off the streets?"

I clinked my glass with hers, and Reese reluctantly lifted her own mug, touching each of ours before taking a sip.

"Fine. I'll let you two have your little secrets," Reese declared. "I don't even care if you were involved more than you should have been. Though, for the life of me, I can't quite fit all the pieces together."

"So, are you going to apply to the BAU?" I asked. "I have a contact there. I could give you a stellar recommendation."

"Gary is going to have a litter of tigers if we both leave," Reese joked.

"I like that. Litter of tigers. That's funny because it has to be more difficult than domestic kittens. You know, there is a dispute regarding the origin of that saying. I tend to believe it makes the most sense that it comes from medieval Britain and the belief that witches turned unborn children into cats that scratched their way out of the womb. Although, the US expression of having a cow makes even more sense because it's far more difficult than having kittens," I added.

Both Reese and Annalise burst out in laughter.

"How about we say hissy fit?" Annalise offered. "I can almost picture that."

By the end of the evening, it seemed as though all the stress from the last several weeks had drained from Annalise's face. I hadn't realized how heavily the case, adjustments to our relationship, and impending career changes were weighing on her. Maybe the prospect of Reese considering a career change allowed Annalise to retain some amount of stability in her work life. There was something to be said about not making too many changes simultaneously, and I suppose I should have recognized that. Even positive alterations added to one's stress level. Whatever the cause, I was grateful to see Annalise smile and laugh without that pinched expression I'd seen more of in the last few weeks than in all the years I'd known her. She was happy. And so was I.

†

When we arrived back at my place, Annalise blurted, "I'm sorry. I should have told you first. It's just that I was afraid I wouldn't follow through if I didn't make the call today. Reese saw me talking to Gary and knew something was going on. She asked me about it, and with all the lying I've been doing lately, I couldn't add one more lie on top of it."

I pulled Annalise into an embrace. "I'm not angry. Quite the opposite. I'm extremely proud of you."

"It was an interesting conversation with Erica. She asked about my confidential informant."

"She did?" I asked.

"Mmhm. I said if revealing my source was a requirement to secure a position with the BAU, I wasn't interested. She assured me it wasn't. All she wanted to know was if I planned on continuing to use that informant."

"Really? And what did you say?"

"I told her I intended to press every available advantage at my disposal, which would definitely include my valuable resource. She seemed satisfied with my answer. I get the sense that all she cares about is results. She may be more inclined to use creative methods to achieve success. Sounds like a perfect fit to me."

I chuckled. "I knew you'd like Erica. The first time I ever spoke with her, I was impressed, but that wasn't the right time. Now it is."

"Yeah, now it is. Seems like it's the right time for a lot of things." Annalise leaned in to kiss me, and the kiss rapidly turned passionate.

"So, you're really okay with everything? I know you had a few trepidations regarding your ability to adapt to all these rapid changes. Studies show that even positive changes like a new job or getting married can affect a person's health because of the increase in stress."

"Getting married," she squeaked.

"Oh, I know we aren't getting married, but we are in a new relationship. It's very similar, you know," I clarified.

"No, it's not. Marriage is a whole new level. Not that I wouldn't consider that with you, because I absolutely have thought about it. Well, fantasized is a more accurate description. But even I know it's way too soon. Besides, we aren't even living together yet."

"We aren't? I just assumed that when you started sleeping in the master bedroom with me that meant we were now living together. Do we need to move your clothes from the guest bedroom into the master? Will that make it clear that we're now living together?"

"Huh? I suppose I do spend all my time at your place," Annalise noted.

"I don't think of it as my place. I can put you on the deed if that makes a difference," I offered.

"I wasn't really angling for that. For someone so opposed to the concept of love a short time ago, you sure are willing to advance our relationship quickly. Even for lesbians, we might be in the top percentile." Annalise chuckled nervously.

"I don't understand. Do you not wish to live together?" I asked.

"No, no, I do. It's suddenly hitting me. I'm getting everything I ever dreamed of, and stuff like that doesn't happen to me. I'm not used to it. First, you discover a miraculous cure for my scars, then you tell me you love me, and finally, we catch a serial killer who's been terrorizing our community for months, which leads to a dream job with the BAU. I'm waiting for the other shoe to drop because it always has before."

"That's superstition. I don't believe in karma, and even if I did, you've done nothing to deserve what happened to you as a child. I also don't believe in a higher power that magically turns water into wine or whatever miracle a person prays for. Life is what you make of it. You work hard. You're a good person. Of course you deserve every positive development. Embrace it."

"I do believe in a higher power. So maybe my prayers have finally been answered," she argued. "At least that is something I'll always be able to count on."

"Your god? Give me a break."

"No, our robust debates. I'd miss that more than any job or other constant in my life. Maybe my god or goddess sent you those alien seeds. I'm willing to concede that the higher power I believe in isn't necessarily male, or any gender for that matter. You have to admit, the effects of those seeds are as close to a miracle as one can get."

"Just because I haven't discovered the science behind the effects of the seeds doesn't mean the science doesn't exist. It's more likely the answer lies in the vast universe. Alien life seems more logical than some mythical being."

Annalise chuckled. "Yeah, keep telling yourself that. Perhaps it will rationalize every mystery in the world that your science has yet to explain. But right now, those brain chemicals you insist represent love are currently going into overdrive. And I feel compelled to act upon them by taking you to bed."

"I can agree to that. We can return to this topic at a later date and time."

## CHAPTER TWENTY-FOUR

*Six Months Later*

I was relaxing in the living room, catching up on some reading, including my daily perusal of the various news outlets. Something caught my attention, and I was reading about another possible serial killer in the serial killer capital of the world, New York. Not New York City, but the state, topped the list as the number one state with eighteen known serial killers. I guessed they were about to add to that list.

Although the cases we worked on together interesting, I found I was easily bored and would occasionally prowl the streets late at night, looking for trouble. Sometimes, I found it, but most of the time, I didn't. What kind of superhero would I be if I wasn't able to help the masses. I wondered if living in a relatively rural area limited our opportunities for doing good. But would moving to somewhere like Detroit or Baltimore, two cities with the highest violent crime rate that weren't located in the South, be something Annalise might consider? She'd already made drastic changes to her life. Maybe it wasn't fair to ask this of her just because I felt like I wasn't reaching my full potential with the gifts provided by the alien fruit. She wasn't either, considering her enhanced strength and other senses.

Annalise barreled into the room, panting and out of breath. Despite my desire to be a better fighter and gain overall improved conditioning, I continually passed on Annalise's offer to join her on her daily run. I'd purchased and promptly ignored the elliptical and exercise bike set up in the room that was now Annalise's playground. She loved those additions to her free weights. The one small adjustment I made was allowing Annalise to train me in martial arts. I insisted that would be an adequate daily workout. It sure felt like it to me. I argued that anything that caused me to sweat counted.

"Wheels up in an hour," Annalise announced through labored breathing.

I raised my eyebrow. "Wheels up? You sound like the BAU actually has a private jet."

Annalise leaned over, grabbing her knees as she caught her breath. "I've always wanted to say that. We need to meet Erica at the airport in an hour. Why are you just sitting there like you haven't a care in the world. Didn't Erica call?"

I shifted my eyes to my phone sitting on the charger. "She might have. Let me take a look." I ambled to my phone and plucked it from the charger, scanning my missed calls. "Yes. It looks like Erica did call. I suppose I don't need to listen to the message now. You'll fill me in."

Annalise shook her head. "Why do you insist on keeping your phone in silent mode? I'll bet that's incredibly frustrating to those who wish to get hold of you. For the record, I'm one of those. I can't believe Erica lets you get away with ignoring her calls."

I shrugged. "We live together, so you always know where I am, and Erica knows you're like my first alert system. She called you, and you'll give me the details I need. Any other call I might receive isn't important. Even if it were something critical, the person could simply leave a message. Eventually, I would get it."

"We better never break up, then. You'd be lost without me," Annalise stated.

I didn't like her even jesting about that. "That isn't a consideration, is it?"

Annalise quickly grabbed me in an embrace. "Nope. Of course not. You aren't getting rid of me that easy." She gave me a quick peck on the nose and took a step back. "Forget your total disregard of your phone as an important communication device. There's a fresh body. It tracks with two other homicides, so they suspect a serial. The mayor is requesting the assistance of the BAU."

"New York?"

"Yeah, how did you know if you haven't checked your messages?" she asked.

"There's a developing story I was just reading about. It's light on details, only that there is a suspected serial killer on the loose."

"I'll fill you in on the way to the plane, but I need to jump in the shower. Then we can grab our bags and go. She was going to send the case file for us to look at."

"All right." I crinkled my nose. "You are a bit ripe. Probably a good idea to shower. The plane is a compact space."

Annalise chuckled. "I'll hurry. For someone who tends to be on the blunt end of the spectrum, you have an incredibly developed ability to lie or tell half-truths when it suits you."

I shrugged. "Superman was the epitome of a boy scout who could keep his identity secret without losing sleep. Why shouldn't I follow suit?"

Annalise continued to laugh as she hurried to our master bath.

†

While waiting for Annalise to shower, I decided to listen to the message from Erica. There wasn't much to it. She relayed that she would like my expertise on a case with a suspected serial in New York, and if I got the message, I needed to call her back as soon as possible, otherwise she'd call Annalise. I smiled. Not that Erica didn't believe in Annalise's skills, but I sensed that she knew we were a package deal. She was also working on adding another spot for Reese, but that was proving more difficult. Erica's budget was constantly being scrutinized. Unfortunately, politics played a significant role in FBI budgets, including the infamous BAU.

Instead of calling Erica back, I texted that Annalise and I were on our way and would be there within the hour. I knew she wouldn't consider that rude since we'd worked on several cases in the previous six months, and she'd become accustomed to my style. After I finished with my quick text, I grabbed my to-go bag and placed it in the car. I was getting ready to fill a plastic bag with some alien fruit, when Annalise emerged from the bedroom, her hair still wet as she finger-combed it with her right hand while readjusting her bag on her shoulder with her left hand.

"Ready to go? Where's your bag?"

"In the car already. But I need to harvest some fruit from the greenhouse."

"Right, right. Let me dump my bag, and I'll help."

"No need. It won't take me long. I'll meet you in the car," I suggested.

After filling a plastic bag with fruit, I stuffed the entire supply inside my sling pack and hurried to the car. Tossing the bag in the back, I climbed into the passenger seat and said, "Let's roll."

Once Annalise had backed out of the driveway, she began to fill me in. "Okay, it's a little gruesome. What else is new, huh? Why can't the serials do something simple like strangle their victims?" she quipped.

"Gruesome? In what way?" I refocused.

"Right. Well, the eyes were gouged out with an unknown instrument. The tongue was removed. Also unclear what he or she used. Finally, there was blood that poured from both ears, as if the killer shoved a knife or some kind of sharp object inside the ear canal."

"Interesting. See no evil, hear no evil, speak no evil," I noted.

"Do you think the killer is trying to send a message?" Annalise asked.

"Aren't they all? What do the profilers have to say?"

Annalise glanced at me and shook her head. "I don't know. Erica only provided those basic details, stating it was a consistent pattern that led them to believe we have a serial."

"I would take a close look at the victims. Guaranteed there is a clue there. If I had to guess, they're all individuals who may have looked the other way regarding someone's crimes or immoral behavior. In the eyes of the killer," I added.

"Hmm, maybe you should change careers and become a profiler," Annalise teased.

"You would have come to a similar conclusion, eventually. Your adrenaline and excitement over a new case usually take you off track. Once you settle, that insightful brain of yours kicks in. Where do you think I learned how to piece the evidence together to formulate a reasonable theory? You've been my mentor in more ways than love and martial arts."

"Aw, thanks." Annalise reached over and grabbed my hand. "Speaking of reasonable theories. I wondered what prompted Tompkins to kill his victims on the day before their birthdays. That was always a head-scratcher for me."

"And," I prompted.

"Scuttlebutt is that he's speaking with a true crime writer and gave up the goods..."

"Stop teasing me. So why did he kill them before their birthdays?"

"Apparently, his father took him hunting every year on his birthday, starting at age seven, and harangued him until he made his first kill. Finally, at age sixteen, he shot a deer and had to watch the poor animal suffer until it died because the shot wasn't a kill shot. In his twisted mind, he was keeping all his victims from turning into the monster he'd become. He had plans to continue killing until he prevented that very first milestone. He had the final victim picked out, a star football player who would turn sixteen in the coming year."

"Why star athletes?"

"Because they were the type of individuals his father respected. His father was a star athlete in high school and college. He believed he would recover from an injury in his final year of college, but no team was willing to chance it. His dream of going pro ended with that injury and turned him into an abusive husband and father. Tompkins wasn't exactly the type of son to pursue sports and become a surrogate for his father's dreams. In fact, he was the exact opposite—an overweight, nerdy computer genius. He snapped on his annual birthday hunting trip. Paying homage to his dead mother, he pushed his father off a cliff and began his killing spree. That is some twisted shit, huh? I almost feel sorry for him."

"A significant percentage of serial killers have experienced trauma in their childhoods," I recited. "And an even larger percentage admit to witnessing or being a part of sexually stressful events. I'm not saying that should excuse their behavior, but it does make you wonder how, as a society, we could have prevented the horrific killings."

Annalise chuckled. "I bet you know the exact percentages." I opened my mouth to cite them, but she held up her hand. "Don't need to know what they are."

I closed my mouth, but the compulsion overtook me, and I blurted, "Forty and seventy percent, respectively."

Annalise broke into a full belly laugh. "Gosh, that was fun. I almost saw your head explode, trying to keep those stats from tumbling out of your mouth. Honestly, I'm surprised you didn't include them when you first shared the information."

I crossed my arms over my chest and, uncharacteristically, pouted.

"Aw, hon. I'm just teasing you. Don't you know how much I love it when you spout facts to me? It's one of the most endearing things about you. Don't change a thing. I've always loved that about you."

"Really?"

"Yes, really."

†

Erica was waiting for us at the gate and waved us over. We'd arrived just in time as the line to board dwindled, leaving only a few passengers ahead of us. She handed each of us a file with presumably different information. Annalise generally received details on the case, and I would obtain a more tailored file limited to any initial forensics that had been done.

"You can view the information en route. I think you'll find the victimology quite enlightening," Erica noted as she took her place in the short line.

"So, we have a good place to start," Annalise responded. I could tell she was itching to open the file and begin reading.

"I'm happy to be here and consult, but from what Annalise told me, you don't need a skin expert."

"In my humble opinion, local authorities made rash decisions about the cause of death. Sure, whatever was shoved into the ear canal would definitely cause death, especially if it penetrated the brain, but I need you to take a look at the pictures and see if you notice anything strange," Erica explained. "The skin just looked off to me. I've seen a lot of dead bodies, and something wasn't right. Plus, we have a fresh body for you to examine."

I nodded. "All right. Anything else you can share about the body?"

"Yeah, there was a symbol carved into the skin, and I thought you might be able to shed some light on that. We need to know what was used, what the symbol means, and was the carving done peri or postmortem. There are pictures you can review, and when we arrive, you can examine the body."

"Fascinating. Did anyone on the forensics team test for particulates?" I asked.

Erica shook her head. "Not on the previous victims. Honestly, I wonder a little about the investigation. Sloppy police work, rudimentary forensics. The local authorities don't seem too thrilled to have us join the investigation."

"Then why were we called in?" Annalise asked.

"The wife of this last victim has connections. She comes from old money. He was also a very influential man in the community. Sorry, we can talk later." Erica swiped her phone and held it under the scanner so the device could recognize her boarding pass.

"Figures," Annalise muttered as she followed suit, placing her phone under the scanner.

We finally made it to our seats, and Annalise helped me find a place for my carry-on after she shoved her backpack into an open space. She slid into the middle seat, leaving me the aisle. I loved that about Annalise. She was always so considerate and gallant. Obviously, I didn't need help with my bag, but I suppose she thought it was easier for her with her height. Before gaining my super strength, securing my bag in the overhead compartment had occasionally been a struggle. Being five-foot-two had its disadvantages.

Once I settled into my seat, I opened the file and began my examination of the pictures taken at the scene. The previous forensic reports were rather sketchy. I could definitely understand why Erica had concerns. I didn't have all the facts, but it didn't take a stretch to surmise that someone wanted things shoved underneath a rug and never uncovered. But why? And who? The picture of the symbol carved into the body wasn't very clear. I reached for my pair of magnifying glasses to take a closer look.

"All the victims were associated with Excelsior Academy," Annalise whispered.

"That must be what Erica was talking about," I said as I donned the glasses and took a closer look. "Mmm. Someone might be out for revenge." I pointed to the picture of the symbol. "This is the double infinity symbol."

"I never heard of that. What does infinity have to do with revenge?" Annalise asked.

"The symbol became popular with that television show, *Revenge*."

"How do you know that? We've never watched the show. I've never even heard of it."

I shot her the look. "I know a lot of things. Do you really question my knowledge?"

Annalise chuckled. "I don't even know why I bother to Google anything. You're like the human equivalent of a Google search engine. I suppose the whole 'see no evil, hear no evil, speak no evil' is definitely a viable avenue to pursue. Something bad happened to someone associated with that school, and people with the authority to address the issue looked the other way. If we discover what happened, we'll find our killer."

"A premature assessment, but certainly a viable theory. Are you going to suggest that to Erica?" I asked.

"I am. Perhaps we'll be able to wrap this up quickly. That would be nice, huh?"

I shrugged. "Maybe. I don't really enjoy having a lot of free time, even if it does allow me to pursue other interests."

"You mean like going on the prowl at night? I really wish you wouldn't do that."

"Most nights are a total bust. You could come with me," I suggested hopefully.

"Oh, you don't need my help, Ms. Invisible Woman. That would just shine a spotlight on me again. You've been doing just fine making those anonymous calls to the police. Did you know that Reese asked me about that? She wondered if the good Samaritan calling the police occasionally was my confidential informant. I had to dodge her question. Fortunately, she let me, but her knowing smirk told the entire story."

I couldn't think of a better opportunity to bring up my idea of moving to a city with more violent crime. "I think we should move."

"Move? Why?"

"To be closer to the action. Like maybe Detroit or Baltimore."

"Ugh," Annalise groaned. "I can't think of any place more unappealing than those two cities."

"Every city has some redeeming qualities. I'm not suggesting we buy a home smack dab in the middle of gangland…"

"Now you want to be like Batman, moving to some dreary place like Gotham City. No thanks. I like where we live."

"Well, I can't fly like Superman, so I need to be closer to where I can do some real good."

Annalise pinched the bridge of her nose. "Can we talk about this later? I'm getting a headache."

I grabbed her hand and squeezed. "As long as you promise that we will talk about it. You have a tendency to procrastinate when something is uncomfortable. I love you."

It was becoming easier to declare my love for Annalise, especially when it softened her for whatever new idea I wanted to spring on her.

"Quit trying to butter me up. You do that to me every time you believe I'm going to fight you on something."

I grinned. "It always works. Why should I change tactics?"

"We'll talk, and I'll keep an open mind. That's all you're getting from me right now."

# CHAPTER TWENTY-FIVE

The case quickly turned into something neither Annalise nor I expected and ended up being the last case we would work on during our short-term stint with the BAU. It wasn't that I didn't have the stomach to work on serials, but this case brought about so many conflicting emotions that, in the end, it proved too difficult for both of us. The only fortunate aspect of the case was that it unraveled rather quickly. We literally hit the ground running once we touched down at the airport.

After deplaning, Erica met us quickly and pulled us away from prying ears. "We've got another body. Follow me. There's a car circling the airport, ready to pick us up. If we hurry, we can make it to the curb on his next drive-through." She began her sprint through the airport to ground transportation with Annalise close on her heels.

I silently cursed my small rolling case. Not only did my short legs have me at a disadvantage, but both Annalise and Erica each had a carry-on bag that they easily slung over their shoulders or attached to their back. Even with my super-speed, it was awkward to run while dragging the bag behind me. Plus, there were so many witnesses to my super-strength or super speed, and I couldn't exactly shove the rolling case under one arm while I caught up with my two colleagues. My arms weren't long enough to wrap around the bag.

One thing that hadn't improved with the consumption of the alien fruit was my lung capacity. I might be able to run fast, but that didn't mean I wouldn't huff and puff at the end of any significant jaunt. No doubt Annalise would tease me about my aversion to running with her and improving my cardiovascular endurance.

I kept Annalise and Erica in my line of vision as I saw them both climb into a black SUV. A man jumped out and grabbed my bag, slinging it into the back while I attempted to catch my breath. The door to the back seat remained open, and I took the empty seat next to Annalise.

"Told you that a regimen of aerobic exercise would do you some good. Sparring with me does not count," Annalise quipped.

"Yes, yes. You know best, but I'm going to need something less disagreeable to me," I answered between my continuing labored breaths.

"Cycling?"

I wrinkled my nose. "Not on that exercise bike. It's boring and uncomfortable."

"How about we look into a bike with a comfortable seat? A recumbent cycle, maybe? You can read your science journals while pedaling. You won't even know you're getting daily exercise."

I considered her suggestion. "Okay, you win. We'll go shopping when we return."

"Are you two done squabbling about exercise routines?" Erica sniped. "So, the most recent victim is a detective with the local police. He's the first victim not associated with the boarding school."

"Wasn't one of the victims some kind of security officer for the school?" Annalise asked.

"Yes, he was the head of campus security," Erica answered.

"Does campus security have a relationship with the local police?" I asked.

"Unknown, but probably. I suspect there would be occasions where they would collaborate on certain investigations of crimes that happen on the campus, especially violent crimes. Before we interview anyone at the school, we need to check out the body. I'd prefer Tamara give her initial assessment before the local police muck things up," Erica directed.

"How about we divide and conquer?" Annalise suggested. "The two of you can go directly to the crime scene. Tamara will be responsible for ensuring the body is thoroughly examined. I doubt I have the same tactical approach to gaining any valuable information from the local police. Erica, you're much nicer to deal with."

Erica smirked. "You can be quite charming when you want to be."

"Not with incompetent law enforcement, then my prickly side comes out to play," Annalise argued.

"Fair point." Erica turned to the driver. "Somehow, I believe the local police will be a lot more cooperative. After all, one of their own just turned up dead. Rick, would you mind dropping us off at the crime scene and then taking Annalise to the school?"

Rick nodded. "Yes, ma'am. I wouldn't want to be on the other end of someone's prickly side."

Annalise chuckled. "You and I are going to get along just fine, Rick."

Rick rolled to a stop beside several police vehicles. Before heading to the melee of police and the forensic team, Erica leaned inside the car and said, "Give 'em hell, Annalise. That school is hiding something, and I want to know what it is before several more bodies show up. Feel free to intimidate them all you want. In fact, I'm counting on it."

Annalise grinned. "You got it, boss. I despise bureaucrats obstructing our investigation as much as incompetent police."

"I know you do." Erica pivoted and walked to the man who was clearly in charge.

While Erica made nice with the local police, I didn't feel compelled to make small talk with any of them as I made a beeline to the body. Flashing my credentials that Erica had provided on the way to the scene, I snapped on a pair of gloves and squatted beside the body.

While there was certainly a small pool of blood oozing from both ears along with what I suspected were tiny specks of brain matter, what caught my attention most was the pink discoloration on the skin. I had a strong suspicion that the cause of death was not whatever weapon the killer had shoved into both ears. Nor was it likely that the removal of his eyes and tongue had caused enough trauma or blood loss to result in death.

"We need to test for cyanide poisoning," I announced.

A technician shifted his eyes to me. "Pretty sure the cause of death is whatever someone shoved hard enough into his ears to leave brain matter behind."

I shook my head. "I suspect the eyes, ears, and tongue were all done postmortem. Very close to the time of death, but still postmortem, which would account for the amount of blood on the scene."

"Who the hell are you?"

"Dr. Tamara Childs, forensic consultant for the BAU."

He narrowed his eyes. "Since when did we hand over jurisdiction to the FBI?"

"I imagine that happened when the bodies started piling up, and I suspect with the police losing one of their own, they'll be more inclined to hand over the reins, considering you've done an inadequate job with the previous autopsies." I spoke without meeting his eyes as I continued to evaluate the body. Pushing aside the man's shirt, I leaned in for a closer look at the double infinity sign carved into his chest. "This was also done post-mortem."

The man stalked away just as Erica approached. "I see you're making friends already." She chuckled. "What do you think?"

"I don't generally like to guess, but I suspect poisoning. Could be a woman. I know that's rare for a serial, but poison is the preferred method for women."

Erica nodded. "Local police are still hiding something, but we have jurisdiction now. I'm no longer in the mood to cooperate much. I need you to make sure a thorough evaluation of the body is done. When you're finished supervising the work of the forensics team, give me a call, and I'll send Rick to come get you and take you to the hotel."

"I don't believe they will be too happy with me supervising their work," I remarked.

"Tough. Find someone competent to work with," Erica directed.

I nodded and caught the eye of another tech who seemed to watch our interaction closely. I only hoped she'd be an ally rather than an enemy. As soon as Erica walked away, the tech approached.

"Are you really Dr. Tamara Childs?"

I squinted in her direction. "Yes, why?"

"I've read all your papers. You're brilliant. I prefer to concentrate on the bones, but skin is important too."

"Thank you. Yes, both specialties are critical to unraveling the mysteries behind death."

The young woman beamed. "I can take you to where they'll be doing the autopsy and help you navigate some of the egos who will be involved in this investigation. Not everyone is like Grant."

I glanced at the tech, who was still glaring at me while in a hushed conversation with another person. "Ah, Mr. Personality over there. To be fair, I'm not known for developing warm and fuzzy relationships with everyone I work with. Although I do okay with those I respect."

She shrugged. "Hopefully, I'll earn your respect."

†

It had been an excruciatingly long day, made especially more tiring until the bone expert arrived. Once I believed the autopsy and forensic examination would be thorough and to my specifications, I left the other consultant in charge. I'd already gotten the answers I needed to satisfy my suspicion that the cause of death was cyanide poisoning. All other wounds were postmortem, as I had suspected.

I was starving when Rick finally dropped me off at the hotel. Annalise met me in the lobby and took me to the suite Erica had arranged for us. Considering how uncooperative the local police had been, she wanted to pull together the small team at our hotel. The suite was the largest space to gather in, and Annalise warned me before we arrived there.

"We have a surprise for you," Annalise said, with a glint in her eyes.

"I hope it's dinner because I haven't had anything to eat since the very underwhelming breakfast on the plane."

We stepped into the elevator and waited for it to take us to the fifth floor. Annalise frowned. "No, sorry. But we can order as soon as we get to the room. I have a lot to share. I wouldn't be surprised if we wrap this up within the next day or two."

"Okay." We stepped off the elevator, and Annalise waved the key over the door. When we stepped inside, I saw Reese lounging on the loveseat, looking over an open file.

"Reese!" I exclaimed.

She smiled at me and answered, "Finally made it into the dream team. Erica called, and I grabbed a late flight, but I'm here. Annalise was just about to fill us in."

I sat in a chair across from Reese and Erica, who had both occupied the compact loveseat. Annalise grabbed another chair and pulled it around the table where they had strewn about all the case files.

"Sounds like she's the only person to have dug out useful information," Erica noted. "The local police have continued to stonewall me. It doesn't take a crack investigator to know they're hiding something."

"Most of the school officials did the same to me, but I finally caught up with one of the campus security personnel who was willing to talk," Annalise shared. "I noticed the guard watching me when I approached the headmaster to interview him. He's the school's interim replacement. He couldn't or wouldn't tell me much, but the guard had some very interesting information to share. He's been at the school for over twenty years."

"Well, don't keep us hanging. Annalise always does this. Like she's reciting a story to build the suspense," Reese teased.

"I do not. Do I?" Annalise asked as she caught my eye.

I nodded. "Sometimes, yeah."

Erica sighed. "Please continue."

"Right. Okay," Annalise began, "some of the young men who come to the school are less than honorable. Apparently, the school has had some issues with boys from the more prominent families engaging in sexual assault. The school likes to handle these issues without involving the police. Typically, the guard wasn't involved in any of those situations. But on one occasion, he was on duty early in the morning and came across a young woman who was very distraught. He noted her torn clothes and the bruises on her wrists. He'd been directed that if there was ever a suspicion of sexual assault, he was to bring that to the head of campus security. So, he took the young woman to his supervisor."

"When did this happen?" Erica asked.

"Seven years ago," Annalise answered.

"That's a long time to hold a grudge," I noted.

"Perhaps. I think we need to dig a little deeper," Annalise declared. "The guard didn't know the young woman's name, but he did remember that she was a scholarship recipient who lost her scholarship shortly after the incident. He wasn't sure which boys were involved, either, but he suspected that whoever they were, it was likely they came from influential families. The guard mentioned hearing a rumor that the young woman's mother eventually went to the police. He assumed that the two detectives assigned to the case were following up because he saw them talking to the headmaster. One was a woman, and the other a man. After the incident, he occasionally saw the man come to campus but never saw the woman again."

"Well, isn't that interesting?" Erica remarked. "The guy we found dead today was a detective assigned as a liaison to the school. I did manage to wriggle that out of the Chief. I want to know who his partner was seven years ago. Annalise and Reese, why don't you follow up on this? Tread lightly. We need that name without showing our cards. I'd very much like to talk to that detective."

"Can I go too?" I asked.

"I don't think that's a good idea. Sounds like you ruffled a few feathers today. Let Reese take the lead on this. She has a softer touch," Erica answered. "Why don't you do some internet research? See if you can find anything on what might have occurred seven years ago. Maybe find a class list. There can't have been too many scholarship recipients, especially someone who lost their scholarship."

"The school seems to toot their own horn by announcing prior graduates who have made good," Annalise noted. "That might be an interesting angle to explore. Undoubtedly, those success stories are young men from prominent families. Just

240

tossing spaghetti on the wall. But what if one of those less than honorable young men had a recent success, and that's the trigger?"

"Good thought. Tamara, is that something you could explore?" Erica asked.

"Sure. Now, can we eat?"

## CHAPTER TWENTY-SIX

---

The next day was a flurry of activity for all of us. While Reese and Annalise visited the local police, Erica and I started digging into the news archives and past yearbooks. Apparently, Reese had the magic touch and managed to wiggle the former detective's name out of an unsuspecting local police officer.

I stumbled on an article in the local paper about an alum making history as the youngest person elected to Congress if he won in November. The young man was from a prominent family. Check. And he was in the same class as the young woman we now suspected was the girl who had lost her scholarship. Erica scoured through yearbooks and found a missing senior year picture. We needed to find Catarina Reyes before the local police and before she struck again.

Reese and Annalise returned in the late afternoon with not only the name of the detective, but more information after tracking her down. This time Reese provided a summary in her more succinct style of reporting.

"Detective Laney Smith resigned nearly seven years ago after her efforts to hold three boys accountable for the brutal assault on Catarina Reyes went up in a haze of smoke. She received virtually no support despite her insistence that the young woman was a credible victim. The school cared more about its reputation and alumni support than the health or safety of its students."

"Let me guess. Jonathan Carlson the third was one of those boys," I interjected.

Reese tilted her head in my direction. "Yes. How did you know?"

"That's the trigger," I proposed. "I suspect Catarina's life has not been as rosy as his. Mr. Carlson is about to make history as the youngest congressman ever in the state."

"I don't think Catarina is done," Annalise stated. "Tamara has a theory that this is all about everyone looking the other way. 'See no evil, hear no evil, speak no evil.' There were more individuals at the school and local police who were involved in this cover-up, as well as other instances where the school ignored wrongdoing. Actually, wrongdoing is an understatement. What happened to this young woman was truly horrific. They took turns and assaulted her for hours. I suspect the local police know exactly who is responsible for these killings. They aren't going to let her live. We better track her down before they do."

"Agreed," Erica said. "Any idea who is next on her list?"

"The school counselor," Annalise blurted. "Unless Catarina turns her rage toward the boys."

243

Erica shook her head. "No, I believe at this point, she's concentrating her wrath on those in authority who let her down."

"This is all so sad. If only the authorities had listened." I wiped away a tear, surprised at how much this case affected me. I knew we had to stop Catarina from striking again, but she was the original victim. What about justice for her?

"One person did. Detective Laney Smith. Unfortunately, they shut her down. Nothing about this case is good. It won't be a satisfying end when we catch her," Annalise added.

"No, it won't. But it isn't our job to right past wrongs," Erica noted. "We need the address for the school counselor. Something tells me we don't have a lot of time to stop the next killing."

"What's going to happen to her when we catch her?" I asked.

"This may be a tough case to prosecute," Erica answered. "I suspect Catarina will make a very sympathetic defendant. Although the pieces all seem to fit, we don't have a lot of hard evidence yet. The prosecutor may try for a plea deal. Or her attorney may attempt to have her committed in lieu of jail."

"I hope she gets the help she needs." Everyone nodded, and I suspected they all felt as crappy as me about how this case was unfolding.

†

I knew there was no legitimate reason to accompany the team to the counselor's house, but I needed to be involved lest I ruminate over the case even more than I was already doing. As soon as they left the room, I became invisible and utilized my special abilities to travel to the address provided by the data tech. It was the first opportunity to apply my talents to this case.

Miraculously, I arrived before the rest of the team, which was a very good thing. I recognized Catarina right away from her yearbook picture. She was wearing a brown UPS uniform and carried a small package in her hand. I had to stop her before it was too late.

Before she lifted her hand to press the doorbell, I approached from behind and put my hand over her mouth to keep her from screaming. I'd perfected certain aspects of my invisibility, allowing only my arm and hand to be seen. She struggled a little but stopped, realizing whoever had detained her was a lot stronger. It wasn't much of a feat, considering Catarina was a slight young woman, barely a wisp.

"Don't do this. The FBI are on their way and will be here soon. It's over. I promise, they'll listen to your story. You won't be ignored, Catarina. But if you try to escape, the local police will track you down, and you won't get the justice you deserve."

"Who are you?" she mumbled through my hand.

"Someone who wants to ensure that all parties are held accountable for their actions. Unfortunately, that means you too."

Catarina grew limp in my grasp, and I loosened my hold on her, keeping her in front of me. "I don't care what happens to me. Do you promise everyone will get what they deserve?"

"I promise to do my best to ensure that happens." A siren blaring in the distance grew close. "I'm going to let go now. They'll be here soon, and I can't be here when they arrest you, but remember I'm going to do everything in my power to ensure justice is served for all, including those three young men."

As the car screeched to a stop, I let go entirely and slipped into a fully invisible form as the three agents scrambled from the car and announced their presence. I watched as they took a compliant Catarina into custody.

It was at that moment I decided the BAU no longer matched my skills. I wanted to help people who had been ignored by law enforcement. I didn't know if Annalise would join me, but I just couldn't forget what I believed was my true calling. In addition to prowling the streets and taking cases where the reward would be enough to pay the bills, I would be like *The Equalizer* and take on those lost causes. Annalise had already made so many changes. I didn't know if I could ask her once again to uproot her life. At least I had softened Annalise to the idea of moving, and it wasn't like she didn't have any notion of my desire to start our own firm.

†

I was waiting for Annalise when she returned. After so many years together, even if most of them were as good friends, she could read every minute change in my facial expressions. Carefully removing her gun and setting it on the table, she cocked her head and shot me a questioning look. I watched as she approached the bed.

"You okay?"

"Remember when you promised me that we would talk again about moving?"

Annalise groaned. "Now? Can't this wait?"

246

"No, I don't think so. I want to tell Erica that this will be my last case with the BAU," I blurted as I set my tablet on the side table by the bed and looked her in the eye.

Annalise sat heavily, facing away from me, before slipping off her shoes, swinging her legs onto the bed, and turning to meet my gaze. "This case really got to you, huh?"

I nodded. "I know what she did was wrong, but I can't stop thinking about how different her life would have been if only she hadn't been a victim herself. How many other people are traumatized every single day? And no one is there for them. Even worse, sometimes the systems we have in place to help them after the fact fail miserably. That counselor was supposed to help her. The police are obligated to get justice for victims, not turn them into vigilantes. I'm not saying we can't help law enforcement. I'd just like to do it by following a set of rules and a code of conduct we establish for ourselves." Holding up my hand, I continued, "Yes, I know law enforcement has its own rules and professional conduct the agents are supposed to live by, but unfortunately, some of them don't."

"Erica runs a tight ship and has been nothing but professional. It wasn't like the BAU was responsible for this poor woman's trauma. We simply clean up the mess after the fact."

"The BAU is reactive, not proactive. I want to move to a large city, too. Preferably one with a high rate of violent crime."

"You've made up your mind. No dialogue. No discussion. This isn't a conversation. It's you telling me what you plan to do. An edict," Annalise spat out.

"It's not an edict," I defended. "I'm not your superior. I would never tell you what to do. If you feel like the BAU is the perfect fit for you, I won't ask you to quit. I admit that I'd love for you to join me. If you don't want to move, I'll pick a city that's close. You can keep the house and stay there so you don't feel like I'm forcing you to uproot your life. It doesn't have to mean the end of our relationship. I don't want that," I insisted.

Annalise leaned back and smacked her head against the wall. "I'll move with you, but I want a say in where we move to. Detroit and Baltimore are out. And I'd rather not move to a red state."

"Albuquerque or Oakland?" I suggested.

"I can work with that," Annalise agreed.

I launched myself into her arms. "Thank you. I love you so much. I honestly don't think I could have survived another BAU case like this one. Did Erica tell you what will happen to Catarina?"

Annalise kept her arm around my shoulder as I laid my head on her chest. I could hear her steady heartbeat. "Not in detail, but she believes the prosecutor will take her circumstances into consideration."

"And the school and local police? What will happen there? What will happen to the young men who started it all? I promised Catarina she would get justice."

Annalise stiffened. "You were there?"

I pulled away and faced Annalise. "Of course I was. I didn't want some trigger-happy local cop to shoot her like a rabid animal."

Annalise relaxed. "I'm glad she surrendered without incident. I didn't want to have to shoot her, either. You would have never forgiven me," she teased.

"So, will Catarina get justice or not?"

Annalise sighed. "The BAU doesn't have authority over what happens to the young men who attacked her, nor do they have any influence over the school or local police department. Our involvement is limited. You know that."

"Fine. Then this will be my first pro bono case. I can be quite persuasive. Remember what I did to Tompkins? You haven't seen anything yet. I'll need to get the names of the other two young men."

Annalise grinned. "It would be my pleasure to provide that information to you."

"Can you stay with this unit of the BAU if we move to New Mexico or California?"

Annalise frowned. "I don't know."

"Do you think she would hire you as an independent consultant?"

"No harm in asking," Annalise responded.

"I could offer to stay, but only on a limited basis. My original agreement was that I would pick and choose the cases I wanted to be involved in, but that hasn't exactly panned out. Once you started with them, I've been involved in every case. That has to change."

"It's worth a try." Annalise frowned. "You know you never had to accept every assignment."

"I know, but it kept me close to you."

Annalise smiled. "You were compromising, and I never even knew it. I'm sorry."

Annalise's body language changed, and I could almost feel the excitement build as her heart rate increased.

"What's going on in that clever brain of yours?" I asked.

"Compromise is a good thing. If we can pull this off, both of us will get what we want. I'd even consider joining your unique private investigator company. You'll need me and my contacts with law enforcement. Of course, I'll probably have to establish those once we land in the new city we intend to move to."

"I like compromise." I began tugging on Annalise's clothes. "A good compromise deserves a reward."

"I like the sound of that. We both have too many clothes on."

"Yes, that is a verifiable fact."

# EPILOGUE

Erica wasn't thrilled with our plan to move to Albuquerque, but she agreed to the change in our work status. She didn't want to lose either of us. It turns out that some crime-fighting work can be quite lucrative.

Annalise ended up being the face of our business, and after we assisted in the capture of two of FBI's most wanted, we had plenty of money to continue our pro bono work, which made up the lion's share of our cases. Additionally, we accessed the crime stoppers system for additional income, but compared to the rewards related to those offered by the FBI or income from wealthy customers, it was only a small percentage of our income.

Our reputation grew with our nearly perfect success rate. I justified taking on cases where the clients could easily afford any quoted fee because over seventy-five percent of our cases were either pro-bono or a sliding fee that barely covered travel costs. Although kidnappings with ransoms were rare, with only a hundred cases every year, this became a specialty of ours and a stable income we could count on. It wasn't that only wealthy kidnapping cases were important to solve, but they did provide enough income to keep the company in the black and allowed us to employ a top-notch data tech.

Annalise became proficient at establishing a relationship with law enforcement in areas of the country we hadn't worked in before. It didn't hurt that our information leading to convictions was always rock solid.

I was on the recumbent exercise bike while Annalise was on her daily run when the company cell phone rang. I answered my tablet instead of interrupting my workout by going to the kitchen, where my cell was on the charger. Annalise had been on me to answer the calls versus letting it always go to voice mail as was my previous habit.

"TC Investigations."

"Tamara, it's Erica."

Immediately, my antennae went up. Typically, Erica would contact Annalise first because she knew she had better luck getting Annalise involved when she had a case she wanted us to work on.

"Why are you calling the company cell?" I asked. "Annalise usually has her phone on her even when she's on a run."

"This is personal," she replied, and I could now hear the strain in her voice. "I need your help. You guys are the best at finding kidnap victims. I'll pay you whatever you ask."

I heard Annalise enter and pop her head into our workout room. At this point, I'd stopped pedaling. I waved Annalise inside and pointed to my tablet. "Erica's on the line."

"A new case?" Annalise asked.

"Not exactly. Erica, Annalise is here now. Who's been abducted?" I asked.

Annalise raised an eyebrow.

"My niece has been missing for twenty-four hours. My sister didn't call until this morning. She's only thirteen." Erica had a noticeable quiver in her voice. "No way would she run away."

"Shit," Annalise muttered. "How can we help?"

"Will you take the case?" Erica asked.

"Of course we will," I answered for both of us. "And no way will we charge you."

"Charge her? What are you talking about? Isn't this a BAU case?" Annalise asked.

"No, it's not. Apparently, I'm too close to the situation, and they're passing it off as an unhappy teen running away."

"Send us everything you've got. We'll find her," Annalise assured.

I could hear the audible relief in Erica's voice. "Thank you. I know you will."

"Do you think your sister will let us have a piece of her clothing?" I asked.

"Anything you need. I've learned to trust your unconventional methods," Erica answered.

"How did you know?" Annalise asked.

"Oh, come on. The rumors are rampant. They were there before you joined the BAU. I didn't care as long as you got results, which you always did."

Annalise chuckled. "So, where are we flying to?"

"Seattle. I'll have a car available to you once you arrive, and I've already made the reservations. I took a personal leave. I'll meet you there. I'm sending details now."

"Always the ultimate organizer. How much time do we have?" Annalise asked.

"Two hours."

Annalise nodded and caught my eye. I hopped off the bike on my way to the shower. "All right. Cutting it kind of close, but we'll make it work. See you when we arrive."

Before I left the room, I heard the relief in Erica's voice as she said, "Thank you."

I'd already lathered my hair, when I smelled Annalise enter the bathroom. My eyes were closed, but I felt the rush of air right before she stepped inside to join me.

"You don't mind, do you?"

"No, but you need to keep your hands to yourself, or we won't make our flight," I answered after wiping the soap from my eyes and taking in Annalise's toned body.

"I just thought it would save time to shower together." Annalise grinned. "In case I haven't been clear, I'm glad we started TC Investigations."

"You haven't been clear about that, but better late than never," I quipped.

"Oh, like you admitting to being in love with me."

"Fair point," I conceded.

"So, how much longer before you agree to marry me?" Annalise asked.

"You've never asked."

"I'm asking now."

"In the shower before an important case? Really? Not exactly the best timing."

"It wasn't great timing when you declared your intent to move to a big city and start your own company, but I adapted."

"Yes, you did."

"So, what's your answer?"

"Well," I began, "it's a big commitment. Normally, I would want to collect enough data to make a good decision, but in this one instance, I think I'll go with my gut. It is a logical progression for our relationship, so yes. I love you and can't think of a reason not to."

Annalise shook her head. "I'll take it."

"Do I get a nice ring?" I asked.

"Sure. Anything you want."

"You mean you don't have one for me?"

"It was kind of a spur-of-the-moment thing," Annalise answered.

"Fascinating. Since neither of us are very good with spontaneous change, do you think long-term consumption of the alien fruit is having a negative impact."

"No, Tamara. I believe, as you already stated, it is the logical evolution of our relationship. I can't see myself ever leaving you. Might as well take advantage of all the legal benefits offered to married people. Besides, I'm madly in love with you, and that's the only reason I need."

I offered her a quick peck and replied. "I love you, too. Now hurry up, we're going to be late."

# ABOUT THE AUTHOR

---

Annette Mori is an award-winning author, published by Affinity Rainbow Publications, who lives in the beautiful Pacific Northwest with her wife and their four furry kids. With over thirty published novels, six Lesfic Bard Awards, and one Goldie Award for her fourth novel, *Locked Inside*, she finally feels like a real author. Annette is as much a reader as a writer and is always looking for the next sapphic novel to queue up. She came up with the *One Fan at a Time* tagline, because it rolled off the tongue much better than *One Reader at a Time*. After pondering who she was at her core, she feels it was all about connecting to each reader on a personal level. Annette would be the first to admit she doesn't do well with the masses. If someone picks up her book and it touches them, she believes she has achieved what she wants with her writing by reaching each reader. It is who she is at her core. Drop her a line. She loves to hear from readers.

Email: annettemori0859@gmail.com.

Sign up for her mailing list: http://eepurl.com/cS7nr9

Check out her blog: Everyday Occurrences: https://annettemori0859.wordpress.com/

Visit the Affinity Rainbow Publications website for her books and many other outstanding authors: www.affinityebooks.com

Let the author know what you think about the book - write a review.

## OTHER AFFINITY BOOKS

---

Never Too Late by Glenda Poulter

After the death of her long-time partner, and a scandal at the school where she taught music and art, Janice Halston emerged as a shadow of herself. Feeling shaken, cautious and artistically blocked.

Tam Murphy lost her wife and son within a short time of each other. She tries to fill her emptiness with her daughter Mae, and granddaughter, Ocee.

Janice and Tam are brought together by the precocious Ocee. As their friendship deepens, so do their feelings for each other. Their deepening feelings send both women spiraling…in different directions. One toward what could be, the other away from fear of another loss. Will their spirals lead them back to each other, or further apart?

Nothing But Net by Ali Spooner

Hunter James, a rising star in college basketball, has her career and life sidelined after experiencing a family tragedy.

An opportunity for a fresh start opens the door to return to what she loves most: playing basketball. Hunter rushes through that door to make the most of her second chance.

Back in the basketball arena, doing what she loves, will she open herself and her heart to another chance to forgive herself and fall in love?

The Kitten Trap by Annette Mori

Inspired by the classic movie, *The Parent Trap*, two adorable black kittens, Midnight and Onyx, play matchmakers for their human mothers, Mac and Carmen. Struggling with the complexities of farm life, Mac can barely believe her beautiful girlfriend, Carmen, has agreed to move to the drafty old farmhouse to live with her and her beloved Pops. When Carmen is forced to leave the farm to care for her ailing mother, Midnight and Onyx as well as Mac and Carmen must struggle with the difficult separation. Just when it appears Carmen and Onyx may come back home to the farm, cruel fate raises a further challenge, one that will need the help of two mischievous kittens to overcome.

To Autumn by Katie M Hall

Sixteen-year-old Robyn Gale, along with her younger sister Anne, is sent away for the summer holidays of 1997 to stay with her grandmother at a caravan park in Devon. Robyn's had a tough few months: trying to cope with the fallout of their mother's attempted suicide, messing up her GCSEs, and finding herself attracted to girls. Perhaps getting away from her real life is just what she needs...she can focus on finding a boyfriend, watching *Neighbours,* and swimming. A solid plan, until she meets charismatic Australian lifeguard, Autumn, and her life is turned even more down under.

### Fairytail Farm by Ali Spooner

Dr. Hill McCall and her wife Alice dreamed of developing a sanctuary for unwanted cats and dogs to live out their lives as a retirement project. Hill has secretly worked on the project for months when a wealthy benefactor surprises her with a large donation, allowing Hill to be more aggressive with the project's opening. A group home operator approaches Hill about summer volunteer positions for four girls as Fairytail Farm becomes more than just a sanctuary for the animals. It creates an environment of love and kindness for the animals and all that support the project. Several love stories develop from first love to mature couples who have found their forever person. Fairytail Farm is more than a dream come true. It is a home for happily ever afters.

### The Love Demand by Annette Mori

In the dazzling realm of reality television, where love and drama entwine in a complicated dance as old as time, a groundbreaking series emerges that transcends the ordinary. *The Love Demand* is not your typical reality show. Lacey Fellows isn't sure she wants to subject herself to further humiliation, however, on the off chance her girlfriend may agree to accept a second marriage proposal, Lacey reluctantly consents to participating in the new reality show.

What she doesn't count on is meeting a kindred spirit—one she can't seem to shake from her thoughts. Jaimie would do almost anything for her girlfriend, including following her to the ends of the earth and participating in a conniving television show that puts her in front of a camera, which happens to be her least favorite place. Her girlfriend, Sabina, hasn't met a camera she doesn't like. They couldn't be more opposite, but Jaimie still hopes Sabina will want marriage, kids, and the whole shebang. The last thing she expects is to fall in love with someone else. Let the games begin.

### Sullivan's Trace by Ali Spooner

Micah "Sully" Sullivan has settled into a solitary life at the family horse ranch after her father's death. When her long-term vet, Doc Barton, plans to retire, his granddaughter, Bryn, arrives to take over his practice. An attack on one of Sully's prized horses throws Sully and Bryn into a whirlwind as they fight to save the young animal. Just as Sully is becoming comfortable with her growing attraction to Bryn, tragedy occurs, and her brother and his wife are killed in an accident. Sully's solitary life drastically changes when a family of three is born.

### Love Sins by Annette Mori

Jessica Green's life is predictable and boring. As the chief engineer for Solar Flair, her career is right on track. Her love life, not so much. The last thing she expects is a call from her estranged father's attorney. Too curious to ignore the message, she can't resist meeting with him and discovering more about specific instructions related to his estate, as well as the letter her father left for her. Rattled by what she finds at her father's home, she promptly dials 911.

Special Agent Amanda Forrester is perplexed by a call to join a homicide investigation until she arrives at the scene and learns the victim is not only a serial killer but an elite assassin the authorities have been after for years. To Amanda's increasing irritation, the daughter recognizes a picture of the last target and insinuates herself into the investigation. As the case takes a surprising turn, Amanda finds she has landed smack dab in the middle of a complicated and dangerous situation. The facts lead her to a puzzle weaving together the recent suicide of a wealthy businessman with the activities of several prominent politicians. Amanda must join forces with a mysterious organization and the persistent woman she finds increasingly hard to resist. Her instinct to protect the alluring and vulnerable Jessica Green kicks into high gear, taking the reader on a roller-coaster journey for the last book in *The Next Generation* series.

A Wild Moon Rises by Jen Silver
Successful author, Malory G Holmes, has had a rough year. Wounded by an emotional breakup and writer's block she returns home after eight months travelling to discover the startling results of a DNA test. Apparently, through her mother's side, she is related to a baronet with an estate in Briarbay, Northumberland. She decides to visit the place to find out more about this unknown side of her family.

Selene Wylde is content with life, running a bookshop in the small hamlet of Briarbay. She also looks after her father, Reginald, who is grieving over the recent death of his husband, Sir Alan Guyatt. Reginald is worrying about his claim to stay at Briarbay Hall as the Will of Sir Alan has not yet been found.

With the arrival in her shop of a very attractive, well-known writer, Selene's world begins to tilt alarmingly. Malory and Selene become entangled in a web of secrets and deceptions with the added complication of a rapidly growing attraction.

The Wolf and The Unicorn by Ali Spooner (Erotica)
Ready to explore a steamy, passionate, and tantalizing erotica romance….

Keagan and Celeste have built a solid relationship on trust and independence. A successful surgeon, Keagan understands Celeste's supercharged libido and her desire to experience a variety of sexual encounters. Everything changes when Sky, a new doctor, arrives at the hospital, and Celeste is immediately drawn to the younger woman. Keagan is surprised when she is also attracted to Sky, who shares common interests with Celeste and her. When more than a physical attraction develops, the three women discover a loving relationship beyond the bedroom.

The Blank White Page by Ali Spooner
Tatum Chastain, Corporate Officer of Chastain International, her family's real estate empire, accepts the challenge her father, Charles, has set forth. Charles has tasked Tatum and her brother, Charlie, to survive in the wilderness for six months to prove their skills in taking over the family business once he retires. Charles fails to realize that Tatum would fall in love with the southeastern Alaska cabin he has chosen for her to test her resilience and creativity. Tatum prepares for life in the bush, and shortly after she arrives, Poe, a beautiful raven, becomes her companion and guardian. When River Foster, a designated

hunter for her village, crosses Tatum's path, she finds a different kind of love awaits her.

Love Hacks by Annette Mori

Joy Stiles is adrift. Having finally finished her graduate degree at the National Defense University, the only thing keeping her interest is an ongoing feud with a fellow hacker to gain access to sensitive information. Against all odds, the person snuck their way into her tech and kept leaving taunting messages. It's driving Joy crazy. She doesn't have time for this. Operation Elephant Bites isn't working as The Organization thought it would when they started down that path two years ago. Now they have a new worry. Someone is desperately trying to find out more about The Organization, believing they are behind the attacks on the mines. Whoever that person is has not only ties to the Chinese and Russian governments but also members of the US Government. Top secret files at the NSA call their unknown group The Crusaders. Joy's efforts to uncover the identity of the enemy lead The Organization to a lot more than evil plans, and it's up to The Next Generation, with support from senior members of The Organization, to thwart the inevitable trajectory, perhaps with the assistance of Joy's irritating foe.

Affinity
Rainbow Publications

eBooks, Print, Free eBooks

Visit our website for more publications available online.

https://affinityebooks.com/

Published by Affinity Rainbow Publications
A Division of Affinity eBook Press NZ LTD
Canterbury, New Zealand

Registered Company 2517228

www.ingramcontent.com/pod-product-compliance
Lightning Source LLC
Chambersburg PA
CBHW051539260626
47170CB00003B/1005